Living with NO Regrets

ANNETRA WAGNER PIPER

Recipes by Earnestine Bryant Wagner

Abounding Favor Publishing Company
Houston, Texas

Novel by Annetra Wagner Piper, Copyright 2008
Recipes by Earnestine Bryant Wagner, Copyright 2008

Living with No Regrets by Annetra Wagner Piper
Recipes by Earnestine Bryant Wagner

Abounding Favor Publishing Company
P.O. Box 450515
Houston, Texas 77245
713-729-7168
www.annetrapiperbooks.com

© Copyright 2008, Annetra Piper and Earnestine Bryant Wagner

All rights reserved. No part of this book may be reproduced, stored in a retrieval system, or transmitted by any means, electronic, mechanical, photocopying, recording, or otherwise, without written permission from the authors.

ISBN 0-9820004-0-3

Cover and Text design by Barry K. Henry, Grafikally Speaking

Cover illustration by: Jarvis Jackson

Printed in the United States of America

Living with NO Regrets

Lady Madeline Newton,

Be Blessed!

Anitra ...

ACKNOWLEDGMENTS

It is both a privilege and an honor to acknowledge the people who have had such a great impact on my life and on my being able to complete this book. I thank God for the opportunity to put my thoughts on paper. I could not even fathom doing what I do without God in my life. I depend daily on the Holy Spirit to guide me in all that I do. Thank you my Father.

I would like to begin by thanking my husband, Adrian. Thank you for your understanding and patience as I worked late into the night to finish this project. Thank you for being such a wonderful husband and father, and for taking such good care of us. I love you very much. To our children, Nicholas, Phillip, and Shannyn - thank you for being who you are. Nicholas and Phillip, you are strong, faithful, mighty men of valor. Shannyn, you are a capable, intelligent, virtuous woman of God. I love you with the unconditional love that a mother has for her children. The fact that you make me so proud is icing on the cake. I would like to thank my parents, Henry and Earnestine Wagner. Thank you for your guidance, encouragement, and moral support for this project. I am so happy to be a part of your lives. Thank you for always supporting every project I undertake and making me feel like a winner in all that I do. I love you very much. Mom, thanks for the excellent edits and the wonderful recipes. To my sister, Tonja Jackson - you are not just my sister, you are my friend. You encourage me, you lift me up, and you make me so proud of who you have become. Thank you for editing my book, and also for being so engrossed in the story that I feel successful before anyone even reads it. To my friend Rita Alford - What can I say? You are like a wonderful little sister to me, who is so giving and kind. Thank you for who you are - a wonderful person, mother, wife, and sister in Christ. Thank you also for pre-reading the story, ensuring that it would be easy for others to read. I would also like to thank Thayla Andrews for critically reading the novel and giving me great insight into how the story might impact others. Thanks also go out to my friend Barbara Harris Curtis, author of *Confessions of a Kept Woman*. Thank you, Barbara for your sense of humor, your flare, your contacts, and your critical editing eye. I am glad you are a part of my life.

   I would also like to thank my Pastor and First Lady, Bishop I.V. and Lady Bridget Hilliard. Thank you for the Word that you impart into my life and for standing flat-footed and teaching the Word, loving God and loving the people. I really appreciate you. Dr. Bridget, thank you for all your support and prayers, and for reading over this project. You don't know how it makes me feel to know you would take the time out of your very busy schedule to encourage me.

   Thank you to my book club – Page Turners, Too for all your love and support. Nikki, Tandra, Beverly, Thayla, Steenie,

Tonja, Rita, Karla, Alex, bless you - I love you all. There are so many people in my life I would like to thank. My close family members – Kevin and his wife Shelia and my niece Shelby; Fred and my nephew Tarrick; Tonja and my nephew Jarvis; my aunt Barbara and her husband Wes and my first cousin Krystal, the list goes on and on. I would like to thank everyone who has encouraged me to go to the next level - my sisters-in-law (Karen and Gus); my brothers-in-law (Kenneth and Joe), my father-and mother-in-law (Elwood and Ora Lean); and my nieces that I have not yet mentioned, but who are just as important to me (Demetria, JoNiya, Klarissa, Lanisha, Reneishia, Thelma and Tylan). I would like to thank all of my extended family members (who if I mentioned everyone, I would need as much room as the book takes up). Thank you for your support, love, and prayers. I love you all. I would like to thank my staff in the Grant Department, where we help make the lives of children and others better daily. Adrianne, Elizabeth, Florine, Jacelyn, Jene, Karen, and Robert - thanks for making my life easy. I would like to thank the partners in my Circle of Light for praying for me always - Amaniese, Cammie, Charlyn, Evelyn, Pam, thank you, I love you much. Thanks also go out to my Master Torch Bearers – Minister Gabriel and Sarita Hood. Thank you for always praying for me. Thank you to the Top Teens of America and Top Ladies of Distinction, Inc. – Houston and other Chapters. You continue to support me in all that I do. Thanks to my sorors of Delta Sigma Theta Sorority, Inc. – Houston Alumnae and other chapters. I feel your love.

Thank you all for being a part of my life. If I left anyone off, as the saying goes, "charge it to my head and not to my heart."

I very much enjoyed writing this story. The family members in the story became my own and I was sorry to let them go, but time waits for no one. Until the next book, thanks for your support! To God Be the Glory!

CHAPTER ONE

A Fish Out of Water

March 2005

The phone was ringing. Cherrelle rushed towards it, but the answering machine picked up the line just as she approached it. With her hand over the receiver, she decided to see who was calling. She looked at the caller ID.

"Hello…baby?"

It was Big Mama. She was the only extended family member she was still on speaking terms with. Ever since her fiancé had deserted her on her wedding day, she felt like her family members treated her differently. She knew they were still laughing at her behind her back. Even her sisters didn't call her as often. They said she needed her space, and maybe they were right.

Cherrelle hesitated, her hand still hovering over the receiver. She could always call Big Mama back. She listened to her grandmother leave a message.

"Cherrelle?... This Big Mama. How you doing? You know I hate to talk into these things. We planning a family reunion, and I want you there. Call me... I love you, Cherrelle. Bye, bye."

Cherrelle stared at the answering machine and leaned her head back against the wall. She just bet they did want her there. The last time Cherrelle went to a Carter family reunion she swore she would never go back again. She used to think that family meant something, but she quickly realized that was not true. She had been the subject of too much attention, backbiting, and gossip. Darryl not showing up on their wedding day was bad enough, but to be stared at and whispered about behind her back by her own family made the situation much worse. They made her feel like she didn't belong, in her own family! Like his not showing up at the wedding, with all the guests in attendance, and her getting ready to walk down the aisle with no groom in sight was her own fault. Even worse, the fact that Darryl left her for her first cousin, who literally stole him from under her nose, was the ultimate proof that family meant nothing. She couldn't seem to let it go. She wouldn't let it go. She dwelled on that situation and thought about the hurt that she felt, every day since it happened. She was going to have to make up some excuse as to why she couldn't make it to the family reunion once again. She wasn't going, that much was for sure. It was too much hassle and too much stress.

As usual, whenever her family contacted her or she thought about them, Cherrelle's thoughts went back to her near-wedding day. She didn't want to, but she couldn't seem to help it. Her thoughts just went that way anyway.

She had been so happy that day. She had awakened with a big smile. The weather had cooperated and was totally beautiful. There wasn't a cloud in that bright blue sky. She remembered lying in her bed and looking out of her window thinking of the old wives' tale about rain on your wedding day meaning you would cry many tears in your marriage, or something like that. There wouldn't be any rain on her wedding day and no tears for her. She thought about her fiancé. Darryl was so good to her. They had so much in common. He was her best friend. He had goals for his life, and he had shared them with her many times. She had goals too. As a recent graduate of Dillard University, she was idealistic and excited about her future.

Cherrelle looked up when her mom walked into her room. Theresa stood still and watched her daughter still snuggled under the covers in her pink and blue bedroom.

"Hello, my baby. This is your day." Theresa was smiling her brave smile, but there was a hint of tears in her eyes. Her daughter was so young. Although she had been young when she married Cherrelle's father, she didn't think Darryl and Cherrelle were ready.

"I'm so happy for you. What time do you want to get dressed?" her mom asked.

Cherrelle looked over at the bedside clock. It was already nine o'clock in the morning. Her wedding was at one. She stretched widely.

"I thought I'd start with a big breakfast and time to talk to you. We won't have this special time anymore. I know this is my day, but I'm going to pamper you this morning, Mom. Then you can help me get dressed." Cherrelle threw the covers off and climbed out of bed. She walked over and hugged her mother.

"Besides, we need to talk about me being a good wife. I want to be the perfect wife and mother, just like you. Darryl deserves the best wife he can have. I want to be that," she said wistfully as she smiled and looped her arm through her mother's. Theresa smiled and moved to open the door.

"Let's go."

Theresa and Cherrelle talked earnestly about what a man expects from his wife in marriage. During the discussion her mother opened the Bible and turned to Proverbs 31, starting with verse 10. As they read it together, Cherrelle was amazed at how much helpful information was there. After they finished reading Cherrelle sat back in awe.

"The Bible is so amazing. It actually tells you how a wife should behave in a marriage and at all times. She should support her husband, take care of the household and the children, including feeding and clothing them." Cherrelle loved God and was a long-time follower of His Word. She read over a few more passages and laughed. "Here it's telling you that a woman should mind her own business and not be a busy body so that she will be considered wise. I wonder if most women read this before they get married. If they did, I bet there would be less confusion in the marriage and in the home and fewer divorces." Her mother smiled proudly at her daughter and nodded.

After breakfast, Cherrelle took a long, luxurious bubble bath. Her beautician would be there an hour before the wedding to make sure her hair was still perfectly in place. She had gotten her hair done the day before, but she didn't want to take any chances. After her bath, she lay down to relax a little while. She was getting anxious. She especially did not want to think about her wedding night. She didn't know what to expect. She was a virgin and had promised herself that she would stay that way until she was married. Darryl had made that promise to her as well. Not wanting to be nervous or uptight at her wedding, she decided to rest for a few minutes. Cherrelle thought about calling Darryl but decided against it. They had decided not to see each other for twenty-four hours prior to the wedding. Even though they hadn't mentioned anything about not calling she figured he thought it was best, since she hadn't heard from him.

Her best friend Talia knocked on her door and popped her head in. She was already dressed in her lilac maid of honor dress.

"Time to get dressed, Cherrelle. I'm here to help you and your mother with whatever you need me to do. How's it going?"

Cherrelle sat up. She and Talia had been best friends since first grade. Talia had been through a lot, and they had always stood by each other. Both of Talia's parents had been killed in a car accident, and she had lived with her grandparents most of her life. As a child, Cherrelle had also lived with her grandparents so they felt they had a lot in common.

"Everything's good, but I'm really nervous. I can't wait for this show to be over, so I can settle down with Darryl and we can live happily ever after."

Talia looked at her strangely.

"What about the other day?"

Talia was referring to the recent conversation they had about Darryl and how he had broken down in front of her and cried because he didn't know if he was ready for such responsibility. Cherrelle had been quite shaken up after that incident. It had taken both her and his mother, who had to be called over, to calm him down and help him focus on the future.

"Oh, he's over that, girl. We had a long talk, and he asked me to forgive him for having any doubts about our relationship. We understand each other, and we love each other. Everything's going to be fine."

Cherrelle tried her best to blow the incident off. She refused to accept the fact that Darryl might not want to marry her. Actually, Cherrelle had been so shocked she had cried later in private. Darryl had cried for real tears in front of her, boohooing like a baby. He had gotten so hysterical, she felt she had no other choice but to call his mom to come over and talk to him. She sat quietly in the living room while he and his mother talked. When they finally came out, Darryl was smiling again and all seemed well.

Talia was about to say something else but Cherrelle's mom walked in, so they ended the conversation.

"You girls ready to get started?" her mother asked. Her sisters Camille and Chalice walked in. "Your sisters are here to help as well." Her seventeen and eighteen year old sisters were going to be her bridesmaids. They looked so grown up.

"You all look really pretty. Lilac suits all of you," Cherrelle told the group. Chalice curtsied for the group. She knew she looked adorable. Camille blushed and turned her head away.

Everyone fussed and primped over Cherrelle until she was fully dressed. She was a beautiful bride. People say that all the time about brides, but Cherrelle was genuinely gorgeous. Her long dark hair was swept up from her face. Her skin, the color of rich cocoa looked like silk chocolate. As she smiled, her dimples stood out drawing everyone's eyes to them, making the group want to smile back. Her make-up was flawless, emphasizing her beautiful brown eyes and long lashes. Her best friend and family members stood back and sighed. Theresa walked over to her and began adjusting her veil. Darryl would be so happy when he saw her.

Her father walked in at that moment with his camera. He could barely look at his daughter without tears forming in his eyes. She looked so beautiful, and she would be a wife in a few hours. He couldn't believe how his baby had grown. He still thought of her as the little girl running around the house, chasing her sisters. Calvin lifted the camera to take a picture of the beautiful and memorable sight before him - mother and daughter preparing for the big day. Chalice and Camille saw the camera and ran to be in the pictures.

The wedding party walked outside as the white, decorated limousine pulled up. The driver got out and opened the door to allow mother, father, bridesmaids, maid of honor and bride to enter. The limo already looked like the vehicle that would escort husband and wife from the church. Cherrelle looked at her sisters to see if they were guilty of decorating it. They seemed as fascinated by what they saw as she was. Everyone made room for her in the car so that her gown would not get wrinkled. Cherrelle looked up at the sky and took a deep breath. The sun was still shining, and there was not a cloud in sight. Everything would be perfect. As they drove down her street to the church, she noticed that there were very few cars left on the street. Most of them were already gone. She had grown up on the street, and most of the neighbors were long time friends or family members. They had all been invited to the wedding and Cherrelle was sure they were already at the church. The limo only needed to make one more stop. Cherrelle had insisted that the limousine stop by to pick up her grandparents. They had been an important part of her life, and she wanted to make sure they were driven to the church in style.

The limousine smoothly glided to the curb in front of her grandparents' house. Her father moved to get out and ring the doorbell. Everyone looked past the well-kept, tiny front lawn to her grandparents' house which was painted canary yellow, with green shutters and a bright green door. Bright plastic flowers adorned the flower garden and surrounded the trees. Their home was their pride and joy. The front door of her grandparents' house opened before her father could get out of the car. Big Mama and Pawpaw stepped out looking like proud peacocks. They looked around, hoping some of their neighbors could see them walking towards and getting into the limousine, but nobody was around.

The driver got out and opened the door again to help Big Mama into the car. Her huge purple hat almost touched the roof of the car. She slid over so her husband Clarence would have room as well. He looked very handsome in his black suit, with a white shirt and a purple tie and handkerchief. Thankfully, they only had a few more blocks to get to the church. It was getting very crowded in the limousine. Nobody said much on their way to the church. Everyone was mainly looking at Cherrelle and smiling. The married folks were thinking back to their own weddings and happy marriages. Her grandfather reached over and took her grandmother's hand. Her father smiled fondly and winked sexily at his wife. The single ones were smiling to themselves and looking forward to their own day.

After arriving at the church, the driver let her mother, grandparents, maid of honor and bridesmaids out near the side entrance as instructed. Cherrelle and her father remained in the car as it slowly cruised to the front of the church. He reached over and squeezed his daughter's hand in encouragement.

"You okay?" Calvin saw how nervous she looked. Cherrelle nodded. "I'm great, Daddy. Thank you so much, for everything. In case I forget to tell you," she said referring to one of her favorite movies. "This has been a great day." Her father smiled broadly.

Cherrelle looked out the window of the limo and noticed Darryl's best friend Cory pacing back and forth on the steps in front of the church. He looked extremely handsome in his tuxedo. He had always been the most attractive and sophisticated of the two, but Darryl treated her so well and courted her so strongly, she had fallen in love with him. Although Cory was usually around when she was with Darryl, he had only treated her like a little sister and a good friend.

Cory had a worried look on his face now. He glanced up and saw the limousine. He hesitated then walked towards the waiting car. Cherrelle lifted her wedding dress and stepped out of the car. She didn't wait for assistance.

Cherrelle usually tried not to look directly into Cory's eyes. He was so handsome, and his eyes were very distracting. Then there was the smooth dark skin… and those lips! It wasn't right for her to think that her fiancé's best friend was so gorgeous. But at that moment even his looks could not distract her.

"What's wrong, Cory?" She knew something was terribly wrong. "Is something wrong with Darryl? Where is he?"

Cory hesitated. He knew something wasn't right also.

"I don't know where he is."

Though there had not been a cloud in the sky when she left home, suddenly the brightness of the sun disappeared, like it had gone behind a cloud.

"What?" Cherrelle grabbed Cory by the front of his jacket and looked into his face. She forgot about her rule of not looking directly at him. She didn't even realize she was doing it.

"I don't know where Darryl is. He was talking crazy last night, like he didn't want to go through with the wedding, but when I talked to him this morning he sounded sane, even happy. I told him I'd come and pick him up so he wouldn't have to drive while he's all nervous, and he said that would be fine. When I went to pick him up no one answered the door. I checked where he keeps his emergency key and went inside. He was gone. There was no sign of him or his stuff. At first I thought, maybe he decided to drive himself to the church, but when I got here nobody had seen him. Then, a few minutes before you got here, his little brother gave me this and told me to give it to you." Cory sadly held his hand out to give Cherrelle a sealed envelope with her name on the front of it.

Cherrelle looked down at the white envelope in Cory's hand in confusion for several seconds. Her own hand wouldn't reach out and take it. The name on the front, she assumed it was hers, blurred from the sudden tears that came to her eyes. She took a step back. Her mouth formed the word no and she shook her head, but no sound came out. Her father got out of the car and rushed to his daughter's side. Cherrelle began loudly wailing and crying. She was bent over at the waist. Her father and Cory helped her into the limousine.

"Driver, take us around the block," her father ordered.

Cherrelle was in a world of her own. She looked out of the window and thought back to her own conversation with Darryl just a few days before and how she and his mom had convinced him that he was making the right decision in marrying her. With tears streaming down her face, she silently took the envelope from Cory. She looked at it a long time. Then, wiping her eyes with the back of her hand, she finally, carefully opened it and read its contents.

Cherrelle,

You know I love you. I do love you, but not the way a husband should love a wife. We grew up together and you are beautiful, but I can't marry you. I would be living a lie. I love you as a friend but not as someone I can't live without. I know that sounds cruel, but if I get married, I want it to be with someone who is my soul mate. You thought it was just nerves. I knew it was more of a feeling of being trapped in a situation I didn't want to be a part of. Marriage is forever for me. I want you to find someone who can be your happily ever after as well. I hate to tell you this in a letter, but you'll find out eventually anyway. I have found my soul mate. That's why I cried the other night. I knew if I married you, I could never be with her. Please forgive me. I am so sorry that I let it go this far. I couldn't let you down before, and she finally admitted how much she loves me so I have to see where this will take us. Please forgive me. You and I have been friends a very long time and I'd hate to think that you're out there hating me. Please forgive me.

Darryl

Cherrelle read the letter as tears continued to stream down her face. As she looked up at her father, the hurt look on her face broke his heart. He wanted to cry with her, but he knew he had to be strong for her. Pulling Cherrelle to his chest, he cradled and rocked her in his arms. She let the tears flow long and hard. Cory sat there helplessly, wringing his hands, wanting to help her. He had loved her all his life, but never said anything because Darryl was his best friend and he loved her too. He never would have done anything to make either of them unhappy or uncomfortable. Cherrelle had been so happy knowing she was marrying Darryl. Cory's heart was breaking now seeing her in such pain. He wanted to comfort her but felt it wasn't his place. He could kill Darryl.

When she finished crying, she sat up.

Cory handed her his handkerchief. She wiped her eyes and sighed deeply. He wanted to cry with her.

"Well," she said and took a deep breath. "Well," she said again. It was as if a shutter had come down over her soul. Her shoulders drooped dejectedly and she attempted to straighten them. Cherrelle clasped her hands and placed her fingers over her lips as if she were deep in thought. Silent tears continued to flow. She wiped her eyes with the back of her hand.

"Daddy, do you think you can tell the people in the church that the wedding is cancelled. I don't think I'm ... I don't think I'm up to it right now." Tears flowed again.

Her father's heart ached for her as fiery anger burned in his eyes. He nodded.

"Of course I will. I wouldn't dare put you through that." He called to the driver. "I'm going to go in and take care of this terrible situation. Take them back to the house as quickly as possible. You can come back and pick the rest of us up after that. I'd appreciate it." He got out and closed the door firmly but quietly.

Inside the church, the crowd was beginning to murmur. "Where is the bride?" "Have you seen the groom?"

Her wedding party was waiting in the foyer for the cue to go in. Her mother looked nervously at her watch. She hated late weddings. As things were, they were already almost thirty minutes late. Where was Darryl? She had peeked into the church and did not see a sign of him or Cory, his best man. The minister was standing at the side door of the sanctuary waiting for the groom. He had taken this position when he saw the limousine arrive.

Theresa also wondered what had happened to her husband Calvin and their daughter. She didn't see the car in front of the building anymore. She was about to pull her cell phone from her purse to call when her husband walked in. She looked in his eyes and ran over to him. She knew something was terribly wrong. He looked like he was in shock, and he looked…angry. He was such a kind-hearted, slow to anger man, that she knew something had to be wrong. Theresa tried to read his thoughts through his eyes. Looking into her husband's eyes she asked, "What's wrong?"

He shook his head in disgust. "Darryl is not going to show up for the wedding. He decided he wanted to be with someone else. He told Cherrelle about it in a letter. He left her a note, Theresa. What kind of man is that!"

Cherrelle's mom's eyes filled with water. "How is Cherrelle? Where is she?" All she could think about was her baby and how she must be feeling.

"She is as good as can be expected. Cory took her home in the limo." He paused, "She asked me to tell the guests that the wedding has been cancelled." Theresa put her hand to her heart, feeling her daughter's pain.

"I'll go with you," she told him, placing her hand in his.

Calvin and Theresa walked up the aisle of the church and turned towards their friends, relatives, and invited guests. It was the hardest thing they had ever had to do. When they entered the room, the pastor walked in from the side entrance. The room was so quiet when they walked in, you could have heard a pin drop. Calvin motioned for the microphone, and the pastor handed it to him.

"If I could have your attention: I regret to inform you that the wedding of Ms. Cherrelle Elliot and Mr. Darryl Francis has been cancelled. Please pick up your gifts in the foyer and thank you for coming."

The gasp broke the silence. Theresa heard her cousin Mabel whisper, "I know we better be able to get our gifts back." Theresa cut her eyes at her cousin and walked out on her husband's arm with her head held high. The guests milled around for several minutes talking about what had just happened.

When Cherrelle got home, Cory helped her out of the limo and assisted her in getting into the house. She was so weak she felt like a newborn baby. Cory walked her into her pink and blue bedroom and insisted that she lie down. He pulled the blanket back, took her shoes off, and helped her to get into the bed. He pulled the blanket over her shoulders. She just laid there in a pool of wedding dress. He knew she would fall asleep in her state of shock, and he did not want her to wake up in that dress. Then he eased her up, painstakingly unbuttoned the dress, and removed it from her shoulders. He slid the dress from her body, leaving her slip and underclothes on. She had such a beautiful body, but he wouldn't focus on that right now. He eased her back onto the bed and pulled the blanket over her shoulders. He hung her dress up in her closet. Walking back over to her bed, he saw that Cherrelle had drifted off to sleep with tears still streaming down her face. He placed a light kiss on her forehead, turned out the light, and left the room. When Cherrelle heard the door close, she opened her swollen eyes still filled with tears and whispered, "thank you, Cory."

As she sat thinking about that embarrassing ordeal, her eyes misted over. She had eventually gotten over Darryl. He wasn't the man for her. She realized he was a coward and she was glad she had escaped that. She had not, however, gotten over the embarrassment of being a jilted bride. That's something people don't easily forget, and she hadn't forgiven him for the shame and humiliation he had caused her.

She stared at the blinking light on the telephone and pressed the button twice to delete the message. She'd call her grandmother tomorrow.

Big Mama hung up the phone as her husband walked into the room.

"Was she home?" he asked his wife.

"I don't think so, but with these fancy new machines, you never know. I was hoping I could talk her into coming to the family reunion this time. She never shows up, but I keep hoping."

"She's a busy and important woman. Plus she's got a lot of hurt inside. Give her time, and keep calling her."

Bessie smiled. Everything was so simple for Clarence. They had lived a lifetime together and raised some beautiful children and some grandchildren too. He had other things on his mind, though. He sniffed the air.

"What's for dinner?" Clarence asked his wife. Something sure smelled good. Bessie was an excellent cook.

"You know what the doctor said about being careful about what you eat, so I've come up with a whole lot of recipes made with chicken. Tonight I made Creole Smothered Chicken[1], rice, glazed carrots[2], and turnip greens[3]."

Clarence's mouth began to water. He knew what Bessie could do with some food. He hurried towards the kitchen. His wife followed close behind.

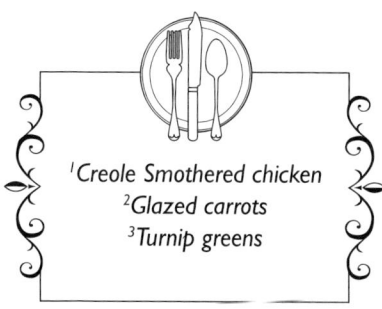

[1] Creole Smothered chicken
[2] Glazed carrots
[3] Turnip greens

CHAPTER TWO

THERE'S NO SUCH THING AS A FREE LUNCH

The next day was really hectic for Cherrelle. She had so much to do. As executive director for a non-profit organization that supported abused children and families, she was always busy. She had certainly followed in her parents' footsteps. She loved giving back to her community. If she wasn't finding new places for shelter and support for the families that came to them, she was looking for funding sources, attending conferences out of town or fundraising events in the city. She had a great staff that assisted her.

"Kathy," she said into the intercom. "Bring me the Norris file. I think I may have found something for them." While she waited, she turned her big oversized desk chair around, leaned back, and looked out of the window. She had a gorgeous view of the city and a large, beautiful office. Her window overlooked Memorial Park, and the trees were in full bloom as they always seemed to be in Houston. The solid wood furniture and overstuffed chairs and sofas in her office made the room comfortable as well as functional. Her computer system was state-of-the-art and perfect for the data she needed to store to help their clients. Just because she worked for a non-profit organization didn't mean that they scrimped on what they did for their employees. They really took care of them. As a result, the employees worked hard. Besides, Cherrelle had a real passion for what she did. She felt genuine empathy for the children and mothers, and some fathers, who came from abusive situations and needed help. She would have done this for free. Thank goodness she didn't have to.

Looking past the park, her view into downtown Houston was fantastic. Everything seemed so green and lush from her viewpoint. She loved living in the city and loved being a part of the thriving and politically active social scene of Houston. One of the best things about living in Houston, to her, was that she had no family members living there, other than a distant cousin. And she knew she could get to New Orleans by plane or car quickly if her parents or grandparents had an emergency and needed her.

Her secretary walked in with the file. Cherrelle turned her chair around with a smile.

"Thanks, Kathy. How is your day going?"

"Busy," Kathy told her. She took a seat in one of the cushioned chairs in front of her boss' desk. "You have three new cases that arrived today. All of them need extended care housing."

Cherrelle nodded. It never seemed to end. Lately, with the

economy as bad as it was, they were getting more and more hard cases. Abuse got really bad when the economy was bad. Tempers are short and patience is low when there is not enough money to support a family, and in some cases, a habit too.

"Just bring them in later. I'll look at them after lunch. I'm meeting Marcus for lunch and I don't want to be depressed when I meet with him. I love this job, but sometimes it's hard to separate my emotions from the situation. Thank goodness we're able to help so many people. If I thought we were doing no good, I think I would quit."

"I know what you mean," Kathy said. "Have you seen how many homeless people there are in the downtown parks and begging at the intersections? Some of the underpasses look like tent city, there are so many obvious signs of the homeless living there. Even though people have been instructed not to give them money, they are still out there begging. So many of them don't come to us for help, either because they don't know about us or they don't want any help. It's so sad. When I'm on my way home, I try to go the other way, just so I won't have to see them. I know it's terrible, but I can't help it."

"Don't worry about it, Kathy. We do the best we can. Now..." Cherrelle started gathering up her files. "I think I'll get busy on these so we can help someone now." Kathy stood up. She was so lucky to have a boss like Cherrelle. Kathy was also passionate about her job, almost as much as Cherrelle was.

"I'll get back to work. Call me if you need anything." She walked back into the outer office to her desk.

Cherrelle was glad she had so much to do, mainly because it took her mind off of her own problems. She hardly had time to think about anything during the day, let alone her current family situation. She made a few more phone calls to arrange housing for the family she was working with. She liked to call the shelter and do a little research on it. When she spoke to the owners of the shelter to find out whether or not there was any availability, and if she was not familiar with the property, she liked to drive by and look at it. She only placed clients in places that she considered safe and that looked clean. She glanced at her watch. It was almost time for lunch with Marcus. She had just enough time to freshen up and get to the Cajun restaurant they had chosen. She would drive by the property after lunch, then contact the family and arrange to take them over there.

At the restaurant, Marcus was sitting at a corner table, impatiently tapping his fingers against the wood. A couple of people had recognized him and asked for his autograph. He had obliged them to pass the time. He really didn't have time to wait for anyone, especially a woman. He was a well-known football player for the Houston Texans. He was only biding his time because Cherrelle was one gorgeous woman. He'd wanted to get with her the moment he saw her at a charitable function they had both attended. He had gone because it made for good publicity for local talent to be seen at such events. She was there because she really seemed to care about the cause and it looked as though she was in charge of the event. He couldn't even remember what the cause was for.

Marcus perked up when he saw Cherrelle enter the room. He looked at her from bottom to top. Long shapely legs, followed by a strong firm bottom, a tapered waist, and generous breasts made every man in the restaurant stop eating and turn to watch her walk by. When he looked into her face, she smiled at him. Long shiny coal black hair, cut just below her shoulders, luscious, smooth brown skin, full lips and beautiful big brown eyes with long, long lashes slighted tilted up in the corners were his undoing. And those dimples! He had to have her. She just hadn't given him the go ahead yet. But she would. He was confident of that. There hadn't been a woman yet who hadn't succumbed to his charm.

He stood up and pulled out her chair. Always the perfect gentleman, at least until he got what he wanted.

"Sorry I'm late," she told him, taking a seat. "I had an emergency phone call I had to take, just as I was walking out the door."

"You know I'd wait for you forever." Marcus told her with a smile. Cherrelle smiled back and picked up the menu that the waiter had put on the table in front of her. She stole a peak at him sitting across from her while she pretended to look over the menu. She ate at this restaurant a lot. It reminded her of home, so she already knew what she wanted. Cherrelle took this time as her opportunity to look at him. He was so fine, with big wide shoulders. He had the perfect football player body. His deep smoldering eyes and big sexy lips made her want to lick her own. He had dimples as well. His smooth bald head was well-groomed as usual. She bit down on her bottom lip. He was so handsome that just looking at him made her heart race. She felt very lucky to be with him, but she was very cautious when it came to a friendship with a man. She hadn't had a real relationship since Darryl. Marcus caught her looking, and winked and smiled at her. When he smiled his dimples showed boldly. She blushed prettily and looked at the menu, trying to play it off.

"Oh everything looks so good. I think I'll have the Shrimp Etouffee[4] and a side salad. What are you having?" she asked him.

Marcus laid his menu down, looked deep into Cherrelle's eyes, and licked his lips.

"What I want isn't on the menu."

Cherrelle's eyebrows rose and her eyes widened as she blushed again and looked away. But she was smiling on the inside. After a second, she looked back at him.

"Marcus, we're here for lunch and to get to know each other better, right?"

He pulled back a little. He didn't want to scare her off before he got what he wanted out of this relationship. Besides, you never know. She could be the one.

"You're right." He picked up the menu. "I think I'll have the Fried Catfish[5] with Jalapeno Cornbread[6], Dirty Rice[7], and Okra and Tomatoes[8]. They also make the best Tartar Sauce[9] I've ever tasted." He smiled showing all of his newly capped and whitened teeth. He was going to be on his best behavior for as long as it took. He sat back to enjoy the company. They spent the rest of the lunch time getting to know one another and planned another date.

[4]Shrimp Etouffee
[5]Fried Catfish
[6]Jalapeno Cornbread
[7]Dirty Rice
[8]Okra and Tomatoes
[9]Tartar Sauce

CHAPTER THREE

THAT TAKES THE CAKE

It was after lunch, and Cherrelle was lost. She had her Key Map out, but she still couldn't seem to find the shelter that she had located by phone for the family. She took out her cell phone and called the contact again.

"Ms. Smithers, I think I must be lost. I've been looking for the shelter for over an hour, and I still can't seem to find it."

"Where are you?" Ms. Smithers asked.

"I'm about two blocks east of St. Thomas University."

"Hold on, you're not too far, let me give you directions from there."

Cherrelle pulled over and wrote down the directions. "Thank you, I'll be there shortly."

She drove up to the shelter and pulled over to the side. No wonder she hadn't been able to find it. She had driven by this spot a couple of times already, and she couldn't believe her eyes. This place didn't look fit for animals, let alone humans. No, it wouldn't do. She wouldn't even need to go in.

She refused to put a family there. She'd write the name of this shelter on her not acceptable list. She would have to go back to the drawing board on this one. She drove off.

Back at the office, Cherrelle had several messages, including one from her sister, Camille. "I wonder what she wants?" Cherrelle thought out loud. She quickly dialed her sister's number hoping everyone was alright.

"Hello."

"Hi, Camille, this is Cherrelle, returning your call."

"Cherrelle, you need to call Big Mama. She's been bothering me all day about you coming to the family reunion. I told her you don't want to be bothered with that, but she keeps calling me, asking me to call you. So I did."

"And how are you doing, Camille?" Cherrelle asked dryly.

"Listen, just call your grandmother." Camille hung up.

"Oh no, she didn't just hang up on me." Cherrelle started to call her sister back and thought better of it. That would just be cause for another argument and she didn't have time to deal with that right now. Besides, she knew Camille was having problems with that husband of hers. When they weren't getting along, she seemed to be in an even worse mood. Cherrelle recognized the symptoms of abuse, but Camille wouldn't admit to anything. She wished her sister would get help. She'd talk to her later. She did decide to call her grandmother.

Big Mama answered on the first ring, like she was waiting for someone to call.

"Hello?"

"Hey, Big Mama, this is Cherrelle. You called me yesterday?"

"I did? How you doing, baby?"

Cherrelle smiled. "I'm doing good, Big Mama. How are you?"

"I'm doing fine." Bessie sat down in her armchair next to the phone. "Pawpaw could be doing better. You know the doctor put him on a special diet to level off his cholesterol. I've had to change the way I cook a little bit."

Cherrelle teased her. "Oh no, you mean, no more Sweet Potato Pie[10] or Buttermilk Pound Cake[11]?"

"No, I'll still cook whatever you all want me to, Pawpaw just can't have too much of that stuff. Which reminds me, our family reunion is coming up, and I want you to work on the committee with us since it's our turn to sponsor it next year. We thought we would get an early start."

Cherrelle began to feel uneasy. Her grandmother was like a dog with a bone. How had they gotten on that subject? She had been trying her best to avoid that particular subject. She didn't like telling her grandmother no, but in this instance, she was going to have to.

"Big Mama, I'm afraid I can't work on the committee this year. To tell you the truth, I hadn't even planned on coming."

"But why, baby?"

"You know why, Big Mama. I don't feel like dealing with all that drama. I'd rather stay peacefully at home, minding my own business, which a lot of them don't do."

"Cherrelle!! You talking about your own flesh and blood. You only get to see them once every other year. Whatever happened between you and your family members, you need to fix so you can be a part of this family again. I know that's why you moved to Houston. I know you were hurt and embarrassed, but you got to forgive and move on. You know what it says in the Bible."

"Big Mama," Cherrelle tried to cut her off. She did not want to hear what it said in the Bible right now, even though she knew her grandmother was going to tell her anyway. She hadn't been to church in a while, and even though she still believed, she was a little upset with God right now. She just wasn't ready to forgive her family members yet and if what her grandmother was going to tell her had anything to do with forgiving them, she didn't want to hear it.

Big Mama continued as if Cherrelle had not interrupted her. "Matthew 6:15 says, 'But if you do not forgive men their sins, neither will your Father forgive your sins.'"

"Big Mama, I don't want to talk about this right now."

"Cherrelle, I know you don't think you're so perfect you don't have any sins that need to be forgiven. Even holding a grudge is a sin. You're mad at your own family."

Cherrelle looked down and saw the light blinking on her extension. "Look, I have another call. I'll talk to you later."

"What about the family reunion?"

"I'll call you later, Big Mama." She hung up. Cherrelle leaned back in her chair, ignoring the blinking light and the other phone call. She knew her grandmother was right, but she wasn't ready to deal with that right now. All she could think about was the hurt she felt.

After Cherrelle had been stood up at the altar she moved to Houston. She needed to get away from her family and friends, and from the whispers and stares that she felt she was the subject of ever since she was jilted. She decided to get her Master's Degree and find a career in the city of Houston. After she had been gone almost a full year, the Carters had a family reunion. Cherrelle had been missing her family and she really thought about going but her schedule wouldn't allow her to go.

Her mother called her and asked her to attend.

"Mom, I would love to be there, but I have to work that weekend." Cherrelle crossed her fingers as she told the lie about wanting to be there. "I have to go to a conference in Atlanta and there's no one else who can take my place. I tried to talk to our cousin Charles to see if he was going, but he moved to New York. His wife Caroline is still in the city, but she seemed pretty out of it. Did you know they separated?"

"Yes, I had heard that. I really wish you could be here though, but we understand." Her mother paused, "You're not avoiding us are you?"

"No, I'm okay, really. And if I thought I could get away to be there, I would."

Her mother was satisfied.

"Alright, I'll talk to you later."

Later that month, Cherrelle was informed that the conference was cancelled, and she would be free the weekend of the family reunion. She decided she would go, but she wouldn't call anyone, she would surprise her family and just show up.

The surprise was on her.

When she first arrived at Big Mama's house, nothing looked unusual. Cars were lined up all along the block. She looked over and saw her uncles Pete and Terrence Sr. playing dominoes at a table under the tree with two of their friends, talking loud and bragging; a group of her male cousins were slapping cards, laughing loud and listening to one another lie; others were sitting around talking. Fun and laughter were everywhere. Some of the women were setting up the tables, and kids were running around playing. No one seemed to notice Cherrelle as she entered the house. Everyone inside the house was crowded around a young man and woman in the center. It looked as if the young woman was holding a baby. Cherrelle couldn't see who it was, but everyone was smiling and cooing. Cherrelle got close to the crowd and yelled, "Surprise!"

She saw her grandmother stiffen and the crowd silently parted. She looked straight into the eyes of her ex-fiancé Darryl. His wife, her first cousin Image, was holding their baby. Her family members had been smiling and gawking over Image, her new husband Darryl, and their brand new six-week old baby. She didn't notice the look of guilt on Darryl's face or the smug look on Image's face as she stared for a few seconds at the baby. He was beautiful.

The big smile that had been on Cherrelle's face melted away

and she turned and ran out of the house. Tears streamed down her face, blurring her vision. She got in her car and backed up. She almost ran over one of the kids playing in the driveway. She stopped quickly and zoomed off once the child was moved to safety.

Cherrelle was so hurt and disappointed that she drove straight back to Houston and didn't look back. She was devastated. Her family, how could they do that to her? She could think of nothing but this ultimate betrayal by her own family. Her mother and sisters, along with her grandmother and aunts, all seemed to adore Image and her little family. Cherrelle spent weeks inside her apartment and even had to call into work sick. Whenever she ventured outside, she walked around like a zombie. When she went back to work, she wasn't the same. She couldn't make herself be passionate about anything. Nothing mattered anymore. She refused to interact with or call her friends. She wouldn't call her family or accept their phone calls. Cory called her a few times, but she refused to accept his calls too. Her parents considered going to Houston to get her, but decided to let her work her way through this. Cherrelle realized she'd had a functional nervous breakdown. She was just going through the motions. She even refused to look up at the sky. Because she wouldn't allow anyone to get close to her, no one realized how bad off she really was. It wasn't so much that she was still in love with Darryl, it was the way he had treated her and the way her family had accepted him with no concern for her feelings. She stayed in this state for months.

When a person is down to her lowest point as Cherrelle was, it is either get over it or get it over with. Cherrelle decided to get over it. One day, she looked up and saw the most beautiful sunset she had ever seen. It shocked her. She realized then that she had not looked up in months. She stood staring at the sky in awe. The sky was beautiful - red, orange, yellow, blue, gray all swirled together. It was a breathtaking picture. When she saw it, she cried. That small sunset made her realize that God was still in control and that good things could still happen for her. It sounded corny in her head, but she didn't care. It gave her hope. She hadn't looked up for months because she hadn't had anything to look forward to. That sunset gave her the belief that things would get better. To her, that sunset represented hope and a beauty that was all around her. She just needed to open her eyes and look up. She knew it was cliché, but that was how she felt. It was then that she realized she was at least partially back to her old self. She decided to see a therapist to help work things out. She spent six months in therapy. That time in her life when she was hanging on to the edge by a thread helped make her stronger. She would not, and could not, stay in that deep, funky depression. Darryl was not worth it. She also realized that her depression was not so much because of Darryl, although that was a part of it, but because she believed her family had betrayed her by accepting him into the family as Image's husband after what they all knew he had done to her. She found that intolerable. That was when she decided to cut them all out of her life. She would never go to another family reunion or interact with her extended family members ever again. Therapy didn't help her with that.

When she was first jilted, Cherrelle's father was furious with Darryl. He swore he would kill him if he so much as came near Cherrelle and his family. But after a while, even he seemed to accept the marriage of Image and Darryl. He tried to explain to Cherrelle that sometimes things work out for the best and that God was still in control, but Cherrelle didn't want to hear that. She wanted Darryl and Image to have a terrible life. She wanted something bad to happen to them. In her heart of hearts she wouldn't mind if they died. She often fantasized about their deaths. That's why she had to leave town. She had to get them out of her mind. As soon as she could, Cherrelle left New Orleans and moved to Houston. She received a partial scholarship to Rice University to work on a Master's Degree in Sociology and worked full time to pay for the rest of her education. She swore she would never go back to New Orleans to live.

"Cherrelle," Kathy buzzed in on the intercom. "I'm sorry to disturb you, but you have a call on line two."

Cherrelle was glad for the interruption. It brought her out of her reverie.

"Cherrelle Elliott, may I help you?"

"Cherrelle, it's your mother."

"Oh God," Cherrelle moaned to herself. "Hello Mother." Would this day never end? She had talked to more family members today than she had all month. They must really want her at that family reunion. Her mother sounded far away.

"Cherrelle, can you hear me? Your grandmother...called me. She ...told us about the ...family reunion and we're so excited about ...it. You know your father and I are ...in Zambia right now, but we are making plans to attend. She said that you were working with her to make it a success. I know it will ...be if you girls are involved."

"Mama, I never told Big Mama that I was working with the family reunion committee." There was a long pause as the connection continued.

"Oh, but you have to. We need you. I'm actually coming ...down early so that I can help. That way ...I'll get a chance to work with my girls."

Cherrelle sighed. She was feeling trapped. "I'll think about it Mama."

Theresa smiled. She knew Cherrelle could never tell her no. After another small pause in the line her mother continued, "Good, really think about it, because your father and I want to spend time with you. I ...will...see you...then." The phone went dead. She hated talking to her parents when they were out of the country. She could never get her point across.

Traffic was horrible on her way home and Cherrelle was tired and irritable when she got there. She ate a salad and went straight to bed. She quickly fell asleep. At about 10:30, her doorbell rang incessantly. She sat straight up in bed. Her heart was beating hard and fast. Who could be at her door at this time of night? She put on her robe and went to the door. Looking through the peephole she saw that it was Marcus. He was standing at the threshold with a bottle of wine in one hand and some roses in the other.

"He must be insane," Cherrelle mumbled. "He doesn't know me like that." She cracked opened the door and peeped through the opening.

"Hi, can I come in?" he asked her, leaning against the wall holding up the gifts. She opened the door. Marcus looked her over from head to toe. Her robe parted and he saw that she had on red shorty pajamas. Her red painted toenails were curled into the carpet as if she didn't want to be seen without shoes.

"Perfect timing," Marcus thought. "She's ready for bed and so am I."

Cherrelle forced a smile to her face.

"Marcus…What are you doing here at this time of night," she paused a beat, "without calling?" She didn't invite him in.

Marcus walked in around her and gave her a peck on the cheek.

"I came to see you, baby. I was lonely tonight. Can you blame a brother for wanting to see the woman he loves?"

Cherrelle's eyebrows rose. She stood there watching him, a real attitude radiating from her face as he walked around her living area and put the wine and roses down. He turned suddenly and winked at her. Cherrelle shook her head and gave him a hesitant smile.

"You should have called first," she told him. Marcus walked towards her, slowly but surely. He reached out to put his arms around her waist, but she ducked just in time, side stepped him and moved to the other side of the sofa.

"Then I could have kept you from wasting your time," she continued. "I like you a lot, but you don't *love* me; you don't even *know* me. We need to spend a lot more time getting to know each other before you can just come by without calling or being invited."

Marcus picked up the bottle of wine he had placed on the mantle, put it on the coffee table and handed her the roses he had brought with him. He smiled his famous *I'm really gorgeous and well-known smile.*

"Can I stay for a little while?"

"No…yes," she sighed and picked up the bottle. He was already there. "Let me open the wine. But just one glass, I'm very tired and I have a long day ahead of me tomorrow."

She took it into the kitchen.

Marcus sat comfortably on the sofa. He looked around. He had never really had an opportunity to actually be inside of Cherrelle's apartment. He usually picked her up at the door, fully dressed. Tonight, she had on the sexiest little robe. He looked around some more. "What is taking her so long?"

When she came back into the room she had changed into jeans and a sweater. He looked into the kitchen. "Another door, man!"

He sat up.

"You didn't have to change on my account."

"I know," Cherrelle said, sitting down beside him. She put

the two wine glasses on the coffee table.

"I just felt it would be more appropriate if I had on clothes."

Marcus leaned back against the couch. He rubbed the back of his hand along Cherrelle's cheek.

"How was your day?" he asked her.

"Long and tiring. I had so many cases that needed shelter today. One of the cases…"

Marcus placed his finger against her lips.

"When I asked how your day was, I thought you would say, 'fine and yours?' I didn't think you would really tell me."

Cherrelle sat up and blinked. He didn't seem to notice as her eyebrows rose.

"Fine and yours?" She parroted, sitting back against the sofa and folding her arms. She didn't smile, but her dimple was showing.

"It's better now that I've had a chance to see you tonight." Marcus leaned in to kiss her, oblivious to her mood. Cherrelle turned her cheek towards him and frowned. He didn't have a clue.

"You know, Marcus. It's really getting late and I have a lot to do tomorrow." She stood up. "Thank you for coming by. I'll call you later."

Marcus stood up reluctantly and followed Cherrelle to the door.

"Can I see you tomorrow?" he asked her.

"I'll call you," she replied, opening the front door. Marcus turned toward her to say something, thought better of it and walked out. Cherrelle closed the door.

"Fine and yours?" she said to the front door. He has some nerve.

"You need to do better than that if you expect to be with me. You're fine and all, but my days of being a door mat to any man are gone." Cherrelle put the wine in the refrigerator, turned off the lights, and went back to bed.

[10] Sweet Potato Pie
[11] Buttermilk Pound Cake

CHAPTER FOUR

SWEETENING THE POT

Cherrelle had no close family near her in Houston. Sometimes that was so hard, and sometimes it was exactly what she needed. There were times though, that she just wanted to be around someone who would love her unconditionally. Then she would remind herself that this was not the case with her family. They wanted to be around her on the condition that she would acknowledge Image and Darryl as man and wife. She refused to do that. How could they expect her to just let the hurt and anger go? They hadn't been through anything like this. Her family didn't understand her, and it was unforgivable that they expected her to accept that marriage. Image stole him from under her nose. In Cherrelle's mind, she and Darryl had been practically married. And Cherrelle hated being judged. She felt she was constantly under scrutiny, and her Aunt Jerry, Image's mother, watched her like a hawk. Cherrelle knew she was laughing and talking about her behind her back. She just didn't feel like being a part of the drama, so she stayed away.

Being alone was easier. She could go home, to her quiet little apartment, and not have to deal with anyone else's drama. She could just close her door and pretend that everything in the world was perfect. She felt like that today. Free. Alone. The only other problem was that Cherrelle didn't have any real friends here. She had quite a few good acquaintances, but no one she felt she could or wanted to confide in.

On Monday, Cherrelle walked into her office and picked up her messages from her secretary. She had had a very good weekend. She had four messages. One from her mother, one from her grandmother, and one from each of her sisters. Uh! Didn't anybody in the world have any emergencies that she could help with, other than her family?

She couldn't decide who to call first. She knew she'd better do it now and get it over with. She decided to call her baby sister, Chalice. She would be the easiest of the four.

"Hi, Chalice. This is Cherrelle. You called?"

"Hey Cherrelle, how are you?" Chalice was always happy to hear from her oldest sister. Being the baby meant she had escaped a lot of the family drama. She could not understand why Cherrelle didn't want to be actively involved with the family. She was so involved she had almost married a cousin. She met him in college and hadn't known he was a relative, until she brought him home. Big Mama almost had a stroke. This was the main reason why they had started having these family reunions several years ago. You need to know who your family members are.

"Guess what?" Chalice broke into her thoughts. She had been babbling on and on about something but Cherrelle didn't hear her. She was thumbing through a report, barely listening. "We had a family reunion meeting on Saturday morning and guess who we chose as our family reunion chairperson?" Cherrelle had an eerie feeling about this. "Who?" She wasn't interested in working with them, but she still wanted to know who would be in charge of this disaster.

"We chose You!"

"What!!" Cherrelle sat up straight in her chair. Surely her sister was kidding her. "You all can't do that!"

"Yes, we can. We want you here." There was a pause as another call beeped through on her sister's line.

"Hold on Cherrelle, I have a call on the other line."

"Never mind, Chalice. I'll call you later. I have some other phone calls to make right now. Bye," Cherrelle quickly hung up and punched in her grandmother's number. It rang several times.

"Come on, pick up, pick up. Somebody be home." Usually her grandmother picked up on the first or second ring.

"Hello?" Finally!

"Big Mama, how could you?" Cherrelle whined into the phone.

"Who is this?" her grandmother wanted to know.

"I'm sorry, it's Cherrelle. I talked to Chalice today. She told me you all voted me to be the family reunion chairperson. You know I don't want to do that. I know nothing about putting on a family reunion and I don't even want to be around those people. Besides that, I'm busy and too far away." Cherrelle was angry.

"I think you would be the best person to have in charge. You know what you're doing and you're always in charge of those big fancy meetings in Houston. I figured the least you could do is plan something nice for your own family." Her grandmother had already decided on the tactic she would take. First she would try to win her with flowery words, if that didn't work, she could always try guilt.

"Big Mama, I don't have time. Most importantly, I'm too far away." Cherrelle was determined not to fall for that old trick. She had known her grandmother far too long and knew her too well.

Her grandmother sighed, "Alright, Cherrelle. We'll see if we can get someone else. We have another month before the next family reunion meeting. But everybody there voted for you. We love you. I'll talk to you later." Actually no one else wanted to do it but she didn't share that with her granddaughter.

Cherrelle grinned into the phone. She felt like she was off the hook now so she could afford to be generous. "Thank you, Big Mama. You know, if I were there, I probably would help you, since you have such confidence in me. As a matter of fact, nothing would make me happier."

"Thank you, baby. I'll talk to you later," her grandmother dejectedly hung up. She was sure she could have put the pressure on her if she had been in town. She really was too far away to be able to do anything with the family reunion committee.

Cherrelle felt so good about being able to thwart her family's plans that she decided to take herself out to lunch. She called Marcus to try to make up to him for putting him out the other night. She hadn't heard from him all weekend.

She dialed his cell phone number. He answered on the first ring.

"Well, well. If it isn't Ms. Cherrelle."

"Are you taking the time to try and rhyme, Marcus?" Cherrelle teased.

"Are you trying to make up to me for putting me out?" he asked.

"Yes, I am," she told him. "Would you like to go to lunch today? I'm in such a good mood that I want to treat you. How about it, is it a date?"

Marcus smiled into the phone and licked his lips.

"Sounds good to me, where shall we go?"

After lunch, Cherrelle had an appointment with the head of a local foundation that wanted to donate money towards the women and family shelter that Cherrelle's company was building on the outskirts of downtown. Cherrelle was in charge of the project and had done a wonderful job soliciting donations and support from companies that wanted to help. The funding for the project was almost complete. This was the last major donor who needed to give for the project. After that, the home could be built and the rest was in the hands of the builder.

She and her boss both met with the donor. After the meeting, her boss called her into her office.

"Have a seat, Cherrelle." She took a seat directly across from her boss, Ms. Tarkington.

"Cherrelle, I am so proud of you. You have done a great job on every assignment that we have given you."

Cherrelle beamed and sat up straight. "Thank you."

Lisa Tarkington smiled.

"We have another assignment for you. We want you to train some associates in another location. We want to branch out and help people in other communities as well. Homelessness and abuse don't just happen in Houston."

Cherrelle nodded.

Lisa continued, "This assignment will mean a promotion, more money, and a temporary change of location. I figure it will take about eight to twelve months to complete the project. You'll have to hire and train a new staff, find the right location, and let the community know we are there and what we are there for. You'll be in charge of fundraising and managing like you are here. You'll also have to oversee the project until the staff there is comfortable enough to operate by themselves. Do you think you're up for the challenge?"

Cherrelle smiled and nodded, "Of course."

Lisa nodded also.

"If you are successful in this endeavor you could be chosen to do the same thing all over the country until we have shelters in place for needy families everywhere."

Cherrelle sat on the edge of her chair, her eyes shining. This was so exciting. To be able to complete the project from beginning to end was her life's dream. To receive a promotion and more money, to do what she loved! She couldn't believe it.

"I'm so excited, Ms. Tarkington, I can't wait to get started. When do you want me to begin and where am I going?"

"You'll need to leave by the end of the month. We feel that April is a good month to start, the weather is good and you can get a lot done during the summer. We want to put our first branch of shelters in New Orleans. You will need to ..."

Cherrelle sat back in shock. What was going on here? Did this woman know her grandmother and had they conspired to get her to New Orleans? She knew that wasn't the case, but she felt trapped. She didn't want to go to New Orleans. But she couldn't refuse the job either. She hadn't heard anything her boss had said for the last few moments. She brought herself back to reality with a sharp shake of her head. Her boss was staring at her.

"Cherrelle, are you all right? I asked if it would be possible for you to get your affairs in order so you can be in New Orleans by the end of the month?"

"Is there somewhere else I could go to get started first and then go to New Orleans later?" she asked tentatively.

"Oh no, we've already decided the path that we want to take in this endeavor. Do you want this opportunity or not?"

Cherrelle nodded with a sigh, "I do."

Back in her office, Cherrelle paced back and forth in front of her desk. She could not believe it! Of all the places in the world she would be sent to set up the shelters, the first place had to be New Orleans. Cherrelle sat down behind her desk and swiveled her chair toward the window. She stared sightlessly outside. Should she call her grandmother and let her know she was coming to town or should she quietly come in, do the job and sneak back out? Maybe she could do what she needed to do for the company and leave before anyone in her family found out she was there. There was no reason she had to call her grandmother or any of her relatives, except that she could never go outside while she was there. She felt the panic rise in her body. What if she ran into Darryl or even Cory? She hadn't seen or talked to either of them since her farce of a wedding day. If any of the people in her parish in New Orleans who knew Cherrelle saw her in town, and told her grandmother, Big Mama would be devastated. New Orleans was a big, but small city. Maybe she could go to a remote area to take care of her business. Or maybe she could never go outside again. She took several deep breaths and closed her eyes. She tried to get back to work to take her mind off of a very difficult day.

She left her office that night, still struggling with whether or not she should call Big Mama, and let her know she was coming home.

Cherrelle decided to sublet her apartment. It didn't make sense to let it go. She still had too many months left on her lease. And she was coming back.

At home, Cherrelle called Marcus to let him know that she would be leaving town for a while.

"Can I come visit you?" he asked her.

"Of course you can. My family would be very excited and very impressed to meet you. I'm sure you'll be a big hit. Even though my family supports the New Orleans Saints, they've heard of you and would be very happy to meet you," Cherrelle assured him. As a matter of fact, Cherrelle thought to herself, he would make a perfect smoke screen for those who still pity me.

"I'll call you when I get there. I want you to meet them all. I'll talk to you later." Cherrelle hung up, formulating a plan in her mind of how to show off Marcus if it was necessary.

CHAPTER FIVE

AS EASY AS PIE

Cherrelle drove through downtown New Orleans, as usual aware of the contrasts. She saw the need with one hand and the prosperity with the other. This city had people in it who needed her. That is what she would focus on. The majority of people who actually lived in the city of New Orleans were black, so she felt she would really be giving back to her own community. She also needed to find a place to live, temporarily. It hadn't taken her long to drive down, about six hours, the roads were good, so she made good time. But she was nervous. She hadn't called her grandmother to let her know she was there. Cherrelle decided she would just land on her doorstep, and hope for the best. She knew her grandparents loved her. She just didn't know about the rest of the family.

The family reunion was a year and some months away. They used a full year for planning. They usually had it on the first weekend in September, the Labor Day weekend. That way everybody could come, and the kids could attend without missing school. Cherrelle felt she would be done with her project from work and long gone by then.

First things first. Cherrelle needed to find a place to live. She had made several calls while at home in Houston for potential rental property. She had an apartment locator working with her. Her locator, Carrie, told Cherrelle she had several prospects for her.

Cherrelle pulled over, parked, and took out her cell phone. She dialed her locator's number.

"This is Carrie, may I help you?"

"Hi, Carrie, this is Cherrelle. I was hoping you had found something that maybe I could look at today."

"Yes, I have. I found some wonderful apartments near South New Orleans."

"No," Cherrelle told her. "I told you I would prefer to live on the north side of New Orleans." To herself, she thought "and as far away from anybody that I know, especially my family and Darryl, as possible."

Cherrelle knew she was going to have to stop by and see her grandmother. The sooner she did so the better. Big Mama would be hurt if she knew she had been in town for even a day and hadn't let her know she was there.

Carrie interrupted her thoughts, "I also have some other properties you could look at. What time would you like to meet me today so you can look at them? Are you in town yet?"

"Yes, I'm here. Anytime is fine. I need something as soon as possible. I'll be staying at the Doubletree Downtown in the meantime. Although my company is paying for my housing, I want to get settled in now."

"Here's the address. We'll meet there and you can follow me to the other properties."

Cherrelle jotted down the information.

"Thanks, I'll see you in a few minutes." Cherrelle hung up and started to put her car into gear. She stopped and stared out of her window. She really should call her grandmother.

"I'm such a coward." She put the car in gear and pulled into traffic.

Big Mama was in the kitchen stirring pots. She always seemed to be cooking. Having a big family was nice, but she was always cooking. Seemed like when breakfast was over and she finished the breakfast dishes, it was time to make lunch. After doing a few chores around the house, like washing and folding clothes, or dusting, it was time to make dinner. The cycle never seemed to stop. But she enjoyed it. Family stopped by at all times during the day, because they knew there was always something cooked or being cooked around Big Mama's house.

Bessie bent down and reached into the oven to check on the crust for her sweet potato pies. The filling was cooking nicely, but she was careful to watch the crust so it wouldn't get too brown. Nothing spoiled a sweet potato pie like a crust that was too brown. She closed the oven door. A few more minutes and it would be ready. The aroma of that pie was filling the house. Bessie chuckled to herself. She could just imagine Clarence having a fit because he could smell the cinnamon, nutmeg, and other wonderful ingredients in the sweet potato pies but he couldn't have any until after dinner. She was surprised he hadn't stuck his head around the corner to try to talk her out of a slice.

Big Mama's phone rang. She picked it up on the second ring.

"Hello?" She answered.

"Hey Big Mama, what you cooking for dinner?" a strong voice boomed through the phone. It was her grandson, Terrence. He was actually one of the oldest grandchildren, but he didn't act like it. Sometimes she wondered why she had talked them out of putting him in the special class when he was in school. He could be so slow at times.

"I can't believe you called first, Terrence. Usually you just stop by."

"I'm hungry, but I'm not close. If you didn't cook something I like, I'm going on home."

Big Mama wanted to laugh out loud. He wouldn't care what it was, as long as it was cooked!

Instead she told him, "I made smothered steak[12] with koochie gravy and rice, and I cooked a big pot of mustard greens[13]. I have cornbread[14] to go with it. Oh, and I'm making some sweet potato pies."

"I'm on my way." Terrence hung up.

Big Mama chuckled and hung up the phone. "I could've told

him chitterlings[15] on rice and if it was warm, he'd be right here. That boy loves to eat, and won't offer to wash a dish. But I love him. I love all my grandchildren, and I'm glad he wants to be here." She went back into the kitchen to get her pies out of the oven, but stopped to take a seat and rest. She knew she should be finishing dinner but she needed to catch her breath. She had been so tired lately. Probably need to get some vitamins, she thought to herself.

Clarence walked in to the kitchen. Bessie got right up. She didn't want him to catch her sitting down, he'd think something was wrong and would make her go lie down.

"You 'bout ready to eat, Clarence?" Bessie asked her husband.

He sat down at the kitchen table and nodded. "I sure am. It's been a busy day, and I'm starved." Clarence worked as a security guard on a construction site. He knew he should be retiring, but he didn't want to give it up.

"Give me a few minutes, it's coming right up."

"Who was on the phone?"

Bessie looked at Clarence strangely.

"I don't know what you're talking about," she told him distractedly. Bessie hustled around in the kitchen, getting the last things together for her husband's dinner. Clarence sniffed.

"Is something burning, Bessie?"

Just that quick, she had also forgotten about the pies. She hurried to the oven. The filling had a black layer over it and the crust was a dark, dark brown. The pies were totally ruined. Her eyes filled with tears. She had been forgetting so much lately. She was probably just tired. Bessie threw the pies away, fixed Clarence's plate and decided maybe she did need to lie down for a while.

¹²Smothered steak
¹³Mustard greens
¹⁴Cornbread
¹⁵Chitterlings

CHAPTER SIX

A Spoon Full of Sugar...

The front door slammed shut. Heart racing, Camille, Cherrelle's middle sister, looked up and saw her husband enter the room. They looked at each other and turned away. Camille took some calming breaths and went back to reading her book. Byron went into the bedroom and slammed that door. Camille shook her head, "Why did he even have to come home?"

Camille got up and went into the kitchen. She stared at the closed door for a moment, looked in the freezer, took out a frozen diet dinner, and stuck it in the microwave. She had stopped cooking for him months ago. He never ate at home anyway. If he did it was with a takeout dinner that he had picked up, for himself, on the way home.

Byron walked into the kitchen. He had changed into his sweats and looked ready for a workout. He reached into the refrigerator and took a bottle of water out.

"Where are you going?" Camille asked him. Byron turned slowly and stared coldly at her.

"Why?"

"I just want to know where my husband spends his time." She said sarcastically.

"Why are you always asking me where I'm going? It's not like you care. If it's any of your business, I'm going to the gym. Don't wait up." He walked out.

"I never do," she mumbled to the closed door. "I never do."

Camille felt her hatred towards her husband grow even stronger. When he treated her like she was not worthy of his time or attention, her heart hardened a little more. Camille hadn't been happy for a long time. She knew he was still playing around as if he wasn't married. She had heard the rumors, and experienced the late nights. She had been the brunt of his anger when he realized she, Camille, was his wife. The woman he really loved had married his best friend a few years ago. Their relationship was on again, off again. When Zenobia and Carl were on the outs, he was calm, peaceful, and absent. When they patched things up and got back together, he was like a roaring bear with a sore paw. So, a lot of nights he went out to bars and nightclubs looking for the feelings that Zenobia made him feel. Bryon and Zenobia had a relationship before she married Carl but Byron got cold feet and wouldn't marry her. Zenobia, pregnant and impatient, married another man who happened to be his best friend. He just happened to be there. Right. Although Carl knew he wasn't the father of her child, he didn't care. He got the prize. He proudly showed off his family as if he had won the lottery. And just like the lottery he was always watching to make sure his dream life didn't get stolen away. Byron had not gotten over her, and he had never forgiven Carl. He continued to contact and pursue Zenobia as if they were both free to do so. A year ago someone told Camille that Zenobia had separated from her husband again. That's when the real trouble began.

The timer on the microwave beeped, and Camille took out her low calorie dinner. She wasn't fat. As a matter of fact, she was bordering on anorexic. Most of her clothes fit loosely or not at all, and the family was beginning to worry about her. She rarely ate, only to keep her energy up and to keep going another day. She didn't hang out with her friends anymore, and she didn't invite friends or family over because she never knew what type of mood Byron would be in that day. She was embarrassed that they might realize how bad her marriage was. Camille ate her dinner and went to bed.

Camille and Byron had only been married a couple of years. The first year was fine, but shortly thereafter, things had gone downhill. They might not speak, except when necessary, for months at a time. Rumor around town was that Byron was still seeing Zenobia, who some say is the mother of his child. Camille asked him about it, but of course he denied it. Camille was not satisfied and did not believe him. Every time she approached him about it, first he would become angry, then all of a sudden he would become lovey-dovey for days. Before long he would be back to his normal self - mean.

Camille remembered the exact day things had changed. They had just come in from dinner. She remembered it distinctly because there was a man at the table across from them who looked at Camille and smiled. She smiled back out of politeness and had turned away. When they got home, Byron was furious with her. He called her everything but a child of God. He threatened to hurt her if she ever left him or even looked at another man again. Then he started breaking dishes in the kitchen, dropping each plate and each glass as if it were nothing, telling her that she didn't care about anything that they had anyway, so she shouldn't care what got broken. Camille was totally stunned and horrified. She had never expected that kind of behavior from him. When his rampage ended he had the nerve to hug her and apologize for being upset, but he "loved her so much and couldn't bear to lose her". After that incident, they stopped going out. What she didn't know was that just that afternoon he had seen Zenobia out with her husband. They had been tightly wrapped up in each other's arms. She hadn't even seen him. He had been furious all day and was determined that he wouldn't lose another woman to someone else. Camille felt he was angry with her because he couldn't have Zenobia. She continued to ask him about his former relationship and had even followed him around town to see where he was going.

One of those times, she and her girlfriend Carol had been sitting around drinking late one evening. They were sitting on the floor leaning against the couch. She poured another glass of wine for both of them.

"You know, I think he's still cheating on me." Camille told Carol.

"What makes you think that?"

"I just feel it. He had a picture of Zenobia in his wallet. I saw it. He doesn't even have one of me in there." Camille took another swallow of her drink. "I bet he's with her now."

"Well, do you know where she lives?" Her friend asked, sitting up on her knees.

Camille nodded.

"Let's go see, then." She stood up.

Camille didn't move at first. She just sat there, staring into space. She debated whether or not she should do that. Did she really want to know if Byron was cheating on her? If he was there, and he saw her, what would his reaction be?

One more swallow of her drink convinced her that she did want to know. She jumped up and joined her friend who was already standing at the front door.

They drove around for a while looking for the car. Camille knew which apartment complex Zenobia lived in, she just didn't know which apartment number. When she saw his car in front of Zenobia's apartment building that evening, she was livid. Camille's first thought was to slash his tires and leave him a note to let him know she had been there, but she realized that that would be stupid. The car was in her name as well as his, and as things stood she ended up paying most of the car notes. Besides that, she would be the one having to get it fixed, so she decided against it. He would know she had done it and that would mean a fight. She left him a note letting him know that she knew where he had spent the evening. She put the note on the driver's seat inside the car and they drove away.

Dejectedly, Camille thought about what her husband contributed to the house. Byron never seemed to have enough money to help with all the bills. She really wanted to insist that he help her pay the bills, but she couldn't let the lights or water be turned off, so she would just pay them. Camille thought about it. She usually paid both of the car notes, the rent and the utility bills. Byron contributed a little, but he usually claimed he didn't have any money to spare, although he had a good job and made a good salary. When Camille checked his checkbook and cancelled checks, there were several hundred dollars written for cash. Her friends thought she was crazy to stay with him.

There were many times when Camille herself wondered why she stayed, and why she didn't just leave him. They didn't have any kids. It wasn't like that was what was keeping them together. They rarely had sex. She couldn't seem to enjoy it like she used to, and he didn't bother to ask her. She was so tense around him, and so angry with him that her body just tightened up and refused to relax. She was basically miserable. But she was afraid to leave. Where would she go? Who would want her if she left? Byron had told her she was worthless and ugly enough times that now she believed it. It was easier just to grin and bear it.

The next evening, Camille got in from work and found Byron at home. He was in deep conversation on the phone with a big stupid grin on his face. He turned around and saw Camille. "I'll call you later," he said into the phone and hung up.

Camille stood there with a frown on her face. She poked out her lip. "Who was that on the phone?" Her head went up.

"None of your business," Byron mumbled.

"This is my house, it is my business!" Her voice was going up. She didn't want to get loud, but how dare he!

"Look, I pay the bills around here just like you do, so I can talk to whoever I want to. Get away from me." Byron's eyes bulged dangerously.

Camille was so frustrated she didn't know what to do. "You are so stupid!" She turned around and went into her bedroom to change clothes. She slammed the door violently.

The door swung open so wildly that it bounced to the wall and back again. Camille looked at the hole left in the wall from the doorknob. Byron advanced on her.

"WHAT IS YOUR PROBLEM!" Camille yelled. She backed away from him. He was acting like a madman. "I'm not afraid of you," she told him backing away.

"You should be," he said as the blows started coming down on her head and back.

Camille valiantly tried to fight back, but she was much smaller at 5'2" and 115 pounds than his 6'0", 185 pounds.

Byron continued to strike her until she curled up in a ball on the floor against the wall.

He grabbed a couple of shirts from the closet and left through the front door. Camille lay curled up on the floor. She must have lain there about an hour before she had the strength to attempt to get up. She moved to get up and a sharp pain shot through her left arm. Her whole body was throbbing. She crawled to the nearest phone to call for help.

Camille called her big sister Cherrelle on her cell phone. When Cherrelle answered, Camille told her she needed her. Cherrelle could tell from her tone that it was an emergency. She told her she'd be right over. Cherrelle called Carrie, her realtor, to reschedule and headed over to Camille's.

It took Cherrelle less than ten minutes to get to Camille's house. Camille was in a state of semi-consciousness and was sitting in the dark. She didn't question how Cherrelle got there so fast. She let her in to the apartment.

Cherrelle walked in and turned on the lights. She turned to Camille.

"Oh, my God! What happened to you?" She ran towards Camille and looked into her swollen, bloody face. Camille's arm hung limply by her side.

"I think my arm is broken," Camille said dully.

"Did somebody break in? What happened?" Cherrelle wanted to hug her, but she was afraid she would hurt her.

"Byron happened."

Cherrelle was shocked and so angry she could feel her blood pressure rising through the top of her head. She knew they were having problems, but she had no idea Byron had become violent. She reached up and massaged the tender spot in the top of her head. She could feel a headache coming. "We're going straight to the hospital, no excuses. I will not take no for an answer. Get your sweater on."

Cherrelle was totally in charge. She picked up Camille's sweater that was lying on the sofa and wrapped it around her sister's shoulders.

At the hospital, Cherrelle filled out the forms and presented her sister's insurance card, while Camille sat limply in a chair in the corner of the waiting room. They admitted her right away.

After the doctor and nurses patched her up and set her arm, they put her in a private room. Camille fell asleep right away. The doctor pulled Cherrelle aside to talk to her.

"She was hurt pretty badly. Does she want to press charges?"

"I certainly hope so. If she doesn't, I will," Cherrelle told the doctor.

"As much as you probably want to, only she will be able to do that. You can't do it for her. Do you know who did it?"

Cherrelle nodded.

"Maybe you can talk her into pressing charges. I will report it. And if she wants me to, I'll give her access to her x-rays and have the nurse give her the pictures we took of her when she came in."

"Thank you, doctor. I took pictures also. Is there anything special we should do?"

"Just make sure she has plenty of rest. She will be sore for the next few days, so I've prescribed some pain killers for her." He handed Cherrelle a slip of paper with the prescription written on it. "She should be ready to leave in a couple of days. I just want to keep an eye on her right now."

When Camille awoke the next morning she was slightly groggy, and in a little pain but other than that, she seemed fine.

"Good morning," Cherrelle leaned over her sister in the hospital bed and kissed her forehead.

Camille smiled weakly and tried to hug her sister, but her broken arm was getting in the way. "Thank you for getting here so fast… By the way, how did you get here so fast?"

Cherrelle looked guilty. "Don't tell anybody yet, but I got temporarily transferred here by my company. I've only been here a couple of days, but I haven't called Big Mama yet to tell her. I want to be the one to tell her. Since I know you can't hold water, I'll tell her tomorrow. Can you hold off a couple of days?"

Camille nodded. "If you can hold off a couple of days telling them that Byron beat me up, yeah I can hold it," she told her wryly. Then she smiled. "That means you can take on your position as chairperson of the family reunion committee. Big Mama will be so happy."

"I didn't say I'd do that, I just said I would be here for a while. That's it. I'm not making any promises. Understand?"

Camille nodded.

Even though Cherrelle often got irritated with her sisters, she did love them and they had all been very close, especially when they were younger. Being the oldest sibling brought a lot of responsibility to Cherrelle. She made sure she looked out for her sisters. When they were growing up during their younger years and into their teen years, they had lived with Big Mama and PawPaw off and on.

Cherrelle's parents were community activists and well known throughout the country. If there was discrimination or any kind of injustice discovered, her parents would be there, no matter where it was. They might be gone months at a time, and her parents had always taken the girls. That was fine in the beginning, but that meant the girls would have to go to several different schools within the year. They had even been labeled 'migrant' students at one point until her mother had explained to the school about their situation. The school didn't care. The school officials told her mother that the girls would continue to be labeled migrant unless they settled down and attended one school. That's when the girls moved in with Big Mama and PawPaw for a while. Many of their relatives had laughed at them and teased them without mercy. It would be different if they had to live with their grandparents because their parents died, or even because of drugs or some sort of abuse. That would have been more acceptable than just leaving your children to make the world a better place. What about your own family? Cherrelle and her sisters got tired of defending their parents' right to leave them and soon started questioning the situation themselves, especially when they were younger. But their parents were always available. And their parents had never forgotten to call or visit their daughters on their birthdays, and they were there for every holiday that they could be.

Cherrelle's parents were famous for the civil rights improvements that they had accomplished. She was very proud of them. Now that she was older, Cherrelle understood what they had been all about. They were focused on making the world a better place for their family and for generations to come. Most importantly, she had needed them and they had been there for her. When the…the thing (the jilting) happened and her life had never been the same, they had been there to help her get through it. So had her sisters. Even though they had been much younger and didn't really understand the hurt that Cherrelle felt, they had stood by her. Every now and then, they tried to talk some sense into Cherrelle about the family, but she wasn't hearing it. That was their one disagreement. Camille and Chalice did not understand why she didn't want to be a part of the rest of the family.

"Listen, I'll come back this evening to check on you. I have quite a few things to do right now. Call me if you need me."

A nurse walked into the room to check Camille's vitals. Cherrelle squeezed her sister's hand and left.

After the nurse left, Camille went back to sleep. She was really feeling the effects of the drugs. Camille had a restless night. Her arm throbbed and the bruises on her face were so painful, she felt she wouldn't be able to sleep. The nurse came in during the night and gave her the morphine that she asked for in her IV. That caused her to have a terrible nightmare. She dreamed that Byron came into her room and leaned over her while she was sleeping. Her heart was palpitating because she couldn't get up to defend herself. In her dream she was unable to wake up.

After the nightmare, Camille slept soundly, almost forgetting about it. When she finally woke up, there was a huge vase filled with beautiful, fragrant red roses on the windowsill. She looked over and saw Byron sitting in the chair in her room. Camille panicked and tried to get up as Byron walked over to her bedside.

"Don't get up," He told her and kissed her on the forehead. "I need to talk to you…"

When he left, Camille drifted off to sleep again.

The next morning when Cherrelle went to visit her sister, her eyes went straight to the big crystal vase with two dozen long stemmed red roses sprinkled with baby's breath sitting on the windowsill.

"Who sent these?" Cherrelle asked her sister suspiciously.

Camille guiltily avoided looking in her sister's eyes as she answered. "Byron brought them. He said he was so sorry this happened and that it will never happen again. He told me he loved me! He hasn't said that in a long time. He asked me to forgive him and I did. I love him so. He had a change of heart. I know things will be different from now on." She looked tentatively up at her sister, finally meeting her gaze. Cherrelle was frowning.

"How can you say he loves you? He just beat you up! If anything, he's trying to keep you from telling the police."

Camille interrupted her, "No, I believe him. I'm going to

give him another chance."

Cherrelle asked her, "Has he ever hit you before?"

"Not like this."

"Has he ever hit you before?" Cherrelle asked again.

Camille nodded. Cherrelle threw up her hands. "Then I can't help you. If you're going to let him do this to you and run back to him every time, things will only get worse not better."

This was the type of thing she dealt with every day on her job. Cherrelle was so mad at her sister, she didn't know what to do, but against her better judgment she kept her word and didn't tell anyone what happened.

CHAPTER SEVEN

CHAMPAGNE TASTES, BEER BUDGET

Cherrelle dialed her grandmother's house. She might as well get this over with. She had been in town for three days, and one of her sisters already knew she was there. She might as well call her grandmother and let her know she was home. There was no telling who else might see her before she got a chance to tell her grandmother for herself.

The phone was lifted from the receiver. There was a pause.

"Hello?" Cherrelle asked. "Hello?" She asked again,

"Can I speak to Big Mama?"

Her grandmother's voice came across the line, "This is Big Mama. Can I help you?"

"Big Mama, this is Cherrelle. I'm calling because I'm in town, and I wanted to stop by and see you."

"That's fine, I'll be here. And I made a big pot of collard greens[16]. I know they are one of your favorites. You coming by today?"

"It'll be a little later on this afternoon, but yes, I am coming by today."

"Good, I'll see you then."

"I'll come hungry. See you later."

"Bye baby." Big Mama hung up. She started humming as she busily moved about the kitchen preparing some candied yams[17] and Sherry Chicken[18] to go with the greens and cornbread that she had already prepared.

Cherrelle's cell phone rang. It was her baby sister Chalice.

"Cherrelle, have you talked to Camille? I keep calling her house, but there is no answer. I called her job, and they told me she hasn't been in for a couple of days. You know that fool Byron won't give me any answers, even if he answers the phone. I'm worried about her."

Cherrelle didn't know what to say. She had promised her sister that she wouldn't mention what happened to her to anyone, but she knew Chalice was concerned.

"Did you try calling her on her cell phone?" Cherrelle asked her.

"Yes and it keeps rolling over to her voice mail. If we can't find her, you're going to have to come down here and help us work this out."

"I'm already here," Cherrelle told her quietly.

"What!" Chalice literally shrieked into the phone. "What are you doing here? I thought you said you wouldn't be coming down for a while."

"It's a long story. What are you doing now?"

"Nothing, come by and see me."

"I'm on my way." Letting Chalice know she was in town had effectively taken her sister's thoughts away from where Camille might be. Cherrelle hung up and looked out of her hotel window to check out the weather, grabbed a light jacket and headed towards her sister's apartment.

Before Cherrelle got there, Chalice ran around picking up things that were out of place in her apartment. Cherrelle always complained about her being messy. She looked around the living room and made sure it was straightened up enough. She finished just in time. The doorbell rang.

"Cherrelle!" Chalice hugged her sister then grabbed her and pulled her into the apartment. "I have really missed you."

"I've missed you, too." Cherrelle looked at her little sister who was dressed from head to toe as usual. She looked around. "It's so neat in here. This is not what I was expecting."

Chalice pouted, "Why are you always so critical of me?"

"I'm not criticizing you honey, but you know how this place usually looks."

Chalice folded her arms together and glared at her sister.

"You know I have a lot of stuff and it is clean now, so let's forget about it."

Cherrelle gave her sister another hug. "And I'm sorry if it seems like I'm criticizing you. I don't mean to."

Chalice rarely stayed angry, especially if she had gotten her way. She smiled at her big sister. "I forgive you. I'll make lunch and we can catch up."

Cherrelle smiled to herself. She knew her sister well. Chalice could never stay angry for long. Her motto was, life was too short to deal with stuff like that. She was too busy having a good time.

They walked into the kitchen. Chalice started pulling things out of the refrigerator in preparation to make a salad. Cherrelle sat down at the kitchen table and watched her sister.

"So, how's it been going?"

"I met a new man a few months ago," Chalice told her shyly, with a faraway look in her eyes, while she pulled the lettuce apart.

Cherrelle stopped just short of rolling her eyes. Her sister was always "meeting a new man". She was a beautiful girl, but she usually attracted the wrong type of man. Oh, they were typically good looking, but that's all they had to contribute. The last one Chalice introduced her to had possessed no personality and thought he was God's gift to women. Jerome. Her lips twisted at the thought of his name. He had really treated Chalice badly. She was such a sweet person, with such a good heart. She was just stupid when it came to men and money. She hated to call her sister stupid, but the only decent guy she had met in her life turned out to be their own cousin. Cherrelle still felt like laughing when she thought about how Big Mama looked when Chalice walked into the kitchen with that boy. At first Big Mama thought the pair were friends who found out they went to school together. They walked in holding hands, looking into each others' eyes. Big Mama looked from one to the other.

"What are you two doing?" she asked them sharply.

They looked at each other questioningly, wondering what was wrong with Big Mama. Chalice was so embarrassed. Big Mama had never met Jackson and she was acting crazy.

"This is my friend Jack. I...I'm bringing him to meet family," she told her hesitantly.

"Why would you bring your cousin to meet his own family? He should already know them." Chalice and Jackson dropped hands and stepped away from each other so fast they almost fell. It was funny then and it was still funny now, although it wasn't ever funny to Chalice or Big Mama. Big Mama sat down with Chalice and Jackson to explain how closely they were related. Cherrelle knew Chalice had really liked him, and was afraid to ask her how far their relationship had gone. Family reunions had become a necessity after that. Cherrelle composed herself and prepared to ask about the new man.

"What's he like?" she asked her sister.

"He's beautiful," Chalice sighed and grinned dreamily.

"He's not a relative is he?" Cherrelle asked her with a straight face and a twinkle in her eye.

"No, he's not," Indignation filled her voice.

"What does he do for a living?" Cherrelle wanted to know.

"Right now he's between jobs, but he has really been looking everywhere. No one will hire him because he says they are intimidated by him. He's really smart as well as handsome."

Cherrelle blinked once. She knew it, another loser.

"Really." Cherrelle could not believe how stupid her sister sounded. She was tempted to tell her about a man who doesn't work, but decided to keep her opinions to herself. "How long has he been looking?"

"Since he got to New Orleans."

It was like pulling teeth. "How long has he been in New Orleans?" Cherrelle continued.

"About two years."

"Two years! How does he support himself?"

"He lives with his mother. She takes good care of him. He stops by here a lot too," Chalice added, her eyes downcast.

"I'll bet he does. If his mom is taking care of him on one end, and you're taking care of him on the other, he'll never see the need to work. Please don't tell me that you're taking care of him too," Cherrelle continued, too mad to stop. "I'm glad he's not my son. You know I believe in tough love. If a man doesn't work, neither shall he eat. That's straight from the Bible."

"Cherrelle," her sister asked her. "I know you are not quoting the Bible. When was the last time you went to church or really read your Bible? And you talk a good game, but you don't even have a man. When was the last time you even went out? Don't talk to me about a man or the Bible. You used to pray and read the Bible all the time. I don't think you even do that anymore. It's like you're different. Harder."

Cherrelle stopped her.

"Hold on. For your information, I do have a man. His name is Marcus and he plays football for the Houston Texans. And you're right. I haven't had much motivation to read my Bible, or to pray. With all I've been through in my life, I don't think God answers my prayers. I don't even think He's listening to me."

"That's ridiculous, God answers all prayers. You just have to know how to ask Him and..."

Cherrelle stood up and interrupted her, "After all I've been through? Please. I don't want to talk about this right now. If you want me to stay, we're going to have to change the subject." She turned her back to her sister. Chalice stared at Cherrelle's back for a while. She walked around and facing her sister, took her hands. "Well, I want you to stay, so I'll change the subject. I'm sorry." She smiled slyly, "Got any ideas about the family reunion, Ms. Committee Chairwoman?"

Cherrelle rolled her eyes, "Change of subject again, please." Both of her sisters seemed to think that was so funny.

"Okay," Chalice told her as she placed the salad she had made in front of Cherrelle. "You want to see what I bought today?"

Cherrelle frowned. None of these conversations were going well. "I thought you stopped spending so much money. Remember our talk last month when you had to borrow five hundred dollars from me to pay your rent? We agreed, no more shopping sprees until you had saved some money. Do you have the money to give back to me that you borrowed?" Cherrelle was mad at her sister. She thought about what she had to give up so that she could help her sister out. This wasn't fair.

"Well no, but, I'm trying. I should have it to give back to you in a couple of months." Chalice sat down at the table and picked up her fork. She just picked at the salad. Her appetite was gone. She mumbled something in a low voice. Cherrelle couldn't understand her. She heard something about a Terry.

"What?" Cherrelle looked over at the downcast expression on her sister's face.

Chalice looked up, "I was saying I didn't spend that much, just a couple of hundred dollars on some shoes, and I bought a new suit for Terry."

"Who is Terry?" Cherrelle couldn't even dwell on the two-hundred dollar shoes right now.

"He's the guy I was telling you about. He needed a new suit for a job interview that he has coming up, and he asked me to charge it for him. He said he'll pay me back."

Cherrelle jumped up so fast, she almost knocked over the table, and bits of lettuce and tomato fell off her plate.

"Are you crazy? You hardly know this person, and you're buying clothes for him? You can barely keep up with the lifestyle that you have. You can't afford to supplement his as well. Look around, you live in an apartment that costs almost one thousand dollars a month and looks like a model home when it's clean, you wear designer clothes and shoes, and you drive a BMW. You are a sales associate at a department store for heaven's sake. Your credit cards are maxed out, and when we talked last, you were complaining because you can barely meet the minimum, let alone pay your apartment rent, car note, and furniture bills. And you have the nerve to buy somebody a suit on your credit card… Wait, I thought you said your credit cards were maxed out?"

"Ok, ok. I used the money I borrowed from you to pay down one of my credit cards so I could buy the suit. Are you happy?" Chalice covered her eyes as tears started to form in the corners.

Cherrelle felt her blood pressure hit the ceiling and her head started pounding viciously at her temples. She wanted to yell and scream at her sister, but she did the only thing she was capable of doing at the moment. She picked up her purse and walked out.

[16]*Collard Greens*
[17]*Candied Yams*
[18]*Sherry Chicken*

CHAPTER EIGHT

OUT OF THE FRYING PAN…

Cherrelle drove away from her sister's apartment fuming. She had a lot on her mind. Her sisters had so much going on in their lives it was hard for her to comprehend what they were thinking, let alone be able to help them, even though she realized they really needed help; they needed her help. Right now though, she needed to think about her own problems. She couldn't deal with what was going on with them. She was too close to the situation, and unable to make a level-headed decision based on the common sense and strategy that she was known for in Houston. Her sister was right about one thing. It had been a long time since she had read her Bible or spent time with the Lord. She knew she wasn't the only one who had ever been jilted at the altar or been betrayed by family members. Although she hadn't read her Bible in a while, she had read it so often in the past that scriptures sometimes popped up in her head. Even now, I Corinthians 10:13 came to her – "No temptation has overtaken you except such as is common to man; but God is faithful, who will not allow you to be tempted beyond what you are able, but with the temptation will also make a way of escape, that you may be able to bear it." Cherrelle sighed. She knew she wasn't the only one, but it still hurt. She shook her head to clear it and turned up the radio. Time to move on. She had only been here a few days and New Orleans was already getting to her.

Pulling up to her grandmother's house, she saw a couple of cars were already there. Cherrelle gathered up her purse and her courage and walked to the side door.

Cherrelle knocked loudly on the pine door. It was still the same bright color. It took a few seconds before the door opened. Big Mama's eyes lit up and she grabbed Cherrelle, hugging her tightly and pulling her into the house. "Cherrelle, what a surprise! What are you doing here?"

Cherrelle hugged her grandmother back, but looked at her strangely.

"Big Mama, I called you earlier today and told you I was coming," she said, when her grandmother let her go. She followed her into the kitchen. Her cousin Terrence was bent over a plate of food. "Terrence, every time I talk to Big Mama, you're over here eating. Did you move in?" she teased him.

"Did you get married?" he responded. Cherrelle almost took a step back. That was so mean. She couldn't believe he had asked her that. He knew like every body else in the family that her cousin and his sister, Image had married her ex-fiancé Darryl and that they had a couple of kids by now. She turned away. "How have you been, Big Mama?" She couldn't deal with ignorance right now.

"I been fine, baby girl. How you been?"

"I'm fine." Cherrelle decided to take the bull by the horns, "How's the family reunion planning coming?" Big Mama looked at Cherrelle with a blank look on her face.

She didn't answer her, but she asked her where she was staying, "Are you spending the night here, or are you going over to your parents' home?"

"Actually, I'm staying at a hotel, although I know I'll stop by their place. I just wanted to stop here first and say hey, give you a hug and a big kiss." Cherrelle bent over and gave her grandmother a kiss on the cheek.

"Where is PawPaw?" Cherrelle asked, heading towards the TV in the den.

"You know where to find him. In front of that TV as usual," Big Mama told her. "Go surprise him."

Cherrelle tiptoed into the room and sat in her grandmother's reclining chair in front of the television.

"Hey, Pawpaw. How are you?"

Clarence looked over at Cherrelle and his eyes lit up. He pulled himself up out of the chair, went over, and gave her a big noisy kiss on the forehead.

"I'm doing fine. What are you doing here?"

"It's a long story, but suffice it to say, I will be here a while," she smiled at her grandfather, then her expression turned serious.

"Pawpaw, does Big Mama act okay to you? She seems to be so forgetful. I called her today and told her I was in town and would be stopping in to see you all this evening. When I got here a few minutes ago, she seemed surprised to see me, like she didn't expect me."

Clarence's eyes darted toward the kitchen door. He sighed.

"She has been forgetting a lot of things lately. Earlier today she burned up a pie because she forgot she had put it in the oven. I'm worried about her." Not wanting to alarm her grandfather, Cherrelle told him Big Mama was probably tired and doing too much. He nodded and looked relieved that the answer could be as simple as that.

"I'll see you tomorrow. I love you very much." Cherrelle got up and went back towards the kitchen. She looked back at her grandfather. His eyes were already glued back to the TV. She smiled and shook her head, honored that he had stopped long enough to talk to her.

When she entered the kitchen, she noticed that Terrence had already gone, and his plate was still on the table. Now that was truly trifling. Cherrelle walked over, picked his plate up, and was about to put it in the sink.

"Put that back!" her grandmother yelled at her. Cherrelle almost dropped the plate. "I didn't tell you to move that."

"I'm sorry, Big Mama," Cherrelle moved the dirty plate back to the table. "Where did Terrence go?"

"He went home already. You want some dinner?" Just that quickly her attitude changed. Cherrelle looked at her grandmother and frowned. Maybe she hadn't let Terrence move the plate. She looked at the pots simmering on the stove. The smells of the candied yams, and Sherry Chicken, along with the greens and cornbread were too much for Cherrelle. Even though she had recently had lunch with her sister, she hadn't really been able to eat. She couldn't resist filling a plate and sitting down at the kitchen table. When she bit into the food, she knew that whatever else was going on, Big Mama had not lost her touch. The meal was delicious. After she finished, Cherrelle picked up the plates from the table, washed dishes, and prepared to leave. This time her grandmother didn't say a word about the plates or the table. Cherrelle attempted to talk to her, but she seemed to be looking for something and didn't even acknowledge her.

"I'll see you tomorrow, Big Mama," she gave her grandmother a hug. Her grandmother walked with her to the door. "You don't need to come out, Big Mama. I'm fine." Cherrelle closed the door for her grandmother and headed to her parents' house.

Once there, Cherrelle used her key to let herself in. The house was quiet. At first she thought no one was home, but she had seen at least one car in the driveway. She walked towards her parents' bedroom and found her mother sound asleep. She tiptoed out so that she would not disturb her and went upstairs to her childhood bedroom.

Cherrelle hadn't been in this room in a long time. She took a deep breath and opened the closet door. There it was. Her wedding dress was still nicely hung up in the closet. She ran her fingers down the fine silk. She had wanted to throw it away, but her mother insisted that they at least try to sell it. It had cost almost three thousand dollars! And here it was still staring her in the face reminding her of what a loser she really was. The thing was, now it didn't hurt so much to look at it. She smiled to herself, maybe she was growing up. She certainly didn't still feel like killing Darryl, although she could still put a hurting on Image. What her cousin had done was low down and dirty, and it would be a long time before Cherrelle forgave her for stealing Darryl from her. They were first cousins for heaven's sake. Image had always been spoiled and had gotten her way in every instance, and she was not about to let the man she desired get away, even if he was her cousin's fiancé.

Cherrelle slowly closed the closet door and went back downstairs. She heard her mother stirring around downstairs. Not wanting to alarm her, she called out her mother's name so that she would know someone else was in the house with her.

"Cherrelle, when did you get in? I'm so glad to see you!" her mother came up and hugged her child.

"Hi, Mom, how have you been?"

"Here, sit down," Cherrelle's mother moved the newspaper off the couch that someone had recently been reading and moved it to the coffee table. Her mother looked older and very tired. Cherrelle looked at the paper and saw that it was open to the city and community section. She smiled at her mother.

"You all are still looking out for the disadvantaged and underprivileged in the city. How is your advocacy work coming? And how was your trip?" Cherrelle's parents, Calvin and Theresa were political activists and attorneys. It all started when Calvin's cousin was killed in prison while being held for a crime the family knew he did not commit. No one came to his defense in what Calvin considered to be the correct way. Theresa, loving her husband, would do whatever he wanted her to do, whatever made him happy. Therefore, the advocacy work was perfect for them because it allowed them to work together and save those that others considered to be lost. They didn't make a lot of money, but they did a lot of good which had also made them a few enemies.

"Where's Dad?" Cherrelle asked her mother.

A shadow crossed Theresa's face, "I don't know."

"What do you mean, you don't know?" she stopped looking at the paper and rubbed her temples. This had not been a good trip.

"I know that everything is fine. He'll be okay. We are busier than ever. But you know how things are here in Louisiana since the election. Before the election, the racism was undercover. Now they are blatantly doing whatever they want to. Last week, the Klan even came out and burned several crosses in front of the homes of some community pastors. It's getting so that we don't know who to trust, and people stop trusting everyone."

"But where is Dad?"

"He went out to talk with some of the pastors a couple of days ago, and I haven't heard from him since. I know he's fine. I think I could feel it if something bad had happened to him. I could feel it."

"Oh Mom, I'm… What are we going to do?" Both women were very quiet as they thought about what could have happened to him and where he could possibly be. Tears formed in Cherrelle's eyes. She looked over at her mother who looked totally dejected and lost. Theresa thought her daughter was fooled by the smile on her face - a smile that did not reach her eyes. When Theresa saw Cherrelle looking over at her, she sat up and put on a brighter smile.

"We're going to wait and pray, that's what we are going to do. You want something to eat? It won't take me long to whip something up," Theresa started to get up, but Cherrelle stopped her.

"No, I just left Big Mama's house and you know she had food cooked. I ate over there…Mama, do you notice something different about Big Mama? Does she seem to be forgetful a lot of the time?"

Theresa nodded and said with a sad smile, "Your grandmother is in the early to mid stages of Alzheimer's. I took her to the doctor a few weeks ago and he told me then. He asked me not to say anything to her, because it is still fairly early and telling her wouldn't do any good anyway, so at this point we are just looking out for her. I haven't even told daddy yet. That's why the family reunion coming up is so important. With this disease, you never know how long we'll have with her or how fast the disease will progress."

"Oh, Mama." The day was getting worse. Cherrelle reached for a tissue as more tears formed in her eyes. She thought about how precious her grandmother had been to her all her life.

"Big Mama really wants me to be the family reunion chairperson, doesn't she?"

"Yes, more than anything else. She seems to be able to remember that," Theresa smiled.

"Then, I guess I have no choice. When is the next meeting?"

"As the chairperson, you set the time and the place."

"Anytime will do." Cherrelle sighed and sat down with her mother explaining to her the circumstances that brought her back home. She apologized for not telling her sooner.

After a while, Cherrelle got ready to leave. She hugged her mother a good, long time before she left.

"Everything's going to be alright, honey," her mom told her. She kissed her daughter's forehead and watched her walk out the door. "Wait, Cherrelle," Theresa called to her. "Where are you staying? Do you want to stay here?"

"No, I am staying at a hotel right now on the company, but I am looking for an apartment temporarily while I'm here. As a matter of fact," Cherrelle looked at her watch. "I was supposed to meet my realtor, Carrie this evening."

Theresa nodded, "I'll talk to you later."

She closed the door and sat back down next to the cordless phone by the window, so she could quickly answer the phone or see her husband when he came home. She had been sitting that way for the last two days. Theresa hadn't wanted to alarm her daughter, but she was worried. A couple of months ago the authorities had found the carcass of a man hanging from a tree. She knew the world thought lynching was over, they had thought so too at one time, but with the new leader of the Klan being wealthy and a leading political figure, the Klan had been able to get away with a lot more lately. Everybody in town knew who the leader was, he was president of one of the local banks as well, but no one was brave enough to turn him in. At the last press conference that had been held to talk about the cross burning on the preachers' lawns, her husband had been very vocal about the injustices people had to suffer at the hands of the Klan and what people should do to stop them. His speech lit up the crowd. She could still hear the cheering in her mind. She had been there, in the background, beaming with pride for her husband. He and a couple of the members of their committee met privately after the rally. Theresa had gone home to see about Big Mama. She hadn't heard from her husband since. He wasn't answering his cell phone, and he had not called her. They had a pact that they would let each other know their location at all times. She had called him several times, leaving urgent messages on his voice mail. Something definitely was not right and Theresa was most certainly worried about her husband. But she had great faith that God was watching over him. She closed her eyes and prayed that the angels of the Lord were encamped all around her husband, keeping him safe from hurt, harm, or danger.

Cherrelle hated to turn down her mother's invitation to stay at the house while she was in Louisiana, but she had experienced just about as much family as she could take right now. She needed her space. She knew her mother needed her, but it seemed as if everyone needed her. Between her sisters' problems, Big Mama's illness, and now her father missing she was worn out. What would have happened if she hadn't come home?

CHAPTER NINE
UPSETTING THE APPLE CART

It had been a long hard day at work. Darryl dusted his feet at the front door, and noticed two things upon entering. There was no smell of food cooking, and there were no little ones rushing to be picked up by their daddy. He wondered where his family was. They could set their clock by his schedule. He'd always come straight home from his job, never stopping off anywhere unless Image asked him to. He brought his paycheck home, and he never did anything that might upset her. He was a good and faithful husband, and he was as miserable as could be. Image had promised him more. He'd left Cherrelle at the altar for her. The least she could do was to try to make his life easier and better. The best thing she had ever done for him was to give him the children. Even then, he had to beg her to keep the first one. When Image found out she was pregnant, she was very upset. She did not want children, claiming they would ruin her figure. She was all set to go to the abortion clinic and "take care" of the situation. He begged her to keep the baby, letting her know that he would be responsible and care for them both for the rest of their lives. And she would never have to work again. All of a sudden, it didn't seem like such a bad deal to her. That baby was as good as an insurance policy against divorce. It got even better when she realized what a fuss people made over her and the baby. The icing on the cake was how upset Cherrelle got when she first saw them with their baby. Darryl remembered also, and he would never forget the look of pain and humiliation on Cherrelle's face when she realized that the people in the center of attention were himself and Image with their baby. That was the last time he saw her.

Darryl thought about Cherrelle often. Only because he felt guilty about the way he had treated her. She'd had no warning that he would not show up at the wedding. Image had said that it would be for the best, and he had followed that advice. Although now he realized the least he could have done was tell Cherrelle the night before. That would have spared her the humiliation and embarrassment of being left at the altar in front of friends and family. His best friend Cory talked about him bad for that. Darryl knew that his friend secretly had a crush on Cherrelle, but Darryl also knew he had been wrong.

He heard a noise outside the front door. Assuming it was his family, he rushed to open it for his wife and kids. When he opened the door, he stood face to face with Cherrelle. Behind her was a woman he did not know.

"Cherrelle," Darryl reached his hand out and took a step towards her. Cherrelle took a step back.

"Hello, Darryl," her heart was beating fast. This was terrible. "I didn't know you lived here."

"Image wanted to move to a better place for the kids." He noticed her wince when he mentioned his wife's name.

"What are you doing here?" he asked her.

"I need an apartment in town temporarily and this seemed like a nice place." Such polite words between them, Cherrelle thought, when she really wanted to scream and punch him in the chest. She turned toward the realtor.

"This is my real estate agent, Carrie Glen."

Darryl shook her hand. "I'll let you two finish then." He turned towards his door, and then quickly turned around, "Can I speak with you alone?"

Carrie opened the apartment door with her key and discreetly let herself in. The door closed with a soft click.

"I have nothing to say to you, Darryl."

"I understand that. If you would just listen to me for a few minutes? I am so sorry. I never meant to treat you badly. Things got out of hand, and I forgot about everyone and everything except my own happiness. Please forgive me."

"What is there to forgive? You embarrassed me in front of my friends and family. I became a laughing stock and example of 'what not to do to keep a man' for them. I saved myself for you. Had I known even a day before… but you didn't care. Neither did your wife." Cherrelle said wife as if it were a bad word.

"So I will never forgive you for that," she turned away from him and wrapped her arms around her body. Darryl placed his hand on Cherrelle's shoulder and turned her around to face him. At that moment, Image and her children came around the corner.

"What is going on here?" she demanded. "Cherrelle, you stay away from my man." Image got in Cherrelle's face and pointed a long-nailed, purple and pink polished finger at her. She was tempted to poke Cherrelle in the chest or scratch her eyes out, but she had just gotten her nails done.

"If I ever find out you are trying to mess with my man, you will regret it."

Darryl quickly opened the door and let his children into the apartment so they wouldn't see their mother's antics. He came back out and pulled the women apart. Cherrelle was not about to let Image treat her that way, and she would demonstrate to them how off she thought her cousin was. She had class, but she was not above letting them know what she thought about them. Darryl pulled his wife away from Cherrelle. Image threatened, "You stay away from my man. Don't ever let me see you anywhere near him."

Cherrelle laughed at her, "Your man was touching me, not the other way around. And that will be pretty hard seeing I'm going to be your new neighbor." She taunted and winked at Darryl, "See you later, neighbor." Cherrelle walked into the apartment, closed and locked the door.

Image was furious. She ran over and kicked and banged on the front door, "Come out of there, I'm not through with you!"

Darryl was embarrassed. He pulled her away from the door

and into their apartment. He had to physically carry her in. A few of the other neighbors had opened their doors and were peeking out when they heard the ruckus.

Cherrelle moved away from the door and leaned against the wall next to it. She couldn't take the beating on the door. She also couldn't believe she had told them she was moving into that apartment. The minute she saw Darryl she had known she couldn't possibly live there, but Image pushed the wrong buttons.

Cherrelle moved around like a zombie while the realtor showed off the apartment. It really was a nice place. Against her better judgment, Cherrelle signed the lease.

By the end of the week, Cherrelle was moving in. A professional moving company and her sisters helped her get moved. Well, Chalice helped, Camille's arm was still in a sling. But she was great at giving directions.

"Camille, where should I put this?" Cherrelle was asking her sister, holding up an African statue.

"Put it next to the sofa on the end table. I think it'll look great there." Camille seemed to be doing much better. Of course, she had allowed that fool of a husband of hers back into the apartment, but her spirits were up. Chalice walked back into the apartment carrying a lamp, her eyes and mouth wide open.

"You will never guess who I just saw outside!" Cherrelle didn't answer and continued to dust off the statue without looking at her sister.

"Who?" Camille asked.

"I saw Darryl and Image along with all those brats of theirs. Image saw me and rolled her eyes. I thought she was going to give me the finger she looked at me so long and hard. I was going to speak to her, but I backed off. I can not believe we are related to her. She has no class and no sense."

"What were they doing outside?" Camille asked turning to look at Cherrelle.

"Oh, didn't I tell you?" Cherrelle told them sheepishly, not looking them in the eyes, "They live across the hall from me."

Her sisters both exploded, "Are you crazy?"

"Have you lost your mind?"

"Why would you want to do that?"

"Did you know they lived there before you moved in?"

The questions were flying so fast that she didn't have a chance to answer them, and really didn't have an answer. Cherrelle just shrugged her shoulders, "It is a nice apartment and a good price, so I took it." To herself she thought, "and I know it will make Image mad to have me living here." Her sisters looked at each other sadly and shook their heads. This could only lead to trouble. They thought she had gotten over Darryl but maybe she hadn't. They hoped she wasn't going to try and get him back. What she really needed was a nice man of her own to have a relationship with. She said she had a man back home, but they didn't know if she really did, and if she had one, had he even called Cherrelle since she had been back? She hadn't mentioned it. If she didn't have a man in her life, they would work on a plan to find someone acceptable for their sister.

Camille and Chalice helped Cherrelle complete the moving process and both went back home, exhausted, but happy that the three of them were back together in the same city again. Even if it was only for a little while.

CHAPTER TEN

HAVE YOUR CAKE AND EAT IT TOO

The phone rang.

"I'd like to speak to Camille."

"This is Camille, may I help you?"

"Yeah, you can. You can let Byron go. You know he belongs to me. For some reason he is afraid to tell you, but I'm not. He is my man, and he always will be."

"Who is this?" Camille wanted to know.

"This is Zenobia, the mother of his children."

"What?" Camille sat down. "Byron doesn't have any children," she said stupidly.

"We have a son, Byron Jr. who is two years old and we have another on the way. What more can I say to you to make you understand that Byron belongs to me. Where do you think all his money is going? He takes good care of us I'm happy to say. We want you to let him go. You don't want him. He told me how you treat him. Let him go, he belongs to us."

"Why are you telling me this? Why doesn't he tell me?" Camille asked her.

"He feels sorry for you and can't bring himself to tell you, but I'm tired of waiting. Let my man go." Zenobia loudly hung up.

Tears stung Camille's eyes but she refused to cry. She would ask him outright if it was true. She had promised herself she would not listen to hearsay, so she would just wait. Camille heard the key turn in the lock in the front door and Byron walked in. She heard his beeper go off. Camille rolled her eyes. It was probably Zenobia calling him. She had to stop herself. She promised she would wait and reserve judgment until he admitted his sins. Byron walked into the den where Camille was sitting. She was lounging on the sofa pretending to read a novel, but inside she was shaking. He took his beeper out of his jeans and turned it off. He laid it on the table and turned toward Camille, "You and I need to talk."

Camille sat straight up, her heart thudding forcefully in her chest. "No kidding," she thought.

"So you're finally going to tell me?" she demanded of him.

"Tell you what?" he asked innocently enough.

"Don't play stupid. Zenobia called tonight. She told me about Byron Jr. and about the little one on the way. You are really stupid if you thought you could get away with this for so long."

"I don't know what you are talking about. I haven't talked to or seen Zenobia in months."

"Are you kidding?" Camille's voice went up an octave. "She just called here, bragging about Byron Jr. and the little one on the way!"

Byron started to deny it, looked defeated for a moment and sat down.

"Alright, I admit it. It was a mistake, but she and I do have a child together, and she claims the one she is carrying is mine."

"How could you do this to me? You know how much I wanted a child and how much I really tried to make this marriage work."

"Look, I said I was sorry. If you spent more time looking out for me and less time with your family or on yourself, we could have made it. Anyway, I'm leaving tonight. I know you're not surprised. I've tried to live this double life, but I can't do it. I really did love you when we got married, but Zenobia wouldn't leave me alone. She loved me more than you did. I tried to make you fall out of love with me, and leave, but you wouldn't. You're either stubborn or stupid, I don't know which, but I'm leaving. I thought I could treat you badly enough that you'd go, but you wouldn't leave. What's wrong with you?" He wanted to shake her.

She wanted to kill him. Her eyes glazed over and her heart hardened, "Goodbye Byron. Have a terrible life. There's no need to pack. I'll put your clothes in boxes. They'll be standing near the front door tomorrow morning. Goodbye." She held out her hand. "I'd like the keys, please."

Byron slid the keys to the house across the coffee table, walked out the front door without looking back, got into his car and drove off.

That was easy. She got an uneasy feeling. Maybe too easy.

Camille once again called her big sister Cherrelle. When Cherrelle answered, Camille told her she needed to talk to her. Cherrelle could tell from her tone that it was another emergency. She told her she'd be right over.

It took Cherrelle less than ten minutes to get to Camille's place. She let herself in. She found her sister sitting in the dark. Cherrelle turned the lights on.

"He finally left," Camille told her sister in a flat tone.

"Good," Cherrelle told her. "He wasn't any use to you anyway. Good riddance to bad rubbish." She knew how badly he had treated her sister.

"Don't get me wrong, I'm glad he's gone, but I feel so unwanted, so ugly. Everybody's going to think I can't keep a man. How do you do it?" she asked Cherrelle.

Cherrelle knew she was just feeling sorry for herself and wasn't thinking right then, so she let the comment pass.

"Camille, this is for the best. I think everyone's going to think you finally came to your senses. We all knew about Zenobia and the boy and wondered how you put up with it. She named him Byron Jr. for God's sake."

"But I didn't know, that's just it. I knew his money was going somewhere, I just didn't think it was on another family. I feel so stupid."

"Don't. He thought he was slick, but no good is going to come of this, mark my words. Zenobia knew he was married, and she continued to pursue him with no shame. You have to live your life without regretting things that have happened to you. You are a good person. It's not your fault. You have to remember that. You have to move forward."

"Thank you."

Cherrelle sat on the sofa next to her sister and held her as she cried like a baby. After a few minutes Camille dried her tears and sat up.

"Are you doing that, moving forward?" Camille asked her sister.

"This isn't about me, this is about you. Anyway, our situations are different. Our family didn't betray you in addition to your man betraying you. We will stand behind you in this."

"Thank you, Cherrelle. You always take such good care of us." Cherrelle hugged her younger sister, still taking care not to harm her injured arm.

Cherrelle had a lot of work to do. Not only did she have to begin establishing the locale for her job, but she also had to begin planning things for the family reunion and find a way to help her sisters get it together, not to mention find her father and deal with living near Darryl and his family. But she could only think about one thing at a time. If she thought about everything that was going on in her life, she felt she might go crazy. Cherrelle thought about her favorite scripture I Corinthians 10:13. She knew God wouldn't give her any more than she could handle, but she felt she must be awfully strong because she had to deal with a lot right now. If she did this family reunion for no one else, she would plan the best family reunion ever for her grandmother. She also decided she needed to go back to church and renew her dedication to the things of God. She was going to need Him, and she couldn't disrespect Him and ask Him to help her at the same time. It just didn't feel right.

Cherrelle called for her first family reunion meeting one Saturday afternoon. She had only been back about three weeks, but she knew she had a lot to do so they needed to get started. They had the first meeting at her grandparents' house.

"I'd like to call the meeting to order." Cherrelle stated, looking around at the members of her family. It looked like almost every one who lived in the city was in attendance. She glanced at Image's mother, Aunt Jerry. Cherrelle's stomach was tied up in knots. Jerry had talked about Cherrelle so badly during and after the almost-wedding fiasco. Seated next to Aunt Jerry were her mother's sisters, Aunt Fran, Aunt Betty, and Aunt Betty Lou. Only Jerry's children were able to participate in the planning of the family reunion. Fran, Betty, and Betty Lou's children were either in rehab for drugs, in jail for stealing, or had long ago stopped speaking to their mothers and other family members. Across the table from Cherrelle were her cousin Image, her crazy cousin Terrance (Image's brother), and her sisters Camille and Chalice. Her grandparents were seated in the reclining chairs near the television; her mother was seated next to her. Big Mama was smiling from ear to ear. Her Cousin Sophie and her husband Howard had not arrived yet. Their kids, who lived out of the city would be attending the family reunion, but were not involved in the planning. Cherrelle frowned when she realized there were very few men in attendance, and very few who were willing to work with the committee.

"I want to thank you all for the opportunity to be the family reunion chairperson this year," Cherrelle cleared her throat as she watched her mother's sisters glance at each other and smirk. "I have some great ideas and plans for our family reunion this year. Before we begin, I would like to begin with a prayer. PawPaw, would you lead us in prayer?"

Her grandfather stood up and began to pray. Everyone else dropped their heads.

"Dear Heavenly Father, we come before You as a family of believers who love You and want this family reunion to be a good one. We know that without You there is no peace so we ask You to be here with us as we make decisions that could make this reunion a success. Thank You for letting everyone arrive safely and we pray for those who are not here or are not able to attend. In Jesus Name we pray. Amen."

Cherrelle passed out the agenda that she had prepared for the meeting. She was going to treat it as she did her regular business meetings. Image and her mother looked at the paper in contempt.

"What do we need this for?" Image asked.

Cherrelle counted to three before answering. She really didn't have time to count to ten. She smiled politely at her cousin and spoke clearly and slowly, through clenched teeth.

"To…keep…us…on…task."

Image shot her a look that could have peeled the paint off the wall. Her grandmother intervened, "This is so good, Cherrelle. I knew you were the right one to be our chairperson. What's first?"

Cherrelle smiled at her grandmother. "First we have to decide on a theme," she began.

When the meeting was over, and everyone had gone into the kitchen for repast, Cherrelle gave a deep sigh of relief. Her mother walked up to her and hugged her.

"You did a great job. Most importantly you didn't let them get to you. I am so proud of you."

"I've dealt with worse than that in some of the meetings I attend at work. I'm not going to let some little country folks get me upset. Let's see what Big Mama made for us."

They walked into the kitchen. Big Mama had prepared a spread. She told them she wanted to try something different. There was Chicken Tetrazini[19], Seven Layer Salad[20], and raspberry tea. For dessert she had made a Pecan Pie[21].

"Oh Big Mama, you have not lost your touch," Cherrelle told her. At least not until Cherrelle bit into the pecan pie and realized that instead of sugar, Big Mama had substituted salt. She gagged and quickly placed the offending piece of pie in a napkin. She took a long drink of tea. Image snickered and Cherrelle immediately took offense.

"Did you know the pie was made with salt instead of sugar?" she hissed at her cousin, not wanting her grandmother to hear. Image simply smirked at her and turned away. Cherrelle was livid. She started to bring Image back into the argument, but her grandmother walked up and asked her how the pie was. All eyes were on her as she told her grandmother, "It was great. Can I take it back with me? It's been so long since I've had your good desserts, I really miss them." About to tell Cherrelle that she had only made one and there were only a couple of slices missing, everyone else said, all at once – "Oh no, she can have it." "No problem, Big Mama." "Okay with me". Big Mama was so pleased with the generosity of her family. She smiled indulgently and wrapped the offending dessert up for her granddaughter to take with her.

[19]*Chicken Tetrazini*
[20]*Seven Layer Salad*
[21]*Pecan pie*

CHAPTER ELEVEN

TOUGH NUT TO CRACK

The next day Cherrelle was settling into her new, temporary office. Her company had leased office space in Metairie on North Causeway Boulevard. She was very serious about making this venture successful and focused on the project all day, not giving one thought to her family or their issues. Cherrelle picked up the phone and began calling the list of possible supporters that she had compiled while still in Houston. She didn't know anyone on the list but had letters of introduction from the many philanthropists and donors she had worked with on projects back at home.

Cherrelle's cell phone rang. She glanced at the caller ID and saw that Marcus was calling. She had been in New Orleans for several weeks and this was the first time he had called. Guiltily, Cherrelle realized this was also the first time she had really thought of him, other than the times she insisted to her sisters that she had a man. Because of her guilt she was extra friendly to him.

"Hello Marcus, how are you? I've been thinking about you. How's the weather in Houston?"

Marcus sat back in the leather chair in his home office and put his feet up on the desk.

"It's fine, I know the weather is nice there as well." Marcus was becoming a little agitated. He hadn't gotten very far with her in Houston and from their stilted, weather-related conversation he could tell he had a ways to go. There was a pause. Though she was not used to manipulating others, Cherrelle knew he could come in handy making her relatives jealous so she encouraged him.

"When are you coming to New Orleans to see me?" she purred and felt like rolling her eyes at herself when she heard how she sounded.

Marcus smiled. This was more like it.

"Anytime you want me to baby. As a matter of fact, our team will be coming there pretty soon to play the Saints. Maybe we can see each other then. I really want to see you." They talked a little while longer, making small talk and vague plans as to when they would get together. When Cherrelle hung up, she picked up the phone again to check on her sister Camille. She had complained the day before about her arm still giving her trouble.

"Hey Camille, how are you?" Cherrelle was also worried about her sister because she had been so distressed when her husband Byron walked out.

"I'm okay. Better today. How are you?"

"I'm doing great…. Have you heard from Byron?"

"No, and I don't plan to either."

"Just call me if you need me," Cherrelle hung up the phone wishing there was something she could do to really help her sister. With all her training and her background she felt as if she should have been able to do something to help her, but she felt helpless in this situation herself.

Camille put the phone on the hook when her sister hung up and walked into her bedroom. She had called in sick again at work today and knew she was in danger of losing her job, but she just couldn't get it together. Knowing she was only feeling sorry for herself, she opened the closet door and looked at the emptiness of Byron's side of it. Silent tears rolled down her face as she looked. His side of the closet was as empty as she felt. He hadn't left a thing. On the surface she knew she was worthy of more than the way he had treated her, but really deep in her heart she didn't feel as if she deserved better. Camille did not realize that she was as beautiful as her older sister. She felt used and ugly and as if she deserved whatever she got. After a few minutes Camille cut off the light and curled in the middle of her bed falling fast asleep in the clothes she had been wearing for the last couple of days.

When Byron left his house he headed straight to Zenobia's. His trunk and back seat were full of his belongings. He looked at his stuff. He didn't realize that everything he owned could just about fit in his car. He couldn't believe Camille had the nerve to ask him to leave. Byron replayed their last conversation in his head. He knew he had only been as calm as he had been, and had not knocked her silly, because he knew he would be back in his own house with Camille soon enough. And because he had promised Zenobia he would be back tonight. He had to make Zenobia believe he was really trying to be with her so he could keep their relationship intact. In reality he knew he couldn't stay with her. Not to live with her. She was sexy as could be, but Zenobia was lazy and couldn't hold a job. Her apartment was a mess. Even now she depended on him for money for herself and the kids. Camille was easy to manipulate. She brought home good money and he could get her to do whatever he wanted her to do, either by flattery or threats. He had worked on her for a long time, and he was not willing to let it go. He chuckled to himself as he thought of his next plan of attack. She shouldn't get comfortable, he would be back.

Byron parked his car in front of Zenobia's apartment, grabbed a few things from the backseat and let himself into Zenobia's apartment with his key. Byron Jr. was the first to run to the door, followed by a smiling Zenobia. Byron smiled at them as he smiled to himself. Life was good.

When Cherrelle pulled into the parking lot of the apartment complex, she noticed Image and one of her kids; it looked like the oldest, coming down the walk. Cherrelle sat in her car and watched her. She wasn't in love with Darryl anymore. She was lucky she had gotten away. He seemed so weak to her now. But what she couldn't get over was how a blood relative could behave the way Image had. Cherrelle felt that she had always been nice to her cousin. They had been as close as they could be considering Image was three years younger than she was. Image had deliberately pursued Darryl. She had even attended one of Cherrelle's bridal showers and brought a gift, so it was no secret that Cherrelle and Darryl were getting married. Image had smiled in her face and then called and contacted Darryl as often and in as many ways as possible. When Image walked closer to where Cherrelle had parked, Cherrelle opened her car door and stepped out. Image stopped in her tracks. Cherrelle could see her attitude change immediately and an ugly scowl covered her face. She really could have been pretty, but all Cherrelle ever saw on her face was a scowl and a frown whenever she looked at her. Image walked over to her.

"Why did you move back here?" She didn't seem to mind that her child was watching and intently listening. He stuck his thumb in his mouth, eyes looking from one to the other. If she didn't care, Cherrelle wouldn't care either.

"Why did you go after Darryl?" Cherrelle demanded.

"You need to go back where you came from. He never wanted you. Why do you think it was so easy for me to get him? He adores me, and he tells me that everyday."

Cherrelle laughed at her. "Then why are you so worried about me? You need to be concerned about your own house and stop worrying about me, sister. You were easy, plain and simple. I wanted to wait until after we got married to have sex, and you could care less. That is what really happened. If I were you, I would keep my eyes on Darryl. He really wants me to forgive him, and I just might find a way to do it." She taunted with a wink as she sashayed away.

Image was furious and fit to be tied. She was so tempted to go after Cherrelle and tell her more of what she thought of her, but she looked down and saw her son was taking in every word. She stormed away and went to get her mail, dragging her son behind her.

Cherrelle's steps slowed as she rounded the corner. Her heart was extremely heavy. She knew she was wrong speaking to Image like that. The past was the past and Image was now Darryl's wife. She had to respect that, no matter how angry Image made her feel, she had to figure out a way to forgive her and treat her better. When she felt up to it, she would apologize to Darryl and Image. She didn't know how she would get through the next family reunion meeting. She could hardly wait to talk to her mother. Image was probably calling her own mother now, complaining to her about Cherrelle and how mean she had been to her. Cherrelle knew her mother would have plenty to say to her about the importance of family and treating one another with love. Cherrelle could hardly wait.

"Cherrelle, how could you!" Her mother was so embarrassed. Theresa continued on her rampage, "Image is Darryl's wife now.

It does you no good to aggravate her. I know she wronged you in the past, but that is over."

Cherrelle rolled her eyes as she listened to her mother rant and rave at her over the phone. When she was done Cherrelle attempted to defend herself, "She approached me. I was not going to say a word to her but she attacked me first!"

"Cherrelle," her mother warned. "Have I taught you nothing? What happened to the sweet girl I raised?"

Cherrelle was genuinely contrite.

"I'm sorry Mom. I will apologize to her. I know with us planning the family reunion we all need to get along to make it successful. It won't happen again."

Her mother sighed, "I know you've had a hard time, but it's not worth the fight. That time of your life is over. You have to let it go. You won't be able to go forward if you don't forgive them and move on. I love you, your father and sisters love you. Let it go."

Cherrelle was quiet.

"Cherrelle, are you alright?"

"Yes, I'll be okay. I really have gotten over Darryl, and I said earlier that I would apologize to them both, but actually, I was thinking about Daddy. Have you heard from him? It's been weeks…I'm scared, Mama. What if something really terrible happened to him? It's not like him to be missing for so long."

"We've gone through worse," Theresa assured her daughter. "Everything will be fine."

"Thanks. It makes me feel better to know you have been

through this before and everything turned out alright," Cherrelle told her mother quietly.

Her mother half-smiled to herself, "You'll be fine. We'll be fine. Talk to you later."

After hanging up the phone Theresa went back to her post by the window.

The next morning Theresa contacted Stan Wallace, one of the attorneys who worked with them on many of their cases. Stan was also a practicing private investigator. He picked up the phone on the first ring.

"Stan, this is Theresa. Have you heard from Calvin? He left weeks ago. At first I thought he was laying low because of the problems in the Ninth Ward, but he hasn't called me or tried to contact me, and he won't answer his cell phone. We've been in situations like this before where we could not contact one another, but it has never gone on this long. Can you help me find him?"

"Of course I'll help you, Theresa. Nobody told me."

"Nobody knows, except very close family. We are trying to keep this low key because of the situation we are…were working on. I don't know what to do; I just know we need to find him."

"I'll do what I can. I'll keep in touch."

Stan hung up the phone with Theresa and dialed another number, "We're in business. She just called and confirmed that Calvin is missing. I'll keep in touch." The phone call ended and Stan turned toward his computer.

CHAPTER TWELVE

NOT LIVING BY BREAD ALONE

Cherrelle opened her apartment door to the frowning face of her younger sister.

"Cherrelle, you have not spent any time with me," Chalice complained. Cherrelle smiled to herself, but she was so distracted she really wasn't listening to her younger sister like she should have. She moved away from the door, "Come in."

Chalice followed her.

"You've spent time with Mama and time with Camille, but none with me," she continued to whine.

"Chalice, do you have any idea of what you are talking about? With Dad missing and Camille in and out of the hospital, I really haven't had a lot of time to think about hanging out." She really wanted to tell her that she didn't care about anything else right now except getting those two issues resolved. Cherrelle walked into the kitchen with Chalice right on her heels.

"You want something to eat?" Cherrelle pulled the fresh Chicken Salad[22] from the refrigerator. She pulled a loaf of wheat bread and some wheat and regular crackers from the shelf. She also put a fresh Marinated Cucumber and Tomato Salad[23] and some potato chips on the table. Chalice could feel her mouth begin to water.

"Would you prefer iced tea or a glass of white wine?" Cherrelle asked her sister. After a while, Cherrelle noticed her sister had been relatively quiet since entering the apartment. After they fixed their plates, Cherrelle and Chalice sat cross legged on the sofa in the living room, facing each other.

"You have my full attention. Talk." Cherrelle took a bite of her sandwich.

"What do you mean Dad is missing? Mom didn't tell me that!" Chalice looked hurt.

"Chalice, when was the last time you talked to Mom, or Dad either for that matter?"

"I guess it's been a couple of weeks. I have been busy. I met a new man."

Cherrelle tried her best to keep from rolling her eyes. How many times had she heard that from her sister?

"You know the Houston football team is playing next week, and several of the players have come into town early to relax and enjoy our city. I met one of them last week at the hotel they are staying in. He is gorgeous." Chalice leaned back with her eyes closed and a dreamy look on her face. Cherrelle smiled at her sister and shook her head. It looked like Chalice was in love again.

"I know someone who plays for the Houston Texans. What is this gorgeous Houston football player's name?" That reminded her. She should call Marcus and find out when he would be coming to New Orleans.

"What else do you know about him? He's not a relative is he?" Cherrelle teased her sister.

Chalice pouted. They just would not let her earlier mistake go.

"No, his name is Marcus, and he is a linebacker. That's all I know." She looked sheepishly at her sister, knowing that she knew nothing else about someone she had spent the past week with. When she looked at her sister the look of shock on Cherrelle's face was terrible.

"Cherrelle, are you alright? What's wrong?" Chalice was alarmed. She stood up prepared to go get help if she needed to. Her sister had turned a very strange shade of green.

"Is his last name Williams? Marcus Williams?"

"Yes, I think so."

"You think so? Did you sleep with him?" Cherrelle knew her sister did not have the same beliefs that she had about sex outside of marriage. After all these years before and after Darryl, she had not had that type of relationship with a man. She was simply waiting for the right one. Chalice went after the one right now. No offense to her sister, of course.

"We spent the whole week together, so of course I slept with him!" She seemed shocked that Cherrelle would think anything else. She was still hovering over her sister. Cherrelle looked up at her sister and told her to have a seat.

"I guess I should not have ignored you. Remember when I told you about this guy I was seeing in Houston, well his name is Marcus. Marcus Williams. I was dating the man you spent the last few days with." Cherrelle looked at her sister strangely.

"Come to think of it, I told you all about him. I even told you his name."

"Aw girl, you know I wasn't listening to you about that. Camille and I thought you were making him up."

"You didn't think to call and ask me when you met a Houston football player named Marcus?"

"No, I didn't." All of a sudden she was contrite. Tears filled Chalice's eyes, "I am so sorry. I would never have talked to him if I thought he was anything to you." She seemed very sorry.

"You are right. He doesn't mean anything to me, not really. It just bothers me that people are able to take my relationships away from me so easily, first Image with Darryl and now you with Marcus." Cherrelle looked her sister in the eye.

"Do you love him?"

When Cherrelle asked her sister that question she realized that she was not now nor ever had been in love with Marcus. She was flattered by the attention he had given her, and shocked by this turn of events, but she did not love him.

"Yes, I love him."

Cherrelle leaned over and hugged her sister.

"Then I wish you good luck with him… By the way, what

happened to Terry? I thought he was the love of your life?"

Chalice shrugged, "He found a job. I haven't heard from him since."

Cherrelle's mouth fell open.

"Are you kidding?" Cherrelle had a hard time keeping a straight face.

"Nope. It's okay. Marcus more than made up for the loss." She looked at her watch. "Look, I have to go. I have a date tonight, and I need time to get ready for it." Chalice hugged her sister for being so understanding, grabbed her purse and keys, and quickly departed.

Cherrelle made a few phone calls for the family reunion, getting quotes to bring before the family reunion committee. After a couple of hours she stretched. She didn't realize she had been working on it for so long. This family reunion planning thing was kind of fun. She was actually enjoying herself. Cherrelle made a note to go to church with her mom and grandparents tomorrow and check on her grandmother after church. She checked the kitchen to make sure she had put all the food away and started getting ready for bed. Her cell phone rang. She looked at the bedside clock. It was after ten. Who would be calling her at this time of night? She looked at the caller information on the cell. Marcus!

Her first thought was – "I thought Chalice had a date with him tonight." Cherrelle allowed the phone to ring a couple more times, and then she flipped it open.

"Hello Marcus, how are you?" She was about to let him know that the woman he was seeing was her baby sister when he interrupted.

"I have missed you so much," he told her in his deepest, sexiest voice. "I just got in town today and I want…no I need to see you."

"Marcus."

"I want to hold you and just breathe your air."

"Marcus."

"They say distance makes the heart grow fonder, and I now know that saying is true. When can I see you?"

Cherrelle was speechless, almost. Her mind was in a whirl. She could not believe his nerve. The thing was, if her sister hadn't stopped by earlier that day talking about him, she never would have known. He could have played them both for as long as he wanted. She wanted to bust him, quick, fast, and in a hurry. If she had had blood pressure problems, she would be able to feel the pressure in the top of her head by now.

"Can we meet tomorrow after church?" she asked in her sweetest voice. "I was going by to visit my grandmother tomorrow. Maybe you can come with me."

"Can I come over now? We can leave tomorrow from your place."

"No, I am exhausted. I have had a very busy day. My grandparents would love to meet you, though. My grandfather was saying just the other day about what a great player you are." She could see his head swelling through the phone.

"Really? Well in that case, we cannot disappoint the oldies, can we?"

"Oldies?" she repeated in her head.

"No, we can't do that. I'll call you tomorrow and we can arrange to meet, or I'll give you the directions to go straight there. Where are you staying?"

He gave the name of the hotel Chalice had mentioned in her conversation.

"Okay, I'll talk to you tomorrow. Goodnight."

"Goodnight baby. Spend your time dreaming of me." He made a kissing sound through the phone. Cherrelle looked at her cell phone like she had never seen it before, frowned and clicked it off.

Cherrelle dialed her sister's cell phone. Chalice picked it up on the first ring.

"Hey girl, what are you up to?" Cherrelle could hear what sounded like club noise in the background.

"I told you I have a date tonight. What's up?"

"What happened to Marcus, I thought you were so in love with him?" Cherrelle was confused.

"I am out with Marcus. He stepped outside to make an important phone call. Here he comes now. I've got to go."

"Chalice, whatever you do, do not mention that I am your sister or that this is me on the phone. Oh, and Mama and I are having dinner tomorrow after church at Big Mama's house. Can you come?"

"Sure, I'll be there. See you tomorrow."

Cherrelle hung up her phone.

"Well, well...tomorrow should be very interesting." Cherrelle was eager to see how Marcus was going to get out of this one. She hated being so deceptive, but her sister needed to see him for who he really was.

The next morning Cherrelle got up early and called her mother.

"Mom, what time are you leaving for church? I wanted to see if I could go with you and if we could ride together." Her mother was so pleased. She knew that Cherrelle had fallen away from the close relationship with God that she previously had. After making arrangements to meet at her mom's house, Cherrelle began to get ready for church.

Standing in the mirror, Cherrelle realized she had never looked so good. She had pulled her most flattering outfit from her closet, along with making sure that her hair and makeup were flawless. She could not wait for church to be over so she could confront Marcus and let her sister know what he was really like. She hated doing it at her grandmother's house, especially if her other family members would be there, but that couldn't be helped.

Cherrelle hurried to her parents' home realizing they would be late if she didn't get a move on.

When she and her mother got to the church, it immediately brought back memories, not all of them good ones. She shook her head and followed her mom to their seats. She looked around the sanctuary. Nothing about the church had changed since she had been there last. The same pianist sat down to begin the praise and worship time. Then she noticed more people filing into the musicians area. A drummer sat down at a set of drums. A couple of young men entered and picked up their horned instruments. Another musician sat down at what looked like an electric piano. She realized things had changed. The praise and worship team entered the stage and the congregation stood as the signal that church had begun.

Cherrelle was really enjoying the praise and worship time. Service went smoothly and the pastor entered to begin his message. He asked the congregation to open their Bibles to Matthew 6:14 and read, "For if ye forgive men their trespasses, your heavenly Father will also forgive you." He talked about how important it was for people to forgive one another, and how God will not forgive your sins if you are unwilling to forgive others. He also asked the congregation to turn to Ephesians 4:32 which declares, "And be ye kind one to another, tenderhearted, forgiving one another, even as God for Christ's sake hath forgiven you." Cherrelle was getting very uncomfortable. She thought about how much she actually hated Image and what she was planning to do to Marcus. She started fidgeting in her seat. She really needed to get away. Maybe she could excuse herself and go to the Ladies' Room. Before she could get away, his final statement stopped her before she could move. "When others sin against us, there is no doubt in our own mind that they owe for what they have done. But rather than make them pay, we need to let it go. For when we don't let it go, we end up running away, leaving relationships in search of things or other people or places that we think will make us happy. But just like looking for love in all the wrong places, we never quite find what we are looking for, and we end up sad and discouraged. So after we have forgiven those who have done us wrong, we need to act like we forgive them, treating them right and acting in love. As it states in 1 Peter 3:9 - Not rendering evil for evil, or railing for railing: but contrariwise blessing." Cherrelle was nearly in tears. "Why had she come today?" she asked herself. She had been very close to God in her earlier years, but with the bitterness and inability to forgive that had been in her heart, she had stayed away from church and had not talked to God in a long while. She realized after hearing the sermon that the hard shell around her heart had cracked, just a little. Maybe she and God would start having more conversations. It looked like He was trying to get her attention. This was much better than therapy.

After church, Cherrelle and her mom were making their way out of the sanctuary. Her mom was looking for Big Mama and PawPaw. Cherrelle was looking around for them as well when she bumped into a solid wall of chest, and he reached out to keep her from losing her balance.

"Cory!" Cherrelle looked up at him. She was so pleased to see him. She hadn't seen him since her 'jilting'. Although he had been the one to bring her the bad news, he had been very kind to her then and always.

"Cherrelle!" He gave her a big hug. She was enveloped in his arms. He smelled so good. He held her away from him and looked straight into her eyes.

"You look great. I heard you were in town, but I didn't know how to reach you other than coming over to knock on your door. How have you been?" He asked with such kindness she wanted to tear up. She was already feeling full because of the message she'd just heard. She felt like the message had been delivered just for her. Cherrelle realized only Darryl could have told him she was back in town, and that thought made her stronger. She cleared her throat.

"I've been fine, Cory. You look great as well." When he dropped his hands from her arms she felt the cold. She looked up at him. He still had those eyes, and he was still as handsome as ever. She tried to keep from looking him up and down, but just looking at his gorgeous face made her weak in the knees. She looked up at him again…those eyes, that mouth. Her eyes roamed over his entire face, and she took him in as if she wouldn't have another chance to see him. Her mother walked up. Neither Cherrelle nor Cory noticed her approach as they continued to stare at one another. Cherrelle felt a strange sensation curling in her stomach. Her heart raced with an urgency she didn't think she had ever felt before. She smiled softly at Cory, her dimple showing. He smiled back. Her mother watched the exchange with one eyebrow raised. She cleared her throat and tried to keep from smiling. Even with all the noise in the outer area of the church where people were greeting one another, Cory and Cherrelle heard none of it. Her mother gently called her name and touched Cherrelle on the arm. She turned to her mother and smiled broadly,

"Mom, you remember Cory? He's a childhood friend of mine and one of Darryl's best friends."

"Of course," Theresa reached up to hug Cory. He leaned over and kissed her on the cheek.

"How are you, Mrs. Elliot?" Cory inquired. They exchanged pleasantries, and then Cherrelle and her mother turned to go.

"Cherrelle," Cory called. "Can I call you sometime? Maybe we can go out to dinner or something."

Again, that fluttering in the stomach.

"Of course you can," she smiled. Cherrelle reached in her purse and pulled out a card. "Here's a number where you can reach me at work. My cell number is there as well." She handed him the card and hurried to catch up with her mother.

"Well, well," her mother teased her. "He certainly is as handsome as ever."

Cherrelle smiled to herself and nodded, looking forward to his call.

Cherrelle felt bad about what she was about to do to her sister, but she knew she had to do it to keep Marcus from getting away with playing her. When she and her mother arrived back at Big Mama's house, Cherrelle went into a back bedroom and dialed

Marcus's number. It rang several times. On the fourth ring, he picked up.

"Hello?" He sounded…distracted.

"Hi Marcus, are we still on for lunch?"

"Um, no. I can't today." He coughed to cover a moan. Then he covered the phone with his hand. "I'm on the phone," he whispered to the woman lying beside him. She rolled her eyes and kept kissing his throat.

"I'll call you later," he hung up quickly.

Cherrelle could tell he was with someone else, and she quickly called her sister. She answered on the first ring.

"Hey Chalice, where are you?"

"I'm on my way to Big Mama's. Didn't you say dinner was after church? You know I am not about to turn down a home-cooked meal. I'll be there in five minutes."

Cherrelle clicked off her cell phone and wondered who Marcus was with. She had been sure it was Chalice. Now she wasn't sure what was going on.

Marcus rolled over and looked at the beautiful young woman lying next to him in the bed. She had just shown up at his door. He was not about to turn away a gift horse.

She could not believe her luck. She could see herself living this life. She knew this was the kind of life she was meant for. She was meant to live in luxury hotels and be able to buy whatever she wanted. She was still young and pretty, and even though she was married that could be easily remedied. When her girlfriends told her about the parties that were going on at the hotel she just had to see for herself. Image put her hand on Marcus's arm to get his attention, and with a smile pulled him down for a kiss.

[22] Chicken Salad
[23] Marinated Cucumber and Tomato Salad

CHAPTER THIRTEEN

A PIECE OF CAKE

The next day, Cory called Cherrelle. He was very nervous. He knew he had felt something special happening between them the day before, but he didn't know how she would react to him calling her to ask her out on a date so soon. After all, in her mind, he was a friend from her past. She had referred to him as her "childhood friend" to her mother. He rubbed his damp palms down the sides of his jeans. Other than at church on Sunday, he had not talked to her since he last saw her lying in bed in her slip after he helped her out of her wedding dress. It seemed like it was so long ago. It had only been a few years, about five or six, but he had never forgotten how she looked or even how she smelled. She always wore this particular scent that reminded him of her. Even if he smelled the same perfume on someone else, he thought of Cherrelle. He never imagined he would have an opportunity to know her on this level, and he was nervous. Women went out of their way to get to know him, and he had been in his share of relationships, but Cherrelle was different. She was his fantasy. He felt as if he had loved her for his whole life. When she broke up with Darryl, he thought he would give her some time and get to know her better when she was ready, but she had virtually disappeared off the face of the earth. Her family would not share any information about where she was or what she was doing. He was able to get her number a while back, and he left a couple of messages, but she never returned the call. Now it seemed she was back, for a while at least, and he was going to take a chance on getting to know her better.

At work the next day, Cherrelle's cell phone was ringing. She reached in her desk drawer and pulled it out. She didn't recognize the number.

"Hello, may I help you?" she asked.

"Hello Cherrelle, this is Cory. How are you?"

Cherrelle sat up. Her pulse picked up.

"I'm good. How are you?" She hoped he couldn't hear the big smile on her face or the excitement she felt.

"I'm doing well also. I told you I would call you soon. Is now a good time?"

"Now is fine. I didn't think I'd hear from you today. How is your family?"

"Everyone is fine. Actually, I called to see if you would go out to dinner with me tonight so that we can catch up on old times. Is tonight okay with you?"

Cherrelle's heart dropped. She had a planned family reunion

meeting this evening. As the committee chairperson there was no way she could miss a meeting she had set up.

"No, I'm sorry, this evening is not a good time for me. I have a family reunion meeting." There was a long pause. When Cory didn't say anything she spoke up.

"How about tomorrow evening? Is that fine with you?"

Cory let out an internal sigh of relief. She wasn't blowing him off. For a minute he thought she had just been polite on Sunday and didn't really want to see him. Now he realized she only had a previous engagement.

"Tomorrow evening is fine." They talked for a few more minutes and decided on a place to meet.

"See you tomorrow." Cory hung up the phone with a big smile on his face, whistling as he went back to work.

Cherrelle hung up the phone with a big smile on her face, humming as she went back to work.

"I call this meeting to order," Cherrelle stated to get everyone's attention. She had begun to be impatient with the inane chit-chat that seemed to accompany all of their family reunion committee meetings. One by one her relatives began to quiet themselves, promising each other to get back to where they left off when the meeting was over.

"We will start with old business," Cherrelle told the group. "The first thing we will finish is the venue."

Terrence snickered and whispered to his sister about Cherrelle always using big words they didn't understand. Cherrelle ignored him.

"Chalice, as the site chair, have you found a place for us to have the reunion?"

Chalice started going through the papers she had brought with her. She laid several sheets on the table in front of her and passed the same information to Cherrelle.

"I found quite a few places. We decided last time that we needed to find a place that had lots of fun things for the children to do, as well as a place that could provide entertainment for the adults. We all know that if the kids aren't happy, the adults will be miserable," she said, glancing down the table towards Image.

"Anyway," Chalice continued. "We have three choices, a hotel near the waterpark, another choice is a hotel with a casino near a park with a covered pavilion, and this one…" Chalice pulled out the next sheet, "…is near an amusement park. If we choose to go to the waterpark or the amusement park there will be an extra cost to the families. If we go to the public park, this will force us to come up with activities that we will have to participate in with each other and the kids. It will force us to spend time together."

"Thought that was the purpose of family reunions," Aunt Emma chimed in.

"It is. The only problem with the hotel near the park is the casino. You know our family from out of town. They will spend more time at the tables and slots than at the family activities, if not during the day, then most certainly at night. If they spend half the night in the casinos, they'll be too tired to participate the next day."

Cousin Elbert spoke up, "That's their business. I think they will do both. Yeah, they'll be tired when they leave, but they sure will say they had a good time. The park will allow us to have fun activities for the kids and adults. I vote for the park."

There was a general murmur of agreement.

"If they want to go to the water or amusement park they can go after the reunion is over. I vote for the park too," someone else said.

"Okay, okay. There seems to be a consensus. All in favor of holding our family reunion activities at the hotel near the park, raise your hand," Cherrelle told the group. All hands went up.

"It is unanimous, motion carried. We will hold our family reunion at this hotel. Chalice did you get hotel room prices? I guess we should have asked that before we voted. Also, how much will it cost to rent the park? You mentioned that it had a covered pavilion, can we get that?"

"I did get room prices. They were very reasonable. And they also guaranteed us a discount on the banquet room based on the number of rooms that we book," Chalice said as she passed around to the group the price of the hotel rooms. Each person looked at the room prices and nodded as they passed the list around.

Chalice continued, "I told them we would need the banquet room on Friday night, Saturday night, and Sunday afternoon. Is that fine with you all?" Everyone nodded.

"I did look into getting the pavilion, and it is available, but I will need a fifty dollar deposit as soon as possible if we are serious about holding it. I know it's early now, but that is a popular park, and it will be taken soon if we don't jump on it. I figure we will need it on Saturday from noon until at least four or five. It costs twenty-five dollars per hour, and we will be able to get our deposit back. What do you all think?"

There was a general discussion among the group as to when the pavilion should be booked. They finally came to a consensus, and the motion was made and seconded. Cherrelle asked the group, "All in favor of having the pavilion from ten to four and putting up the fifty dollar deposit, raise your hand." Again all hands went up. "Motion carried. We will get you a deposit check today. You did a great job Chalice." Her sister beamed.

Cherrelle was pleased. This meeting was going very smoothly. She had not been looking forward to meeting with her relatives, but she was enjoying it. She was in her element - arranging events for large groups.

"Now the hard part. We need to decide on the cost for the family reunion."

"I think it should be the same cost as it was last year," Aunt Jerry, Image's mother piped in. Her posse' nodded, backing her up.

"Alright, Aunt Jerry," Cherrelle began. She pulled out a note pad and a calculator. "This is how much you all charged last time, and this is how many people attended and paid." Cherrelle had come prepared for this argument. She wrote the figures on the note pad and used the calculator to add the figures. "If we add the cost of the banquet rooms, the covered pavilion at the park, and food, drinks, paper plates, cups, napkins, and utensils based on costs from last time, this is how much we will spend." Again using the note pad and calculator, Cherrelle added the figures. "I have a few questions. How many people paid last time? How many people attended without paying?" The room was silent as they looked uncomfortably from one to another. Cherrelle persisted, "Are we going to turn them, our 'family' away if they don't pay? Also how many people make up a family? I won't use any real names, but let's say 'Bay Bay' and her six kids live with her parents. Does she pay separately or are they all a part of her mama's household? Also, did you run out of food or supplies last time? How many times did someone have to go into their pockets or make a 'run' to the store to take up the slack? Did you use all of the money paid in or was there any left? We have to look into all of this before we decide how much we will charge this time. I know it is uncomfortable but we have to face facts. Based on what I calculated, we would be about three hundred and fifty dollars short. Can we afford to come up short? We need to fix the cost based on reality rather than based on what we have done before."

Cherrelle took a deep breath and went even further, "I think people need to take responsibility for themselves and their families. I know this is a family reunion, but it is also like a business when it comes to money. I think we should have those who pay receive a wrist band to show they have paid. That way, they can eat at every occasion. In order to allow family who did not pay to see one another, they can attend events, but they should not be allowed to eat."

"That's not fair. What if they cannot afford to pay!" Aunt Jerry yelled.

Cherrelle turned to her with a tight smile. It did not reach her eyes. "Then some *kind* family member who loves them very much can pay their way. Based on our calculations I propose that we raise the fee by five dollars per family." She looked around the table. Most people were nodding. "All in favor of raising the fee by five dollars per family, raise your hand." Eleven hands were raised. "All opposed?" Three hands went up. "Motion carried. All in favor of those who paid wearing wrist bands to show they paid... raise your hands." Eight hands were raised. "All opposed?" Six hands went up. "Motion carried. We will add an additional five dollars to the cost, and those who pay will wear wrist bands." Cherrelle breathed a sigh of relief. In a way she had railroaded them to get her way, but it had to be done. She would rather have plenty of food and drinks where people would only remember that the reunion committee was well prepared, rather than to appease a few people and run out of supplies because there was not enough money. There were some tense moments there, but it went smoother than she thought.

"We will meet again on Sunday evening in two weeks. Tabitha, could you draft a letter for family members to provide details about the family reunion? You are such a good writer. Make sure you tell them how excited we are to see them and include details. Call me if you need help. Anything else?" Cherrelle turned towards the group.

"Meeting adjourned."

Cherrelle was in a hurry to leave. She felt she had to get out of there. As she was turning to leave she noticed that her sister Camille had not said a word the entire meeting. She was walking over to give her a hug when she was intercepted by Aunt Jerry. "You think you are slick don't you? You know all my kids can't afford to pay for the reunion but we'll show you. They will all be there." She stormed off in a huff. Cherrelle stared after her aunt in amazement. Out of the corner of her eye, Cherrelle saw Camille walking towards the door, with her purse and jacket in hand, in preparation to leave.

"Camille," Cherrelle called out. "How's it going?"

"Everything's fine." She didn't look her sister in the eye and Cherrelle frowned, "Where are you off to?"

Camille sighed, "I'm on my way home." Camille looked up at her sister and saw such compassion that her eyes began to well up with tears. Cherrelle pushed her toward the door. "Hold on, we need to talk. Just let me get my purse." Camille nodded and walked outside to wait for her sister on the porch.

CHAPTER FOURTEEN

BUN IN THE OVEN

Cherrelle followed Camille to a Starbucks not too far from her apartment. Cherrelle ordered a tall coffee, while Camille ordered a Grande hot chocolate. They sat down at a corner table. Camille was quiet for a long time. Her head was down. Cherrelle watched a big drop of water fall from her sister's face and plop on the table. It barely missed Camille's hot chocolate. When she finally looked up, her eyes were filled with tears. She blurted out, "I'm pregnant."

Cherrelle immediately reached out to hold her sister's hand. "Oh, Camille. Congratulations. That is wonderful! I am so excited for you." She knew how much her sister had always wanted a baby.

Camille looked even sadder. "I'm not ready for a baby right now. I…I," she sighed, "I don't want it. I hate this baby's father, and I can not see myself being tied to a baby from a man who virtually raped me. It's not fair."

She put her head on her arms on the table and began to sob quietly. Cherrelle patted her sister's arm and rubbed her hair.

"Everything will be fine, Camille. You can handle this. The Lord never gives you more than you can bear."

Camille sat up and wiped the tears from her face. "I know. I'm sorry for putting this on you. I have been nothing but trouble ever since you came back."

"That is not true. I love you. You are my sister, and I'll do whatever I can to help you."

Camille nodded. After a few seconds, she whispered, "I'm thinking about getting an abortion."

Cherrelle shook her head, "Not that. I cannot condone that. This is my niece or nephew you're talking about. I can't help you do that. I'm sorry."

"I'm not asking you to help me. I just wanted you to know." Camille seemed so sad. "I hate him."

Cherrelle sat back and just looked at her sister. They sat in silence for several minutes, and then Cherrelle leaned forward. "I have some information at home about alternatives. Please don't do anything until we have talked about this some more. Please don't do anything you will regret later."

They quickly finished their drinks and got up to leave. Cherrelle hugged her sister. "I'll call you tomorrow." Camille nodded, but she didn't tell her sister she had already made up her mind.

Camille drove home slowly. She didn't want to even look at Byron. Desperately hoping he wouldn't be there when she got home, she kept going.

Camille could not even remember how Byron ended up coming back home. He had stayed away for a couple of weeks. She'd heard he was living with Zenobia. Slowly but surely, she had gotten her courage back up and had even ventured back to work. She thought he was gone for good. Then one day as she was sitting down eating dinner, she heard a pounding on the door. Her heart immediately started racing. She wasn't expecting anyone. She looked at the clock on the wall. It was a little after eight. Walking slowly to the window, she peeked out. He must have seen the blinds move because he immediately started beating on the door and yelling for her to open up. Camille couldn't believe he was acting so ignorantly. No, that's not true, she could believe it. Afraid of what the neighbors would say, Camille opened the door. He looked high or drunk. Regardless, he was not in a state where she should have invited him in. That was easy to see in hindsight. Leaning against the wall, Byron straightened up when the door opened. Camille was very nervous, but she wouldn't let him see that.

"What do you want, Byron?"

"What do you mean? I came to see my wife!" His speech was so slurred, she could barely understand him. His eyes were blood-shot and his clothes were disheveled as if he had pulled his clothes out of the clothes hamper and put them on.

Before her marriage, Camille might have had a smart answer for him, but she had learned better over the years.

"I'm really tired, Byron. Can you come back tomorrow?" Camille was still standing in the doorway, blocking his entrance.

He brushed past her, almost knocking her down. "No, I want to talk to you now." He wobbled over to the sofa and sat down hard when he lost his balance.

"Why haven't you called me?" He sounded like a little lost, drunk kid. Camille was confused.

"I don't know what you're talking about," she frowned at him slightly, careful not to get him upset. She knew what he was like sober, and he was worse when he was drunk.

"I wanted to talk to you," his voice softened. Camille wanted so badly to ask him why he didn't talk to Zenobia, but she kept her mouth closed.

"Come sit down next to me," he said and patted an area on the sofa close to where he sat. Camille knew better.

"I'm going to fix you some coffee to drink." She headed towards the kitchen.

"No!" Byron demanded. He got up from the sofa and walked slowly and carefully toward Camille. She backed away. Her heart was beating at a tremendous rate. She was so afraid of what he might do. Byron looked into her eyes and saw the fear there. He smiled to himself and grabbed her arm. "I want my wife." He pulled her to himself and started kissing and nuzzling her on the neck. Camille turned her head back and forth, trying to avoid contact. That seemed to turn him on more. Camille started fighting him in earnest, she even considered kicking him in his man parts, but she couldn't do it. She later regretted that. Byron pushed Camille on the sofa and the rest is history. When Byron finished, he zipped up, took a shower, and went back to

Zenobia's. Camille remained curled in a tight ball on the sofa until he left.

For the next few days, Camille walked around in a trance. Byron came back and forth to the house and stayed some nights as if he had a right to be there. She didn't dare say anything to anyone about what had happened and waited anxiously for her period to come the next week. When nothing happened, she didn't panic but decided to take a pregnancy test.

In her bathroom late one evening, Camille looked at the stick and realized that what she had dreaded was true. She was pregnant, and she didn't want to be.

CHAPTER FIFTEEN

THE CREAM ALWAYS RISES TO THE TOP

Theresa quickly dialed Cherrelle's cell number. Cherrelle looked at the caller ID and picked up her phone on the first ring.

"Hey, Mama. What's up?" Cherrelle was relaxing on the sofa, watching TV and going through the channels looking for something to watch. Her date with Cory was not for several hours.

"I've found him." Theresa sounded excited and scared at the same time. She didn't have to tell Cherrelle who she was referring to. Cherrelle quickly sat up.

"Where is he?"

"At General Hospital. The nurse told me he has been in ICU for a couple of days now. I'm going to the hospital to see him."

Cherrelle headed to the closet in her bedroom, phone in her ear, to put on her shoes.

"I'm coming with you. I'll meet you there."

"Thank you. I knew you would come."

Cherrelle looked through her cell phone to find Cory's number from the other day. As the phone was ringing, she backed the car out of the parking space and realized how disappointed she was that she was going to have to cancel their date. He did not answer so she left him a message.

"Hi Cory, this is Cherrelle. I'm sorry to have to do this, but we have a family emergency, and I have to go to the hospital with my mother. My father was recently admitted, and I can't let her go by herself because we don't know what condition he is in. I'll call you later."

Theresa and Cherrelle reached the hospital almost at the same time. Cherrelle waited in the hospital lobby and watched her mom walk up the sidewalk. She looked defeated and excited at the same time if that were possible. Cherrelle's heart went out to her. She knew this had been hard on her mom. Her father had been missing for almost a month. Even though Cherrelle was just as distressed as her mom, she knew she had to be strong so that her mother could be strong. Theresa walked into the lobby, saw Cherrelle and immediately her countenance changed, as if everything was fine.

They approached the smiling receptionist and told her they were looking for the ICU area. They were directed to the correct floor. Going up to the room in the elevator they were very quiet.

Both were engrossed in their own thoughts of what his status might be.

They passed several beds in the intensive care unit. Calvin was in the last bed at the end of the row. He was lying still and quiet, with several tubes coming out of his body. His handsome face was badly bruised. Theresa grabbed Cherrelle's hand for support and swayed slightly. Cherrelle held tightly to her mother's hand as they looked down at her father.

Theresa lightly touched his shoulder and whispered his name. His eyelids fluttered, but he did not open his eyes. The nurse informed them that only one family member at a time could be with him.

"Mom, you stay first, of course. I will go back to the lobby and stay there until you are done, then I'll come back to see him."

Theresa silently hugged her daughter and took a seat next to her husband. She was so full she could not speak. Calvin was alive!

Cherrelle went back to the lobby. When she walked into the room, Cory was at the reception desk asking about her father's condition and whereabouts. She walked towards him. He turned and saw her and had eyes only for her. He rushed towards her and hugged her.

"Are you alright? How is your father?"

Cherrelle was so grateful that someone else was taking charge for a change that she let him take care of her. Cory went to the cafeteria and brought her a cup of coffee.

"When was the last time you ate?" he asked her.

She couldn't remember, but she told him that she couldn't eat anything just then. She hadn't eaten much earlier that day because she was so excited about them going out to dinner. They sat and talked for about an hour before her mother came down so that she could sit with him for a little while. Cherrelle had also called her sisters and they were on their way.

Cherrelle approached her father on the bed and looked down into his bruised and swollen face. She loved him so. He had been a solid rock for all of them their whole lives, and she was not willing for him to go away right now. She would do whatever was in her power to help him get better. Cherrelle took a seat and watched the monitors as they indicated that he was still alive.

After a while, he moaned in pain. Cherrelle was instantly at his side. She held his hand and called for the nurse, who gave him more pain medicine. After about an hour, her sister Camille came up to relieve her. They hugged, and she went back to the lobby.

While she was gone, Cory had taken the opportunity to get her and her mother and sisters some food. He had a spread waiting for her when she returned. He was so thoughtful. Even if Cherrelle had not been a little bit in love with him already, his actions were bringing him closer to that goal.

When Cory got ready to go, he pulled Cherrelle to the side. "I know this was not an ideal first date, but when your dad is better, I'd still like to see you. I like you a lot. You are very special to me." He kissed her on the cheek and left. Cherrelle stood in that spot for several minutes before she realized how much time had passed. She lay her hand against her cheek in the place where he had kissed her and went back to sit with her mother and sister.

They stayed until the nurses told them that the ICU was closed, and they would not be able to stay with him until he was in a room. Theresa immediately told them she wanted him to have a private room and reluctantly left with her daughters.

She was back the next morning, as soon as ICU was open for visitors, and stayed until the end of the day. He remained in ICU for five days.

The doctors moved Calvin to a private room. Now the family could begin the twenty-four hour vigil.

Calvin was very weak, and although he had been moved out of ICU he spent most days in and out of a drowsy sleep. Theresa spent most nights with him, although her daughters alternated in shifts to allow her to go home and rest and get cleaned up for the next visit.

Cherrelle was sitting with her father when he became fully conscious. She was reading a novel by one of her favorite authors when he stirred. Although she was engrossed in the story, she quickly put it down and sat up. Her father was lying in the bed looking straight at her.

"Cherrelle, how long have I been here? Where did you come from?"

Calvin was looking so much better. Most of the bruises and swelling had disappeared. He was looking more like himself.

"A while, Daddy. How do you feel?"

"Like someone beat me up."

"Do you know who did this to you? I don't want to distress you by bringing it up, but the police have been asking questions about who could have done this."

"Oh, I know. And they will not get away with it."

"Be careful, Daddy."

"Aren't I always?"

Neither commented on the fact that he wasn't "always" careful, otherwise he would not be in this hospital, beaten half to death.

"I'm just glad you are going to be fine."

"Me too."

Cory came to visit almost as often as Cherrelle did. He would only stay a few minutes, but he would make his presence known. He always insisted on making Cherrelle comfortable and seeing to her needs before he left. Her parents commented about what a nice young man he was.

"He seemed like a nice young man the first time I met him, right before your wed…."

Theresa tried to get her husband's attention when he started speaking, but he had almost finished the sentence before he realized what he was saying.

"I'm sorry, sweetheart."

Cherrelle smiled, "It's okay Daddy. I'm over that now. God sent Cory to help me get over it." Theresa and Calvin looked at one another with no comment and smiled.

Calvin was finally released from the hospital, after several weeks of care. He was back to his old self, although the doctors cautioned him to take it easy.

◈ CHAPTER SIXTEEN ◈

THE APPLE DOESN'T FALL FAR FROM THE TREE

Calvin was able to attend the next family reunion meeting. It was being held at the hotel where most events would take place so the committee could tour the hotel when the meeting was over. Everyone seemed so happy to see him up and about. After much fuss being made over him by family members, the meeting was called to order.

"Good afternoon. Thank you all for your patience and understanding that we had to postpone the last meeting because my father was in the hospital. During this meeting we are going to take care of quite a few very important details, namely the menus for each of the days, the program set up, and the assignments of which family members will do what. We also need to review the letter that Tabitha wrote. I've already looked at it, and it looks very good." Cherrelle had made copies of the letter and passed them around for her family members to review.

"As you can see it lets our family know that we will be hosting this year, it tells the dates and beginning times so they'll know what time we will start. It also tells them the name of the hotel we will be staying in and the cost of the reunion and hotel. Does anyone see anything else we need to add?" Cherrelle asked.

Calvin beamed with pride. He was very proud of his take-charge daughter.

"The hotel is too high. I don't know nobody who can pay that," Terrence bellowed.

Cherrelle frowned. "Terrence we agreed on this hotel as a group and voted on it at a previous meeting. I don't see what the problem is. If you can't afford to stay at the hotel, just stay at home and drive in everyday. You live right here in the city."

"You saying I can't afford to stay here?"

"You said it, not me."

"Hey, hey. Come on kids. Can't we give them the names, addresses, and prices of cheaper hotels close by in case people can't afford to stay in the main hotel?" Calvin asked. His voice of reason brought Cherrelle back from what was surely about to become a true confrontation. She had told herself she wouldn't let them get to her. She turned to Terrence. "I apologize, Terrence. I do not think you could not stay here, I was just giving you an option."

Terrence didn't say a word, he just glared at her.

"Do we need to make any other changes to the letter other than providing information about cheaper hotels in the area?" Cherrelle asked.

Everyone agreed that if that were added, the letter was ready to go out. Cherrelle turned to Tabitha with a smile. "You did an excellent job. Can you make the changes and get it ready to be mailed? We don't need to mail it now, but it needs to be ready to go at least nine months before the event to give people time to plan." Tabitha nodded and made notes on her copy.

"The next thing on our agenda is the menu. Any ideas?"

Big Mama chimed in, "Cream Cheese Pound Cakes[24] for dessert on the first night." Everyone nodded.

"How about a fish fry and seafood on Friday night?" Theresa suggested.

"Oh, that sounds good. What kind? And of course we'll need to have a Seafood Boil[25] with crab, shrimp, and all the trimmings. Too bad it'll be too late for crawfish."

"How about fried catfish? I also think we should have a Seafood Gumbo[26]."

"My mouth is watering already." Everyone laughed.

Food always got the group going.

Cherrelle wrote down all the suggestions. Things were going great. Except for her little confrontation with Terrence, everything was perfect.

"Next we will need someone to be the chairperson of the food committee."

"How about Big Mama?" someone suggested.

"And I will be her assistant," Theresa added quickly, knowing that her mother would need help, especially with her being so forgetful lately. That salt in the pie thing was enough to make her very watchful. Everyone breathed a collective sigh of relief when Theresa volunteered. Big Mama's other children had noticed a change in her as well. Even though everyone would be responsible for helping with the cooking, she would definitely need some help.

"Good. Can the men be in charge of the seafood boil? Who wants to volunteer to make the gumbo? We can have a couple of people make it and either put them all together, or leave them separated."

"I'll make gumbo, but I want to leave them separated. I don't want to mix my good ingredients with someone who may not be able to make it as good as me. I want my credit." Aunt Jerry told the group.

"I'll make some too." Aunt Betty Lou said.

"We'll need a couple more people to volunteer. From what you all told me, if it is anything like last time, about two hundred people will be in attendance." Cherrelle got a couple of more volunteers. "Make sure you keep all your receipts so you can be reimbursed for the ingredients. Thanks."

Cherrelle continued. "Okay, the menu for Saturday. We will provide two meals on Saturday and let everyone do breakfast on their own or sleep in late. Since we'll be at the park on Saturday, how about barbecue? Or would you all prefer grilled hamburgers and hot dogs?"

"Let's do both!" her mother said. "We'll have grilled hamburgers and hot dogs at the park, and while we're there we can begin cooking the barbecue. That way, the guys cooking the barbecue won't miss out on the family fun. They'll just have to keep an eye out for the food."

Cherrelle jotted all suggestions down.

Someone else suggested, "I like the idea of having the grilled burgers and hot dogs at the park, but why can't we order the barbecue from a restaurant or caterer and make the side fixings ourselves. Barbecuing is hard work."

"Really what I thought we would do is have something light on Saturday night, since it's mostly a time for games and gathering. I thought we could have barbecue on Sunday."

After much discussion the group decided to barbecue the briskets[27], ribs[28], chicken[29], and sausage on Saturday night for dinner the next day and have hamburgers and hot dogs at the park, and salad and different kinds of casseroles on Saturday night. They made sure to include homemade barbecue sauce[30].

They decided who would do what and Cherrelle adjourned the meeting and told the group, "We'll decide on the program next time. I am exhausted."

After the meeting, Chalice was furious. She and Camille had ridden with Cherrelle to the hotel. "Terrence is so ignorant. He knows he doesn't even have a job. How is he going to stay at the hotel, let his mama pay for it? He has some nerve."

Cherrelle and Camille agreed with her.

[24]Cream Cheese Pound Cake
[25]Seafood boil
[26]Seafood gumbo
[27]Barbecue Brisket
[28]Barbecue Ribs
[29]Barbecue Chicken
[30]Barbecue Sauce

CHAPTER SEVENTEEN

A FEW SANDWICHES SHORT OF A PICNIC

Cherrelle was in her element. She had formed a team of people around her at work who were dedicated to the cause – helping others. There was already talk of her going into Atlanta next with a team to improve things there.

With all the things going on around her, both personally and professionally, Cherrelle had completely forgotten about Marcus until she received a phone call from him that afternoon.

"Hey baby, this is Marcus. Why haven't you called me? You know I've been missing my Boo."

"Hello Marcus. Actually I've been so busy I hadn't thought about you for a while. I hear you have been busy." she told him, referring to all the women he was involved with.

"I have, but the season is officially over now, and I am on hiatus until late summer, early fall. I thought I might come up there and see you."

Cherrelle decided to be up front with him. She wasn't into game playing. Besides that, she and Cory were getting closer and she didn't want to do anything to jeopardize that.

"Look Marcus, I am seeing someone else. Besides that, I know you've been seeing other people too, so let's just end this now and move on."

"Baby, I have been faithful to you. Who have I been with? What would make you think that I have been doing anything else other than working and thinking of you? And who is this clown you're seeing? I bet he can't do the things for you that I can."

Cherrelle couldn't believe him. He really thought she was that gullible.

"I'm in town now, staying at a hotel in the Quarters. Could we meet for dinner so we can talk? I really want to see you," Marcus was being his most persuasive.

"Alright Marcus. I'll meet you so we can talk. What time do you want to meet?" Cherrelle got the name and address of his hotel and hung up the phone.

After work, Cherrelle went straight to his hotel. He was waiting for her in the lobby. Marcus pulled her in his arms and gave her a hug. He attempted to kiss her, but she turned her face and gave him her cheek.

"I thought we could have dinner in my room and talk afterwards." Marcus told her.

"No, if we are going to talk it will have to be in the hotel restaurant." She looked him boldly in the eye.

His hands went up defensively. "Okay, let's go."

In the restaurant they were seated near the window. There was a clear view of the beautiful evening sky. Cherrelle's phone rang.

"I apologize, I need to answer this," she told him as she reached for her phone and answered the call. "Hello? Yes. Yes. Okay." She ended the call.

"Marcus I need to go to the Ladies' Room to wash my hands. I'll be right back." Cherrelle eased herself from the seat and exited the room. She had been gone about a minute when Chalice slid into her vacant seat.

"Hi, Marcus. What are you doing here?" she asked him. Marcus's eyes darted to the doorway that Cherrelle had just exited through. "You do remember me don't you? My name is Chalice, and we were together the last time you were here."

"I remember, but I am here with a friend right now, and I can't really talk."

"Oh, I'm here with a couple of friends too." At that moment Chalice's friends Tanisha and Danielle walked up. Marcus began sweating profusely. He had been too busy last time he was in New Orleans, and he was about to be busted if he didn't get rid of them.

"Hi Marcus, remember us? We had a good time together, didn't we?"

Marcus turned to see if Cherrelle was still in the bathroom so he could make a quick exit, and saw her heading back towards the table with a big smile on her face. He couldn't understand that! Why was she smiling? She walked right up to the table, and Chalice stood up. He knew it was about to be on. Then they hugged!

"Marcus, you invited my sister to join us. How sweet!"

He choked on the water he was drinking to help ease his dry throat. He had been with Cherrelle's sister? Oh it was about to be on alright. On him. He had to get out of there.

As he sat there coughing the sisters turned to look at him. Chalice sat back down in the seat she was occupying. Cherrelle pulled up a chair from the table next to them. Not caring whether or not she made a scene, Cherrelle told him. "I think you have some nerve thinking you can play me. I knew months ago that you had been with my sister. We found out later you had been with her friends too and no telling who else. So don't come around here pretending to want me. Yeah you wanted me alright, and you would have discarded me as soon as you got what you wanted. I do not ever want to see you again. If you do try to contact me, I will put an ad in the paper about you so that other innocent women will know what a player you are." With that, Cherrelle gathered her things and walked out of the room. Chalice followed close behind her.

Tanisha and Danielle turned to him. "We're still free, and we want to be your friends." Marcus looked disgustedly at the women and called the waiter.

"Check please."

Outside, Chalice turned to her sister. "I'm really sorry Cherrelle. I am so stupid about men. What can I do to change?" Cherrelle hugged her sister and told her, "We'll talk later. In earnest. I'm just sorry I had to bring you into this, but he needed to learn a lesson. He may not have learned a big one, but he'll be more careful from now on. I love you and I'll see you later."

"Mama, what are we going to do about Big Mama?" Cherrelle was sitting at the kitchen table in her parent's home. They were nursing cups of tea and talking about the family. Her father was on the computer in his home office.

"Right now we are watching her carefully. Eventually we'll have to call someone in to take care of her, because PawPaw can't do it by himself."

"I am so sorry about this and so sad." Cherrelle was deep in thought. "Is there any medicine or anything that can be done to help her?"

"I'm sure they are coming up with something, and there are some experimental drugs, but I don't want to put her through that. If you read the side effects you would see what I mean."

"I read some information about Alzheimer's on the Internet, and I read those brochures that you gave me earlier. It doesn't really say how long she has. It only basically tells us what to expect. It almost seems as if every person is different."

Her mother nodded. "You know what? Let's go visit her. I haven't seen her this week and I need to check on her anyway." Theresa let her husband know that she was leaving.

Cherrelle and Theresa gathered their things and went to check on Big Mama.

When they arrived, they noticed that the front door was wide open. Family members that came to visit usually entered through the side door, so it was quite unusual for the front door to be standing open.

"Big Mama?" Cherrelle called. She asked her mother where her grandfather was. She had forgotten that he worked on some Saturday mornings. They walked around the house, but everything seemed to be in order. Nothing was missing, nothing was cooking on the stove or in the oven. As they walked around the kitchen, they noticed that nothing was cooked. That was really odd. Big Mama always had something cooked or cooking in her kitchen. Big Mama couldn't drive, and they only had one car anyway, and PawPaw had taken it to work. "Where could she be?"

Cherrelle walked back through the front door and looked down the street. There in the distance was her grandmother, walking towards the house. Cherrelle called to her mother and ran to meet her grandmother. When she reached her, Big Mama was breathing heavily and had huge patches of sweat on her clothes and rivulets of sweat dripping from her face. She was soaking wet.

"Big Mama, where have you been?" Cherrelle hugged her, not caring that she got wet in the process.

"I went to the store."

"What store?" Cherrelle was confused. There wasn't a store within three miles of Big Mama's house. Cherrelle looked down and sure enough she had bags from a local grocery store that was more than three miles away and certainly further than she should have walked.

"I'm so tired. Here Cherrelle. Take these bags for Big Mama."

"Of course." Cherrelle took the bags. "Did you walk there and back? Why didn't you call someone to come and take you to the store? Anyone would have been willing to do it."

"It was too early to call someone. I needed these ingredients for my pies so I walked."

"What time is 'too early'?"

"I don't know, but it was dark. PawPaw had just left for work."

Cherrelle knew her grandfather usually left for work at about six o'clock in the morning. It was almost two o'clock in the afternoon now. Her grandmother had been gone for almost eight hours, and apparently her house had been open for those eight hours. Worse than that, the summers in New Orleans were unrelenting with the heat, and her grandmother could have had a heat stroke. Cherrelle guided her into the house, put the bags down on the table, and helped her grandmother into her bedroom. She and her mother helped Big Mama out of those wet clothes. Theresa ran a bath of tepid water for her so that she could cool off. Once Big Mama was cool and dry, she put on a gown. Cherrelle and Theresa helped her get into bed so she could rest.

In the kitchen, Cherrelle put away the groceries and told her mother, "Well at least she didn't get lost. She found her way there and back. That's something anyway."

"Now you see why I think someone needs to be here with her at all times. She left the house wide open and walked to the store. And really, we don't know if she got lost or not. Eight hours is a long time to be gone from home."

While Big Mama slept, Theresa called her siblings and brought them up on what was going on with Big Mama. She invited them to come to her house that evening so they could discuss what they planned to do to help Big Mama.

Cherrelle and Theresa stayed until PawPaw came home. Theresa explained to her father what was going on with his wife. She let him know what the doctor told her and what they should be doing to help her. She also let him know the kids would be meeting that evening at her house to discuss what they would need to do to assist her and him and get them through this.

Clarence grabbed his daughter's hand. "Theresa, all I ask is that you do not talk about putting her away. She needs home. She needs to be surrounded by the people and the things she loves. She needs me, and I need her."

Theresa nodded. They peeked in on Big Mama to ensure she was still sleeping comfortably and left.

Since only the actual children of Bessie and Clarence would attend the meeting to discuss Big Mama, Cherrelle went home with an extremely heavy heart.

CHAPTER EIGHTEEN

A Different Kettle of Fish

Sunday dawned bright and early, and Cherrelle decided to go back to her parents' church. She was also hoping that she would see Cory again. She needed to pray for her family, because everyone had so much going on. Her younger sister was pregnant by an abusive, cheating husband she wanted to leave. Her baby sister would sleep with any and every man who showed her the least amount of attention. Her grandmother was slowly losing herself to Alzheimer's, and her father was home recuperating from being beaten by prejudiced hoodlums. The life she thought was so bad, that had her feeling sorry for herself, seemed like nothing in comparison. Actually she was ashamed of herself. She needed to be thanking God for keeping her from marrying Darryl. That alone was proof that God knows your end from your beginning. He knew Darryl was not the man for her. Just from the small length of time she had lived across the hall from Darryl and Image, she realized she had truly dodged a bullet. Even though he was a nice enough man, Darryl was weak, and Image walked all over him. He looked miserable. No matter what he did for her, it was never enough. Some nights, Cherrelle could hear the fights and screams as Image rammed into him about what he wasn't doing for her. Cherrelle felt so sorry for him. They had three kids now, and rumor had it that Image was pregnant again. Whew! What a life.

Cherrelle continued getting ready for church. She glanced in the full length mirror. She looked very good. She would be watching for Cory at church.

When the services were over, Cherrelle walked over to Pastor Thomas to let him know what a good service it had been. Out of the corner of her eye she spotted Cory, waiting for her. After she shook the pastor's hand, she made her way over to him.

"Hey, you."

Cory kissed her on the cheek. "Hey, you back."

"I've missed you."

'I've missed you too. Sorry I didn't get in touch with you sooner. There were some problems with the manufacturing plant that I work for. I was so consumed with getting that taken care of so I could get back that I didn't think of anything else." A little look of guilt crossed his face as he told her about the manufacturing plant, but it was quickly gone.

Cherrelle saw it, but quickly dismissed it. She really wanted to trust him. "It's okay. You want to go to lunch? My treat."

Cory smiled, "Let's go."

Over lunch, Cory and Cherrelle talked about old times. They laughed about how they used to look when they were younger and Cherrelle teased Cory about how goofy he used to look when he first learned to dance. They omitted speaking of Darryl.

"How's your father doing?" he asked her.

"Much better. Thank you so much for taking the time out of your busy day to come check on him and me. My parents are very impressed with you."

"Good, because I was trying to make a good impression," he told her, taking her hand.

"I'm impressed." They looked at each other for so long, the couple next to them smiled. After a while Cherrelle looked shyly away.

Cory continued to hold Cherrelle's hand. "I'm really having a good time. Thank you for asking me out to lunch."

"Thank you for going out with me, and you're welcome."

"Can I see you again, soon?"

"Yes."

When Cherrelle drifted off to sleep that night, the last thing she remembered was the tender kiss she received from Cory when he walked her to her car in the parking lot.

When Cory drifted off to sleep, the last thing he remembered was that he had not been totally truthful with Cherrelle. And he thought about the kiss.

The next day Cory showed up at Cherrelle's job with a picnic lunch. He had a huge basket filled with two kinds of sandwiches, chips, fresh strawberries in a light glaze[31], Homemade Oatmeal Cookies[32], Deviled Eggs[33], and a light fruit punch[34]. Cherrelle felt like a princess. They walked outside to the patio area of the office and he opened up his basket and put out the spread.

Cherrelle ate until she could hold no more. Everything was delicious.

"Cory, you are spoiling me. This is wonderful."

He had been smiling the entire lunch, but he smiled even brighter under her compliment.

"You deserve it. I know you work hard trying to make life better for the homeless and less privileged. I am so proud of you for all the work you do to make life better for others."

Cory wouldn't let her lift a finger. He cleared away the food and debris and sat back down. Cherrelle put her elbows on the tabletop and placed her chin in her hands.

"Tell me what you do. You know, I really don't know that much about your job."

"Well the company I work for manufactures pipes and other supplies for oil drilling. It is a pretty lucrative business."

"Sounds interesting."

"It is. When I graduated from college, I went to work for the company before…anyway I really like what I do."

"I know you went to LSU on a football scholarship."

"Yep, you get it while you can. I was more interested in learning than in football, but it paid my tuition so I did what they asked me to. I think I did alright."

"I used to read about you in the paper while I was at Dillard. I would tell everyone who would listen that you were my friend."

Cory walked Cherrelle back to the side door of the building. "Thank you for a wonderful lunch." She wiggled her fingers as she waved goodbye and then blew him a kiss. He didn't move until she disappeared from sight.

Cherrelle went back to work, full of food and thoughts of Cory. He was a wonderful man. The more she thought about her life, the more she was convinced that God must really love her.

When she arrived home, she was just changing her clothes from work when she got a phone call from Camille. She felt guilty when her sister's number showed on her cell phone. She hadn't talked to her all week. She flipped open her cell.

"Hey Camille, how are you doing?"

"I'm okay I guess. Can I come over and talk to you? I have

a lot on my mind and I need to talk to someone."

"Of course you can. Are you hungry? Do you want me to fix you something to eat?"

"No, I haven't really had an appetite lately."

"I'll see you soon." Cherrelle hung up. That meant she probably had not had anything to eat all day. She was pregnant, and she needed to keep up her strength if for no other reason than to have a healthy baby. At least, Cherrelle hoped Camille was still pregnant. She hadn't talked to her all week.

Cherrelle usually cooked on the weekend for the week because she was so busy. On Sunday she had made a Lasagna[35], Garlic Bread[36], and had the fixings for a salad. All she needed to do now was heat the Lasagna and bake the bread. Dinner would be ready by the time Camille got there.

When Camille arrived, the smell of the Garlic Bread got to her. She sat down to eat dinner with her sister. They ate in silence until they were both full. Then Camille spoke.

"You know I really wanted to get an abortion. I even went to the clinic to get more information. But with the situation with Dad when he was in the hospital, I didn't think about myself and when I went to the clinic the other day, they told me I was too far along to have an abortion. So now I will have to have it."

Cherrelle grabbed her sister's hand, "I know you may not think so now, but this baby will be a real blessing for you. You've always wanted a baby. Maybe subconsciously, deep down inside, this is what you really want. I am so happy for you. I'm going to be an aunt! Have you let Mom and Dad know they are about to be grandparents?"

"Not yet." She looked so dejected.

"What's wrong?" Cherrelle asked her sister.

"I'm just not sure this is for the best."

"Let me say this to you. God doesn't make mistakes. This baby is meant to be here, no matter how it happened. We will surround him or her with love and care and this baby will not even be remotely like its father. Can I give you a baby shower?"

"Oh Cherrelle, you always look at the bright side of everything. No wonder the family depends on you so."

"So how far along are you?"

"Almost four months."

"Wow."

"What?"

"I've been here almost four months. It doesn't seem like it." She looked carefully at her sister, wanting to lift up her top. She could barely see a bump. "Are you showing yet?"

"Not really. I haven't even told Byron yet, but I will have to tell him soon. I figure I'll be showing for real in a couple of weeks."

"If he comes home tonight, you have to tell him in person. Otherwise, call him and tell him over the phone that he is about to become a daddy." Again was unspoken.

When she got home, Camille paced up and down in her living room. She was actually hoping Byron would not come home that night. This was something she would much rather tell him over the phone. But Cherrelle was right. She had to tell him, she was just dreading it.

After a while Camille stopped pacing. She decided to make a salad for dinner since she had eaten earlier at Cherrelle's. Camille sat down to eat and had begun cleaning the kitchen when the front door opened. It was after eight by this time. Her reprieve was over. She had to tell him. She met him at the kitchen door.

"Hi."

He looked at her and frowned. "Hey," he said suspiciously. He wasn't used to being greeted when he walked in the apartment. "What's up?" He started rifling through the refrigerator.

"Can I talk to you when you get a chance? After you've had a chance to settle down."

He pulled out the milk and started drinking from the carton. Camille made a note to make sure she didn't drink any more milk at home. She didn't know he did that.

"Aaah," he sighed and wiped his mouth with the back of his hand. Camille could not believe she had married this crass man, but she did not make a comment and kept a neutral face. When he put the milk back in the refrigerator she asked him, "Is it okay to talk now?"

"What?" he asked as he turned to go sit in the living room.

"I have some news. I don't know if it will be good news to you, but it is to me." She had no choice since it was too late to end it. She had to accept her fate. If God wanted her to have this baby, then she would be happy about it.

Camille followed her husband into the living room. He sat while she stood and started pacing.

"What?" he asked again.

"I'm pregnant."

Byron stood straight up. "What?"

It entered Camille's mind that that was about the third or fourth time he had said 'what', but she was too distressed to dwell on it.

"I'm pregnant," she repeated.

"Is it mine?"

Camille looked at him like he had lost his mind.

"Of course it's yours." How stupid can he be?

"How many months?"

Camille sighed, "Almost four."

Byron did the calculation. This baby would arrive about a month after Zenobia's baby. She would be livid when she found out.

"Is it too late to do anything about it?"

"Yes."

"Then congratulations." Byron got up, went into the bedroom and closed the door.

Camille was afraid to move. She didn't know what to do, but that was not the reaction she had expected. He was too calm. She continued to pace and think. What did this mean? Was he happy about the baby? Planning her demise? She had no clue and that worried her more than anything else. She sat down, picked up the remote and turned on the TV. After about an hour, Byron came out of the bedroom. He had changed into a pair of sweats.

"I'm going to the gym. Don't wait up."

Camille went to bed at about ten o'clock. When she awoke the next morning, Byron had not returned.

³¹ Strawberry Glaze
³²Homemade oatmeal cookies
³³Deviled eggs
³⁴Fruit punch
³⁵Lasagna
³⁶Garlic Bread

CHAPTER NINTEEN

ICING ON THE CAKE

It was the beginning of August and one of the hottest summers they had had in a while. Cherrelle laughed at the kids running through the sprinklers on her grandparents' block. She made a habit of coming by to check on Big Mama at least once a week, but it usually ended up being more often than that.

Her mom's siblings decided that for the present, they would take turns going over to check on Big Mama throughout the day. Since PawPaw was still there and her grandmother had not progressed to the next stage, right now they felt it was best. They had also come up with a plan of next stage readiness. They needed to be prepared to help her if they needed to, including rearranging work and other schedules. Cherrelle had done a lot of research on Alzheimer's.

She found out that there had been a study done to see if hormone therapy would decrease the risk of developing dementia in older women, years after menopause. This study was stopped when scientists found that the participants taking the hormone therapy had an increased risk of heart attack, breast cancer, stroke, and blood clots, compared to participants on a sugar pill. They also discovered that women taking the hormone treatments also had twice the risk of dementia, rather than a decreased one. The risks were as bad as or worse than the disease. There were other experimental drugs on the market, but the family was hesitant to use them.

Right now they were using a memory loss therapy that Big Mama's doctor had her doing. Cherrelle went to the doctor with her mother, and she paid close attention to everything the doctor and therapist said. She had been to the therapy session with her grandmother a couple of times. The technique had her grandmother use a small pocket calendar divided into several daily events, like a things to do today list. The list does not have a time attached to the events, but the activities are listed on the day it should be done. The person is encouraged to look at the calendar several times per day. Cherrelle had a lot of questions for the therapist about her grandmother's illness and the therapy.

"Doctor, how is my grandmother doing?"

"Right now she is in early stages of Alzheimer's. She has a cognitive impairment that is slowly degenerating. Mild cognitive impairment is a transition stage between the cognitive changes of normal aging and the more serious problems caused by Alzheimer's disease. It often includes the memory loss problems common to Alzheimer's, but doesn't meet the qualifications for full-blown dementia."

"How is this therapy going to help her, and how will she remember to use the calendar?"

"We work with our patients for six weeks, so that it becomes a habit. It's kind of like driving a car. You don't think about all the motions involved in the process. You don't say to yourself, "OK, the light turned red so I'm going to put my foot on the brake and stop the car. You just do it. In addition to writing things in the calendar, we also ask our patients to look at their calendars at least two or three times a day. At breakfast, they can look over what they're supposed to do that day. They need to check the day before, too, to see if there are any unfinished tasks that need to be carried forward. We also tell them to check things off right when they do it. So even if they don't remember doing something, if it's checked off, they must have done it. Also writing things down help them stick in your memory. Saying it out loud as you're writing it down can also help cement it in your memory. I tell people to use all their senses to help jog their memory, even drawing if necessary. The good thing about this calendar is that it can work the way you work."

"Okay, one final question. How is it working for the people in your study?

"Almost every person in the study has said that it has helped them. That has been good news. Some people are still at it after more than a year. That's really something, to have people change the way they do things and have it stick. Every person who participates in this study is accompanied by a support person, usually a spouse or child. And these support people often say,

'It's so nice not to have to answer the same questions over and over'."

"Thank you, Doctor. You have been very informative and very kind. Thank you for taking the time to answer our questions."

"Thank you for asking. Many times people want to know what to do to help their family member, but they don't know what to ask. Your grandmother is in good hands with you all." They all shook hands and Cherrelle, her mother, and grandmother left the doctor's office.

In the car, Cherrelle turned to her grandmother. "Big Mama, you want to stop and get something to eat?"

Her grandmother sat in the front seat with her arms folded and a huge scowl on her face, "No."

"What's wrong, Big Mama?"

"You all were sitting up in that doctor's office talking about me like I'm nothing."

"Mama," Theresa leaned over from the back seat and put her hand on her mother's shoulder. "We weren't talking about you. We just wanted to ask the doctor a lot of questions so that you can get better. We love you. We would never talk about you like that. You are too important to us. Now, what do you want to eat?"

They decided on a place to have lunch, and Cherrelle drove them to the restaurant. When they found a good parking spot, Theresa got out to help her mother out of the car. Cherrelle came around from her side of the car to assist her. When her grandmother got out of the car she looked around and asked.

"What are we doing here?"

Cherrelle and Theresa looked sadly at one another and escorted Big Mama into the restaurant.

The waiter handed them their menus and as they began ordering, Big Mama seemed to be back to her normal self. She laughed and talked with her daughter and granddaughter like old times. When they finished lunch they decided to go shopping. One of Cherrelle's favorite discount department stores was right across the street, and they decided to go in.

"Is that okay with you, Big Mama?" She asked her grandmother.

"That's fine. I need something for Sunday myself."

Big Mama, Theresa, and Cherrelle enjoyed a leisurely pace as they milled through the clothes in the store. Cherrelle found a few cute things, and she helped her grandmother find a few nice outfits as well.

"Mom, Big Mama and I are going to go into the dressing room to try on these things we found. We'll be right back."

Theresa nodded and kept looking through the racks. After a few minutes, Cherrelle came out to get another size. The jacket she had picked out was a little too big. After a minute or two, Theresa looked up and asked, "Where's Big Mama?"

"I left her in the dressing room. She had quite a few outfits and I knew it would take her a while to try them on." Cherrelle found the jacket in a smaller size and headed back to the dressing room. When she entered, the dressing room attendant asked her, "Are you here with you grandmother?"

"Yes, is something wrong?"

"An older lady came out a few minutes ago, saying she thought she was here with her granddaughter, but she wasn't sure which one. When I asked her for the name of her granddaughter she said she didn't know, but she thought she might be here with Camille. Is that you?"

"No, but that is my grandmother. Where is she?"

"We took her to the manager's office. She was quite upset."

Cherrelle and her mother rushed into the manager's office and found Big Mama sitting calmly on the chair going through her purse. Cherrelle and Theresa rushed over to her and hugged her like she had been missing for days. Big Mama brushed them off.

"What is all the fuss about?"

"Big Mama are you alright?"

"Of course I am? Where have you all been?"

"Let's go home, Big Mama. I am really tired." Cherrelle and her mother helped her grandmother up and they left the store, forgetting about the shopping they wanted to do.

At the next family reunion meeting Cherrelle kept a close eye on her grandmother. She didn't know if her mother had mentioned the incident to Camille and Chalice. Cherrelle most certainly had not.

The meeting was being held at Big Mama's house. Looking around the table she saw that everyone was in attendance. Nobody wanted to miss an opportunity to provide input on what would happen at the family reunion. Only Darryl was conveniently missing. Probably at home watching the kids. Today they would be planning the program. Cherrelle considered this to be the most fun part. She had done research on types of activities for family reunions. Everyone agreed that the activities should be kid-friendly because if the kids aren't happy, no one else will be. Cherrelle brings the meeting to order.

"We'll need some really good ideas for our family activities. Let's start with Friday night."

"Well we know that Friday night is registration and fish fry. Why not just sit around and eat? Find out who's here," one of her aunts suggested.

"No, we need something to do. What about playing cards and dominoes?"

"I thought we were going to do that Saturday at the picnic and that night?" Cousin Paul asked.

"Boy, you know we could play cards and dominoes everyday if we had to," Uncle Terrence told him with a laugh.

Big Mama got up to go into the kitchen. While the men ribbed each other about who could beat whom at cards and dominoes, Cherrelle watched her grandmother disappear into the kitchen. She was relieved when her mother got up and followed Big Mama.

She turned her attention back to the subject at hand. "We'll also need something for the kids to do. It may be pretty late that night by the time everyone gets in and they might be pretty tired, but we still need some activities for them. Camille can you look into more activities for the kids for that night for us?"

Camille nodded and already had some ideas. "What about the beanbag game? It won't take long and it will be the perfect ice-breaker for the kids and adults."

"How do you play that?" Image asked her.

"We stand in a huge circle. We'll probably need to use one of the large meeting rooms at the hotel. An adult starts off the game by tossing a beanbag or ball to someone in the circle and asking a question at the same time - like 'What's your name?', 'Do you have a brother or sister?', 'What's your favorite color?' and so on. The person who catches the ball or beanbag has to answer the question and then throw it to another person and ask that person a question. The game works better if you keep it moving quickly, so we may have to step in and help really young kids."

"That sounds like fun. What else could we do?" Cherrelle asked her sister.

"We could have everyone make their own name tag. We would provide the paper and markers for all our family members so they can make their own nametag. They can include hobbies, favorite colors and foods, or other information about themselves on the tag. Once everyone is done, we could have them present their nametag before they put it on and explain why they included the information about themselves that they did. Then we can provide them with a lanyard or something like that so they can wear the nametag."

"Oh, that's good too. Can we do both?" Chalice asked.

"I don't see why not," Cherrelle told them. "I think that's enough, don't you all? We can spend the rest of the time talking and getting to know one another again, renewing old acquaintances. We can also have tables set up for cards and dominoes. Is that okay with everyone?" There was general consensus all around.

"Okay, let's talk about Saturday."

Theresa and Big Mama walked back in from the kitchen. Big Mama caught the tail end of the question, but asked the group, "Are we going to have a family reunion T-shirt?"

"I think that's a good idea. But do you think we can get some shirts printed out of the money for registration? They're pretty expensive, at least five to seven dollars each. A big family would eat the registration fee in T-shirts alone." Cherrelle pulled out her calculator.

"That's true. Could every family get one shirt free with the registration and then we could include the price of the shirts so other people who might want one can pay? Maybe we could even charge a dollar more than they cost to take up the slack for the free shirts we'll give away."

"Tabitha, that is a great idea. Does everyone agree with that?" Cherrelle asked. There was a short discussion because some people wanted everyone to get a free T-shirt and others wanted everyone to pay and not provide anything free. After discussion they decided to go with Tabitha's idea and provide one free T-shirt with registration and include the price plus one dollar in the information letter to the family.

"Okay, let's get back to Saturday activities." Cherrelle pulled her pad closer.

"I want to play volleyball," Image told the group.

Cherrelle wrote down volleyball.

"I want to have a softball game," Terrance said.

Cherrelle added softball to her list.

"For the little kids, I'd like to have games like 'Red Light, Green Light and Fish Pond. Everybody could play sack races and three-legged races. We could also play musical chairs and have a scavenger hunt. My girls used to love to play those games when they were little," Theresa thought out loud.

"Ooh, that sounds good. I would even do some of those," Aunt Jerry said.

Cherrelle was writing fast and furiously.

"We also need to make sure that we have a lot of board games around. We also have to have bingo – we have a lot of elders in our family; and tables could be set up for cards and dominoes," Theresa said.

"This sounds like so much fun, I'm glad I'll be there." Chalice laughed. Everyone nodded. Cherrelle noticed that Camille was still very quiet and said to her sister, "Are you writing this down too, Camille? You're in charge of games. Make sure you get a strong committee. You all have a lot to do."

Camille got a lot of people to volunteer to work on her

committee to assist her with games. Everyone continued to talk, excited about the fun people would have at the reunion.

Cherrelle tapped the table, "Can I get your attention again? We need to at least finish Saturday's activities. On Saturday night, you know we have to have a talent show." Someone groaned.

Aunt Betty Lou told the group. "I'm sorry, but you know the kids love it. I've had people call me and tell me their kids have started practicing already, and the family reunion is a year away. We'll talk about other things to do, but we have to have a talent show." Everyone knew that was true.

"Okay, but after the talent show, can we have a cards and dominoes tournament?" Terrence asked.

"You all ought to be tired of playing cards and dominoes."

"I could play all night and every day."

"If you all want a cards and dominoes tournament, we will include it. But what will the kids do? We still have to have something for them to do. It can be something pretty quiet, because they'll be tired from the afternoon in the park, but they still need constructive activities to do." Cherrelle made sure to include dominoes and cards on the list as she spoke.

"After we eat and after the talent show, let's have board games set up for the kids to play. We'll also need someone to be the DJ or to play music for us while we meet and greet," Theresa suggested.

Cherrelle excitedly wrote down all of the suggestions. As she looked around the room, she realized she was enjoying these people she swore she would never look at or talk to again. She even had a slightly warm feeling for Aunt Jerry, but she had yet to warm up to Image.

"We're almost done. Let's talk about Sunday. We'll need a program."

Calvin chimed in. "Can we have a special time of honoring the elders? We don't know how much longer we'll have them with us and I think this is a perfect time for the kids to learn their history and for us to give a special honor to them. Do we have any one of our elder relatives who wouldn't mind telling what life was like for them when they were young?"

Cherrelle looked at Big Mama. She might be able to do it, but a year was so far away. When Cherrelle thought about the changes that could occur for their family in a year, she got really sad and shook her head to clear it.

"Uncle Buddy wouldn't mind doing it. His mind is sharp as a tack. He remembers everything and enjoys talking about it. Let's ask him," Aunt Betty suggested.

"That's good. He's a good story teller too. He makes you feel like you are there, like you can see what he's talking about," Theresa smiled and remembered sitting enraptured as she listened to Uncle Buddy talk about his life as a child and young adult. She had asked him so many questions about his life.

Cherrelle was asking the group about activities for the Sunday program. "Can we have certificates for different contests, like the oldest and youngest family members; who traveled the least and greatest distances to attend; who has attended the most consecutive reunions; and the person with the most children or grandchildren?" Everybody laughed when she asked about who had traveled the least distance.

"I thought we could also present the winners of the different activities from the picnic and the domino and card tournaments at the dinner as well. And of course we need to see if we could get our pastor to come and say a little something, just a few words since we will not have gone to church that morning."

By this time everyone was so tired they would agree to anything. The meeting was adjourned, and everyone headed to the kitchen to see what Big Mama had whipped up.

Calvin and Theresa walked up to Cherrelle and gave her a long, hard hug.

"What was that for?"

"We are so proud of you, you're doing such a good job. And we missed you." They stood around talking a few more minutes. Theresa looked around.

"Where is Camille? She has been so quiet lately. Is everything alright with her? Has she said anything to you about what could be wrong?"

Cherrelle didn't want to tell her sister's business so she just shrugged. "You'll need to talk to her." She walked off. "Something sure smells good," she said as she headed to the kitchen.

CHAPTER TWENTY

NO USE CRYING OVER SPILT MILK

When Cherrelle got home she was stuffed. Her grandmother's memory may be fading, but thank goodness she hadn't lost her touch with food yet, although someone usually stayed in the kitchen with her while she cooked. She and her mother were saying earlier that they better get Big Mama to write down her recipes while she could still remember them. Her mom had already started writing down recipes for her. Tonight Big Mama served Meat Loaf[37], Mashed Potatoes [38], and Stir Fry Green Beans in Garlic[39]. For dessert she made Lemon Bars[40].

Looking at the clock, Cherrelle realized it was too late to call Cory, but she had been thinking of him all day. She looked at her answering machine and saw that she had three messages. Two of them were from Cory.

"Just thinking about you and wanted to hear your voice. Even if it is just on the answering machine."

"Hey, call me tonight. It doesn't matter how late it is when you get in."

Cherrelle looked at the clock. It wasn't too late, a little after ten, so she eagerly dialed Cory's number. He picked it up on the first ring as if he were waiting for her to call.

"Hi, how are you?" she asked him when he picked up the phone.

"I'm better now"

"Why, what happened?"

"I haven't talked to you all day. I missed you."

Cherrelle smiled into the phone. "I missed you to."

She settled deeper into the couch as she began to tell him about her day and find out about his. When she looked up at the clock she saw that it was after midnight. They had talked for more than two hours, and she could have talked longer but she knew she had a very busy day tomorrow and didn't want to be tired at work.

"Cory, I hate to be the one to say it, but I'm going to have to say goodnight." She heard him groan into the phone. She hated to end the call but needed to get at least five or six hours of sleep or she wouldn't be able to concentrate the next day.

"I know you need to get your rest. Can I see you tomorrow?"

She thought about how tight her calendar was but also knew she really wanted to see him. So she told him, "Yes, I'll see you tomorrow. Goodnight." She hung the phone up with a huge smile on her face. She was smiling even as she drifted off to sleep.

The next day, Cherrelle had meetings back to back. She and her staff were wrapping up the acquisition of a property that could possibly be the headquarters of the New Orleans location for the non-profit organization. They were also pulling data for an approximate number of homeless that lived in the city, and Cherrelle received an update from her staff on several shelters in the area that she would research later. She was just ending the last meeting before lunch when she was called to the phone. Cherrelle turned to her secretary standing in the door.

"Can you take a message and let them know I'll call them back at my earliest convenience? Wait, on second thought, find out who it is. It might be Ms. Tarkington. She said she might call today."

Her secretary came back with the message. "It's Cory Reynolds. He asked if he could hold."

Cherrelle's eyes lit up and she smiled and nodded. She turned to the group, "We'll continue our discussion after lunch. Are there any questions so far?" When there were none, the meeting ended and Cherrelle went to answer the phone. She went into her office and closed the door.

"How are you?" she asked him.

"I'm fine, but I wanted to ask you for a favor."

"Sure, what is it?"

"I made reservations for us to go out to dinner with Darryl and Image tonight."

"Have a good time."

"I want you to come with us."

"No."

"Please."

"No. You know how I feel about them. I don't see how you could even ask me that. They are not my friends and I have no desire to make them my friends. Besides, Image hates me."

"You know Darryl is still my best friend. I don't want to have to give up that friendship. And if you don't still have strong feelings for him, I don't see why you won't just forgive him, let the past go, and move on."

Cherrelle crossed her arms and sat back in her chair. "I said no and I mean no. I don't think you've considered my feelings in this."

"By now you know how I feel about you. I wouldn't choose him over you, but he is my best friend. Can't you do this for me?"

"No Cory, not even for you. Goodbye." Cherrelle hung up feeling very sad and heavy hearted.

Cherrelle had essentially lost her appetite for lunch, but she ate a small salad to keep her strength up. She was quiet the rest of the afternoon and noticeably distracted.

"Cherrelle, do you want to do this later?" Irene asked her referring to the paperwork in front of them.

"No, I'm fine. Let's finish this up."

Her staff tiptoed around her, completed the day's assignment, and left quietly at the end of the day. Cherrelle continued to work a couple of hours more, then she turned out the lights in her office and walked slowly to her car.

When Cherrelle entered her apartment, the phone rang. She hesitated before looking at the caller ID and answering the call. It was her sister Chalice.

"Cherrelle, I really need you to come over here. Somebody broke in and took all my stuff!" Chalice cried.

"Have you called the police?"

"Not yet."

"Call them. I'll be right there. Lock the doors."

By the time Cherrelle arrived at her sister's apartment, the police were there. They were asking Chalice a series of questions. One of the officers spoke, "It looks like this may have been an inside job. There was no forced entry, so either the door was left unlocked, or the suspect used a key. Have you given out your key to anyone?"

Cherrelle turned, looked at her sister, and saw the look of guilt creep over her face. "Well, just my boyfriend, John," Chalice told them. "And I gave a key to my boyfriend before him. His name is Timothy. And Terry has a key. He was my boyfriend before him." The police officer had stopped writing as he listened to her rattle off the names of the men in her life who still had keys.

Cherrelle couldn't believe what she was hearing. She knew her sister wasn't stupid, but she sure sounded like it right now. She wanted to shout at Chalice to stop calling out the names, there were too many of them, but she didn't. One of them could actually be the thief. Cherrelle looked around. It seemed as if everything of value was missing. Her sister's doll collection, which she had recently started collecting with some of the dolls valued at up to fifteen hundred dollars each. All of her jewelry. Even some of her shoes and suits. This person was serious.

The police were leaving. They advised her to change the locks and told her they would get back to her as soon as possible.

Cherrelle turned to her sister as soon as the door closed, "Are you crazy? How could you give so many men a copy of your apartment key? Anything could have happened at this point."

"I forgot I gave them a key. There's been so much going on in my life that once we broke up, I didn't think about the keys, I just wanted them to be gone. I cannot believe somebody took all my stuff." She sat down heavily on a chair. She couldn't sit on the sofa. It was gone.

Cherrelle leaned against the wall. She felt sorry for her sister but she was furious with her as well. "You know, we never got a chance to have that talk you wanted to have with me."

Chalice shook her head, "This is not a good time. Right now, I cannot deal with a lecture." Both sisters were silent. Cherrelle looked at the dejected expression on her sister's face and decided to hold her comments until later.

"Chalice, I'll help you put back as much of this mess as I can, then you and I are going back to my apartment. You can spend the night there until you get the locks changed. I don't want you here by yourself until that is done."

Chalice wanted to refuse, but she was more than a little afraid to spend the night by herself. She nodded and started putting things back that were in disarray. Her heart was heavy as she wondered who would do something like this to her. She had been so good to each of them.

When they got back to Cherrelle's apartment, she made up the sofa for her little sister. After Chalice had said her prayers and gotten beneath the covers, Cherrelle came in to turn out the lights. "I'm sorry you had such a bad end to your day. Are you okay?"

Chalice nodded, "Yes. But would you pray for me, Cherrelle?"

"Of course." She told her sister and turned to flip the light switch.

"I mean now. Could you pray with me and for me now?"

Chalice sat up, and Cherrelle walked over and sat next to her sister. They joined hands and bowed their heads.

"Dear Heavenly Father. Thank you so much for who you are and what you have done in my life and my sister's life. Thank you Father that you are great and worthy to be praised. I ask Father that you place a hedge of protection around Chalice and that Your angels are encamped round about her, protecting her at every turn. Thank you Father, that she has no need to fear and that no weapon formed against her shall prosper. I thank you Father that those who would cause her harm are exposed, revealed, and removed from her presence.

In Jesus' name, Amen."

Chalice hugged her sister really tight. There was a sheen of tears in her eyes. She cleared her throat.

"Thank you. That was just what I needed to hear."

"You're welcome, now go to sleep." She got up and turned off the lights."

It took Cherrelle a long time to get to sleep. She kept thinking about the importance her sister placed on things that could so easily be taken. She thought about her sister Camille who didn't place a big enough value on herself and her safety. She thought about her grandmother and how precious life could be, at any age. And she thought about how important Cory was becoming to her and how selfish she had been earlier that day, not considering his feelings. Cherrelle tossed and turned, and eventually fell asleep.

Cory was wide awake as he watched his bedside clock change to two o'clock in the morning. He wasn't obsessive, nor did he have stalker-like tendencies, but he had called Cherrelle more times than he wanted to think about tonight, and she had not answered, nor had she called him back. He was worried about her because of their disagreement earlier in the day. He really cared about her. He didn't consider that he might be falling in love with her because Cory knew he had loved her since the first time he had seen her. He and Darryl had met her at the same time, but he could see that his friend was smitten. Technically, Cory already had a girlfriend, so he sat back and watched his friend make his move. It had always been easier for him to get women than his friend Darryl. Cherrelle had been gorgeous, even as a teenager. He could tell then that she would be a beautiful woman, and she had turned out to be even more so than he had imagined, but more importantly she was beautiful on the inside. When they first met, he was entranced by her. The more he was around her, the worse things got for him. He soon dropped his so called girlfriend; no one else could measure up. He felt like a third wheel though, because Darryl always asked him to hang out with them. When he looked into her eyes, when she would let him, he felt like he was in a tunnel. He could see and hear nothing but Cherrelle. He would devour her face with his eyes. At night he would dream about them having a future together. But he never told Darryl. He could not hurt his friend. That was one of the reasons he was so angry with Darryl for standing Cherrelle up on their wedding day. He felt cheated, like he could have been the one courting her and having her fall in love with him, instead of standing on the sidelines letting his friend have the prize. Now that he had an opportunity to be in her life again, he was not going to blow it. He would let her know, if she was still talking to him, how he felt about her, and that he wouldn't let anyone else come between them. With that thought, Cory drifted off to sleep.

Cherrelle took the morning off to help her sister take care of things in her apartment, including getting the locks changed on her front door. At noon she left for her office.

When she got to her office, she looked through her messages and saw that she had four from Cory. She smiled to herself. At least he was still speaking to her. She dialed his cell phone. He picked up the line. He didn't say hello, but went straight to an apology, "I'm sorry, Cherrelle. I should have thought about how you would feel when I asked you to spend time with Darryl and Image. I should have known how you would feel."

"No, I'm the one who should apologize. I was being selfish. I've gotten over Darryl, and Image is my cousin. I can spend a few hours in their presence."

"We won't even talk about that anymore. How have you been?" They talked for a few more minutes and set a date for dinner that night. After she hung up, the day seemed to fly by.

Cory and Cherrelle spent the next few weeks getting to know one another in a way they had never done before. Cherrelle knew that her feelings for Cory were getting serious. She thought he might feel the same way, but she was afraid of getting hurt, so she still kept a distance with her feelings. Cherrelle told Cory everything about herself, from the way she felt when she was left at the altar, to how she was able to finally forgive most of her family members. At every turn, Cory listened patiently with understanding of what she went through, because he had witnessed her devastation. When she had finally purged herself of that event, Cherrelle decided she was done with it and would not bring it up again. She turned to Cory to find out how he was doing and what was going on in his life.

"That's enough about me, I'm done with it. Let's talk about you. How is your project going at work?"

"It's okay. How about going to get something to eat? I'm starved."

Cherrelle was a little taken aback. She realized that every time she brought up his job, he brushed her off or changed the subject, but it was getting ridiculous. She didn't want to be suspicious of him, and she also was hoping that everything was alright. He might be avoiding talking about it because there might be layoffs in his company. She was noticing that a lot of people had gotten laid off recently.

"Is everything alright at work?"

"Everything's fine," he told her as he pulled her to him and kissed her forehead and then her cheek. Cherrelle lifted her face towards him, and he kissed her deeply. Cherrelle melted into him and forgot for the moment what they were discussing. After a few minutes, they pulled apart and smiled into each other's eyes.

"Food," Cory stated hoarsely.

Cherrelle laughed and pulled out her binder filled with take-out menus.

When Cory left later that evening, Cherrelle thought back to their very first kiss. It had been so tender and so sweet. They had been walking hand in hand down Bourbon Street one afternoon, just talking. It was early in the day, so there were people out, but not too many. She had not been expecting it, and Cherrelle didn't think Cory had been expecting it either, it just happened. She was laughing up at him, teasing him about something he said. They stopped talking, leaned toward one another, and kissed. Slowly at first, tenderly and tentatively, with more assurance as the kiss increased. They broke apart when someone passed by them saying, "Get a room!" Cherrelle was so embarrassed, she quickly pulled away. After that first kiss, Cory and Cherrelle couldn't seem to stay apart, but Cherrelle had insisted that she wanted to remain a virgin until she married. Cory understood and respected her boundaries. He found himself respecting her more and more every day.

The next Sunday they went to church together. After listening to the message about getting back in right standing with God, Cherrelle stood up and went to the front to rededicate her life to Christ. She was whole again.

Cory was really disturbed about the half truth that he had told Cherrelle about his job. He could tell it was bothering her too, and she had brought the subject up more than once. He decided that he had to tell her the truth, that evening. He would have to trust that she loved him for himself, and that nothing could change that. He showed up at her front door unannounced. Cherrelle was very happy to see him. She immediately let him in.

"Cherrelle can we have a seat? I really need to talk to you. I haven't been totally honest with you and it is really bothering me. I want to be up front about everything in our lives."

Cherrelle's heart began beating fast. Telling her to have a seat meant that it might be so devastating to her that she shouldn't be standing when he told her. Did he have children, a girlfriend, a wife? She couldn't imagine what it was so she sat.

"Cherrelle, I'm just going to come out and say it. I'm what most people would consider rich. I'm worth more than fifteen million dollars. That manufacturing plant that I told you I work for is mine. I own two in this state and more in a couple of other states. I started with nothing and worked my way up and out, so I am proud of my accomplishments, but I was afraid to tell you because I didn't want you to be intimidated by me. I have been in so many relationships where the women were only interested in my money. I didn't want us to be like that. I wanted you to love me for me, not my money. Please forgive me for the lie."

Cherrelle heard two things. One – there wasn't someone else, and two – he wanted her to love him. She only addressed one of them.

"You want me to love you?"

Cory nodded, "Yes I do."

"Why do you want me to love you?" Cherrelle pressed.

"Because I love you. More than I love myself. I saved myself for you. I wouldn't consider marrying anyone else knowing you were still free and could possibly, maybe, one day be mine."

A lone tear dropped from Cherrelle's eyes as she smiled at him.

"Oh Cory, I love you so much. Your money doesn't matter to me, although it doesn't hurt," she teased.

Cory pulled her up and laughed at her attempt to make a joke. He kissed her until she was breathless. "You are gorgeous, beautiful, and mine. Marry me."

He saw the sudden fear in her eyes and kissed her soundly on the mouth. "We'll talk about it," he told her, backing off. He knew where the fear came from, and he was determined to help her overcome it. Cherrelle couldn't say yes, but she didn't say no.

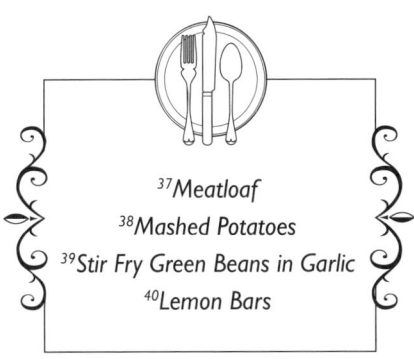

[37] Meatloaf
[38] Mashed Potatoes
[39] Stir Fry Green Beans in Garlic
[40] Lemon Bars

CHAPTER TWENTY-ONE

WAKE UP AND SMELL THE COFFEE

Cherrelle and Cory were inseparable. When you saw one, you saw the other. Today, though, Cherrelle had a lot of personal family matters to take care of, so she was alone. She decided to call her mother to find out how Big Mama was doing.

"Hey Mom. How are you?"

"I'm doing fine now that your Dad is home. He is doing so much better."

"Good, I am so glad. I wasn't really worried about him, because I know how strong he is, but you never know."

"That's true."

"How's Big Mama doing?"

"She has good days and bad days," her mom sighed.

"I need to go by and see her."

"Yes. Have you talked to Camille lately?"

Cherrelle didn't answer.

"Did you know she was pregnant? She came over last week to visit me and your Dad. I looked at her and I knew. When I asked her, she didn't bother to deny it. I was so happy for her, but she didn't look happy at all."

"No, she's not as happy about it as she should be, but she'll be fine. I think I'll call her or go by and see her today, too."

"Good. Have you seen the news today? They were talking about a storm approaching. It has already hit the coast of Florida."

"No, I've been so busy I haven't had a chance to look at television at all. What's going on with it?"

"The news said a Category 1 hurricane hit just north of Miami. So far about ten people have been killed because of it, and it spawned quite a few tornadoes, although they reported the tornadoes didn't hit any buildings."

"Do you think it's coming this way?"

"No, I don't think so. I hope not anyway."

"I'd better start listening to the weather, just in case. Listen, I'll talk to you later. I want to go check on Big Mama." Cherrelle hung up and turned on the TV.

The weather report predicted that the city of New Orleans could possibly be in the cone of uncertainty, so people needed to stay close to news reports. When Cherrelle stepped outside, she looked up into the sky. The weather was beautiful. She could not believe a hurricane could possibly be on its way. Cherrelle got in her car and drove to her grandmother's house.

When she got there PawPaw was sitting in his favorite chair watching the weather channel. He was concentrating on what the meteorologist was saying. "The storm has been named Hurricane Katrina. It is currently in the Gulf of Mexico and has strengthened into a formidable Category 5 hurricane. Currently it has winds of 175 mph and minimum central pressure of 902 millibars. As you can see from the Storm Tracker, the sheer physical size of Katrina might cause devastation far from the eye of the hurricane. It is possibly the largest hurricane of its strength ever recorded. As you can see from this projectory, it seems as if Hurricane Katrina is on a straight path to Louisiana, specifically New Orleans." As she listened to the newscaster, a small amount of fear rose up in Cherrelle, but she quickly pushed it back down. She turned to her grandfather.

"PawPaw, it looks like the storm is heading this way after all. Do you think we should leave town?"

"I have lived here all my life and I never met a storm that could make me leave. I might call one of the boys to come over and help me board up the house, but we staying."

Cherrelle nodded. She realized the storm was only in the middle of the Gulf of Mexico, and if anything major happened, they would get out of town when the time came.

"I'm going to check on Big Mama. How has she been doing?"

"She seems to be doing fine today. Yesterday wasn't her best day," her grandfather said sadly. He seemed like he wasn't doing so well himself. Cherrelle realized that her grandparents had been married more than sixty-five years. They had married when her grandmother was sixteen; her grandfather had been seventeen. All they had ever known was each other. She thought he might feel like he was losing part of himself as Big Mama slowly lost her memory. Cherrelle went into the kitchen to check on her grandmother.

Big Mama was bustling around the kitchen. She was busy preparing dinner for her family. Cherrelle stood in the door of the kitchen and watched her grandmother work. If she didn't know any better, she would swear there was nothing wrong with Big Mama; that her memory wasn't fading. Big Mama turned around and spotted Cherrelle. A huge smile came over her face. "Cherrelle, I am so glad to see you, when did you come back in town? We have really missed you." Big Mama hurried over and hugged Cherrelle. Cherrelle told her gently, "You know I have been in town for a while now, Big Mama."

Her grandmother ignored her as she released Cherrelle and went back to stirring pots. "Are you hungry?"

"As a matter of fact I am," Cherrelle sniffed. "What are you cooking?"

"Chicken Spaghetti Casserole[41] and a tossed salad."

Big Mama fixed Cherrelle a plate. She sat down to the kitchen table and ate every drop. "Big Mama this is delicious. You wouldn't happen to have any dessert, would you?"

"I made Butter Roll Dumplings[42]. Here try some." Big Mama gave Cherrelle some of the dessert.

"Ummm." Cherrelle licked her spoon and wanted to lick the bowl. When she was done, she rinsed her dish and put it in the dishwasher. Cherrelle turned towards her grandmother and hugged her.

"Big Mama, there is a big storm coming this way. If it gets too bad, I'm going to come by and pick up you and PawPaw so that we can get out of the storm's way." Her grandmother nodded. She went into the den and let her grandfather know as well.

The next morning, as Cherrelle drove through the Quarters, she could see the property owners starting to board up the windows of their shops and buildings. It was Saturday. In contrast, the tourists were out as if there was no storm on the way. Cherrelle parked her car, got out, and walked the couple of blocks to the spot she and Cory decided would be a good place for breakfast. There was a line of people at the beignet shop picking up the delicate donuts and famous coffee. The place was crowded. She spotted Cory sitting in the corner of the room, reading the paper. He looked up when she approached. A smile spread across his lips, and he stood up to greet her.

"I'll go and get our breakfast," he told her. Cherrelle took a seat at the table and picked up the paper he had been reading. The hurricane was the major news. There was a picture of the size of the storm and an article that was telling the people of New Orleans that they may need to get out of town. Cherrelle eavesdropped on the people at the next table. The three of them were discussing the storm.

"I'm not leaving. I have been through too many of these so called hurricanes and nothing ever happens. I'll just board up my house and ride it out."

"The news says it's the biggest storm we've ever had."

"And last night the news said the hurricane turned toward us," another one of them said.

"Hurricanes are always changing course. I'll believe it when I see it."

Everyone at the table agreed. They continued to talk about other things, but Cherrelle got to thinking. She really needed to have a plan to help her parents get her grandparents out of town or at least keep them safe during the hurricane. Things were happening pretty fast. She had gone to work yesterday, never dreaming she might have to have an alternate plan for the week.

"Here you go." Cory put the plate of beignets[43] and cups of coffee on the table. Cherrelle immediately dug in. She always loved these powdery confections and could eat more than she should. She ate with gusto. Cory watched for a minute with a satisfied smile as she ate, then he dug in as well.

When they finished eating, Cherrelle wiped her mouth with the napkin. "Those were so good," she sighed. Cory reached over and wiped the corner of her mouth with the pad of his thumb to remove the last of the powdered sugar.

"Have you thought any more about what we discussed the other day?"

Cherrelle smiled at him, "I haven't thought of much of anything else."

"Well?"

"Well what? I'm not ready to make any decisions about us if that's what you mean. I really love you, but that's the best I can do right now."

Cory grabbed her hand and held it in his. "I understand and I'm willing to wait for you, no matter how long it takes." He kissed the back of her hand.

"I think we should leave town during the hurricane. I made reservations for a couple of rooms in Houston. Will you go with me?" Cory asked her.

"I sublet my apartment, but the people moved out last month. We could stay there. If I can convince my family to go with us, I'll go. Otherwise I'll need to stay here to help my mom with Big Mama and PawPaw."

"I'll do whatever you do. If you don't leave, you know I won't go either. Just let me know what's going on. Keep your cell phone on at all times." Cherrelle nodded, and they got ready to leave.

As Cherrelle drove away she saw two men putting shutters on a shop on Bourbon Street. She turned on the radio in the car and heard the mayor of New Orleans, Ray Nagin warning citizens to evacuate because Hurricane Katrina was threatening landfall in New Orleans within the next day or so. Cherrelle pulled out her cell phone and called her sister Camille.

"Hey Camille, how are you? How's the baby?"

"We're fine so far. What's up?"

"Well, I'm thinking with this hurricane coming we should round up the family and get out of town. I just need one other person to agree with me, and we're gone. What do you think?"

"I've been watching the news all day. My TV hasn't changed from the Weather Channel since early this morning. They say it's definitely headed this way. I agree."

"Good. Start gathering up your things or whatever you are going to take. Cory and I will meet you at Big Mama's. You might as well ride with us so we won't have so many cars going."

"Alright, I'll start getting things together. Cherrelle… thanks for being my big sister and always taking care of me." Cherrelle smiled and hung up. The next person she called was Chalice. The phone rang with no answer. She hung up and tried Chalice's cell phone. Her sister answered on the first ring.

"Hello."

"Chalice, pack your bags. We are going on a road trip."

"What are you talking about?"

"I'm just trying to make a joke about this hurricane situation so I won't be so nervous. I'm sorry. This is nothing to make light of."

"I know. Do you think we should go?" Trust Chalice, who always thought about the family as a unit, to make sure the family stayed together during this crisis.

"Yes. I just told Camille that Cory and I will meet her at Big Mama's later today. What time do you think you could be ready? I figured you and Camille could ride with us, and Mom and Dad could stop by and pick up Big Mama and PawPaw and follow behind us."

"That sounds good, have you talked to Mom or Dad today?"

"Not yet. Is anything wrong?"

"No they're fine. I just know how strongly they feel about not wanting to leave town during a storm."

Cherrelle dialed her parents' number. Her father answered.

"Hey Dad. How are you?"

"Getting better every day. I'm glad you called. Your mother and I were just about to call you girls. I know we usually don't like to leave during a hurricane, but this one looks serious. We were hoping you all would leave with us and we can follow one another."

"Most definitely, I was just calling you for that same reason."

"Good. We are going to get our things together and go by and pick up your grandparents. You know we can't leave without them, especially with your grandmother's illness. How soon can you contact your sisters and meet us over there?"

"I'm way ahead of you. I already called Chalice and Camille, and they are riding with me and Cory. Big Mama and PawPaw can ride with you all."

Calvin nodded. "Can we meet you at your grandparents' house in, say, the next two hours?"

"Yes." Cherrelle hung up and called her sisters to tell them the plan. They told her they would meet her at their grandparents' house. On her way home, Cherrelle also called Cory. He told her he would meet her at her apartment, and they would ride over to her grandparents' house together.

41 Chicken Spaghetti Casserole
42 Butter Roll Dumplings
43 Beignets

CHAPTER TWENTY-TWO

FEELING HER OATS

Cherrelle turned on her television when she arrived home to keep an ear on the weather and plugged in her cell phone as she gathered her things for the trip. She didn't know how long they would be gone, but she wanted to take at least a couple of changes of clothes. She also packed toiletries, water, and some snacks.

Cory came in and helped Cherrelle put the items she had packed together in his truck. He had brought his Suburban because he didn't know how many people would need to ride with them. As they were putting the final items in Cory's vehicle, Darryl and Image walked out of the apartment. They had all of their kids in tow and were heading towards their automobile. Cory walked over to help them; their hands were full and the kids were under their feet. He took the items from Image so she could tend to the youngest child. She picked the child up and told the other two to follow. Cherrelle stood helplessly aside as she watched him. She knew she should help them, it was downright selfish not to. But it was as if she were rooted to the spot.

When everyone was securely in the car, Cory stepped aside and waved. The poor car looked as if it wouldn't make it to the corner, let alone a far enough distance to make it to a safe place. Darryl turned the engine and she heard it make a grinding noise. He tried again and nothing happened. He tried one more time. The engine started smoking, but it would not start. She looked at Cory, and he had a pleading look on his face. She knew what that meant. She shook her head. She could not see them riding together for whatever time period without her wanting to strangle Darryl, Image, or both. Cory walked over to her.

"We have to help them. He's my best friend and she's your cousin. If anything happened to them or one of their children, I would never forgive myself." Cherrelle sighed and nodded. She helped Darryl and Image unpack everything from their car and put it in Cory's truck. Image didn't say a word. She knew she was there by the skin of her teeth.

Chalice pulled together as much as she could. She was having a hard time deciding what to bring. She didn't know how long they would be gone, but she wanted to be comfortable and chic. She pulled a few outfits out, put them in a suitcase, and turned out her lights so she could head to her grandmother's. Before she left, she remembered to unplug everything and grab a flashlight.

Camille was in the middle of packing when she heard the front door open and Byron walked in. He had a goofy grin on his face. "Somebody told me you were really pregnant. Am I going to be a daddy again?" He didn't bother denying that he already had kids by someone else.

Camille looked at him like he was on crack. She had already told him herself earlier and his reaction was to close her out. She couldn't figure out what had happened differently to make him act as if he was so happy now.

Camille crossed her arms protectively across her stomach. She had already begun to show. She didn't answer him. She turned back to the matter at hand. She put a few more items in a bag. Byron started thinking back. He couldn't remember the last time he had touched her. Maybe it wasn't his baby.

"It is mine, isn't it?"

Camille still refused to answer. She knew he was trying to start an argument with her.

He stood close behind her as she continued to pack.

"I'm talking to you." He forcibly turned her around to face him.

Camille knew he was crazy. But she was so tired of the abuse. She had decided that wherever the storm took her, she was going to stay there and never look back. She just looked at him and continued to be silent.

"You …" He slapped her so hard she fell against the wall against her almost healed shoulder. She grabbed the upper part of her arm.

"Answer me, and the answer better be yes or I will kill you!" He growled. Byron grabbed Camille by the arm she was nursing and yanked her into an upright position. She cried out again, as this time it felt as if the shoulder had become dislocated again.

"Yes," she screamed. "I already told you, it's yours."

"I don't believe you." The look in his eyes was monstrous. Camille was so afraid, she almost fainted. The next thing she felt was a tremendous blow to her stomach. She doubled over in pain and passed out.

Byron panicked. When he saw Camille lying there, he attempted to get her to wake up. After a few minutes she did rouse. He brought her some water and helped her get comfortable, but he refused to allow her to leave. She rubbed the ache in her stomach.

It took Cory and Cherrelle almost an hour to get to her grandparents' house. By now, most of the people in the city who could, had heeded the mayor's warnings and started to leave, en masse from the city. The outbound arteries of the city were filled with cars. The four adults in the car looked out on the scene before them in wonder. They had never seen this many cars on the highway before in their lives. Cory pulled off the highway and went down some of the side streets that would take them to her grandmother's house. It would take a little longer than it normally would, but it would be much better than trying to travel in that mess on the freeway.

They arrived at the house at the same time as her parents. Her father pulled his car behind the Suburban. Chalice pulled up behind him. Everyone got out. Cherrelle walked over to her parents. Her father told them, "We need to hurry and get Clarence and Bessie out of here, because if we wait too late, we'll get trapped on the road during the hurricane, in all that traffic. If that's the case, it will be safer to stay here. At least we'll all be together and have a roof over our heads."

"Did you call and let them know we were coming?" Cherrelle asked her mother.

"Yes, I spoke to my father and my mother to make sure they both understood the seriousness of this hurricane and that we are leaving with them regardless of what they say. They both said okay."

"Good. We'll help you put their things in your car," Cory told them.

Theresa didn't ask Cherrelle how she ended up with Darryl and Image.

When the group walked in they saw PawPaw in the back room of the house, putting things in bags to carry with them. The men went to the back to help him. Theresa and Cherrelle went into the kitchen to see if Big Mama needed any help. Image sat down with her kids and turned the television to cartoons to distract them. Theresa and Cherrelle quickly came out of the kitchen.

"Have you seen Big Mama?" they asked Image. She shook her head no.

Cherrelle started running from room to room, calling her grandmother's name looking all over the house. Image got up to help them look. The men heard all of the commotion and came out to see what was going on.

"Dad, have you seen Big Mama?" Theresa asked her father.

"Last time I saw her she was in the kitchen. Claimed she was making Oatmeal Bars[44] for the road."

"Cherrelle, run into the kitchen to see if they have any oatmeal," Theresa told her daughter in a frightened voice. Cherrelle quickly went into the kitchen and came back with the expected report.

"They don't have any oatmeal."

"She went to the store!" Theresa cried despairingly.

"She's done it before." Cherrelle agreed.

"How could she get to the store? She doesn't drive." Image told them.

"No, but she can walk, just like she did before. We have to go find her. She couldn't have gotten very far."

The group spread out. Cherrelle, Cory, and Darryl went in one vehicle, Theresa, Chalice, and Calvin in another. Image and PawPaw stayed at the house with the kids. He was to call them if Big Mama returned before they did.

They looked for Big Mama for hours. After a while, dusk became dark. They called the police and were told that because she was an adult, she would have to be missing for twenty-four hours before a formal report could be filed.

Theresa was furious, "Anything could happen to her in twenty-four hours. We have to keep looking for her."

The group went out to look for her again. It was after midnight when they stopped looking for her for that day. They decided they would continue their search in the morning because they refused to leave without her. Theresa and Cherrelle rationalized that Big Mama had been gone for more than eight hours the time before. They kept telling themselves that she would be fine. The crisis of finding Big Mama had distracted them from the fact that Camille had not yet arrived at Big Mama's house.

That night, everyone spread all over Big Mama's house in an attempt to get some sleep. Clarence went into his bedroom. Theresa and Calvin went into the other bedroom. Image, Darryl, and their kids made a pallet on the floor in the den. Chalice curled up on the sofa. Cory and Cherrelle found a spot and spread blankets out on the dining room floor.

Right before they fell asleep, Cory was tempted to tease Cherrelle about the fact that they were finally getting a chance to sleep together, but she was too upset to appreciate the joke, and he decided now was not the time.

CHAPTER TWENTY-THREE

FISH OR CUT BAIT

The next morning, the group got up to face another day of searching. They knew that Big Mama was out there somewhere; tired, hungry, and more than a little confused. They had to find her and refused to leave without her.

Theresa got up and fixed them all a good hot breakfast so they would be strong for the search. While she was in the kitchen preparing breakfast, everyone else took turns in the one bathroom in the house taking care of personal hygiene.

Cherrelle had been the first one up after Theresa, so she was dressed first. She walked into the kitchen. Her mother had really cooked a lot of food. That told Cherrelle more than anything else how worried her mother was about Big Mama. Theresa had prepared Salmon Croquettes[45], scrambled eggs, grits, and Homemade Biscuits[46]. She had taken out two kinds of syrup and jelly. Everyone else soon filed in and filled their plates with the delicious breakfast. PawPaw took his plate into the den, sat down in front of the television, and turned it on.

The news was bleak.

"It's Sunday, August 28, and the National Weather Service has issued a bulletin predicting 'devastating' damage will be caused by Hurricane Katrina. The mayor has issued a mandatory evacuation for everyone in the city of New Orleans." The news cut to the mayor of New Orleans as he spoke. "Ladies and gentlemen, I wish I had better news for you but we are facing a storm that most of us have feared," Nagin said during a news conference after reading a mandatory evacuation order. "This is a threat that we've never faced before."

The report went back to the weatherman as he continued. "Currently, Katrina is a Category 5 hurricane with sustained wind speeds of one hundred seventy-five miles per hour and gusts of up to two hundred fifteen miles per hour. I repeat, a mandatory evacuation has been issued." The weatherman continued to show pictures of how large the storm was, but the family couldn't take any more, and they turned the channel.

Everyone finished breakfast and prepared to go out and look for Big Mama one more time. Before they left, Calvin sadly told the group, "As much as we all love Big Mama, if we don't find her by one o'clock, we'll have to stop the search and get on the road. You heard them say we are under a mandatory evacuation. We will leave before three no matter what." Everyone solemnly agreed, although you could see they did not want to. As the group walked out, the day was still so pretty, it was hard to fathom that a storm of the magnitude that they said Katrina might be, was approaching.

They searched everywhere. They went to her friends' homes, but they had already left. They searched side streets, major streets, shelters, and stores. There was no sign of Bessie anywhere. At one o'clock, the group dejectedly returned to the house. While they were out, they had noticed that traffic was so bad it would be unwise to leave now. They decided to wait it out. Calvin, Cory, and Darryl begin the process of boarding up and securing the house.

In the kitchen, the women began preparing lunch.

"Maybe Big Mama caught a ride with one of her friends, and they took her with them. That's possible," Chalice told her mother wanting to encourage her.

"Maybe, but unless the house was so far out of the way, they would have brought her back, come back for PawPaw, or at least called," Image stated gloomily.

Cherrelle glared at Image for being so negative. "We need to look on the bright side and think positively. Even though we haven't found her, there have been no reports to say something bad has happened to her, so we'll assume that she is fine." Everyone was quiet for a while after that.

Theresa finished up with the part of the meal she was preparing, washed her hands and dried them on a dishtowel hanging on a rack. "Has anyone heard any recent reports about the storm? I'm going in to keep Dad company. I know he is so worried."

When she walked out, Cherrelle turned on Image. "Why

are you here? If you can't say something positive, don't say anything at all."

Image's neck swerved and she turned around so fast she almost knocked Chalice, who was standing next to her, to the side. She put her hands on her hips.

"I know you didn't." Image yelled at Cherrelle.

"Keep your voice down. You don't have to be ghetto everyday," Cherrelle whispered roughly.

"Look, you just wanted my man and he chose me, so you need to get over it. I don't care what you think of me. Big Mama is my grandmother too and I can say anything I want to. You need to keep your opinion to yourself."

"I am way over it. I am so glad Darryl chose you. If I had married him, I would have ended up just like you. Broke, busted, and disgusted." Cherrelle was looking around for someone to give her a high five for finally telling Image off, but when she looked around, all she saw was disappointment and shock. Especially on the face of Cory. She didn't realize he had walked in and heard her giving Image a piece of her mind. Darryl looked so dejected. He already felt that way, but now he realized other people thought it too. Image was about to retaliate, but when she saw Darryl, she ran into his arms and burst into tears. Cherrelle couldn't believe it. Could those be real tears or tears for Darryl and Cory's benefit? Cherrelle stepped forward and touched her cousin on the shoulder.

"Look, I'm sorry. I think everyone is just upset right now, and I apologize. Although I do not want to be with Darryl anymore, …I do, …I do want you all to be happy." Cherrelle took a deep breath and said softly. "I really am sorry. Can you forgive me for this and all the other times I've been mean to you?" Cherrelle turned to Darryl. "Darryl, I have already forgiven you. But I have to actually say it. For the longest, I blamed you for how my life turned out, but the truth of the matter is, my life isn't so bad. I know that God wants me to be happy. And no offense, but we never would have been happy together. You made your choice. You were meant for Image, and Cory was meant for me." Cherrelle turned toward Cory and smiled. "And although he was right there under my nose, I was afraid to see him, because I didn't want to hurt you. I loved you like a brother, like a friend. But I loved him as something else, which is why I would never look him in his eyes, or go anywhere alone with him. He made my stomach do funny things. Now I know what it was." He hadn't moved before, and this time she smiled tentatively at Cory. He walked over to her and took her hand. He pulled it and her to his heart and kissed her cheek. Image looked up at him with new eyes. When Cherrelle stepped away from him, she saw Image looking at Cory with renewed interest. She turned to her cousin. "I also forgive you, Image. I'm sure you had to plot and plan to get Darryl alone so you could work your magic and you did it. I'm sure you have the life you deserve." Image frowned at that, but she didn't reply.

There seemed to be peace truce between Darryl, Cherrelle, and Image, especially since it seemed they would be stuck with one another for a while. After a few minutes, everyone was called to eat. The family sat down to Shrimp Creole[47] served on rice, and a salad. After their full day, everyone had a hefty appetite, and finished it all.

After the dishes were done, and the kitchen was cleaned up, they went into the den to listen to the weather news, play cards, or read. Chalice was bored, so she went into the kitchen to make a Banana Pudding[48]. Theresa went into the bedroom to lie down.

"What's the weather doing?" Clarence asked Calvin.

"Still on its way. It's already done some damage to the areas not protected by the levees. Some of the low lying areas are already covered with water caused by the high tide."

The helicopter cameras showed a picture of the gridlock on the freeway of people trying to get out of town.

"Wow, look at that. We were almost in that mess. I'm glad we decided not to go. We are safely here at home, and they are trapped in hot cars, trying to move forward like turtles." Five year old DJ, Darryl and Image's oldest son, heard his father say turtles and came over to see what he was talking about. DJ climbed on his father's lap and watched the TV, thumb in mouth.

"It's still pretty early. What do you all want to do?" Image asked.

The news flashed to Mayor Nagin. He was ordering those who could not leave town to go to the Superdome for shelter during this "state of emergency". The anchorman then went to a shot of a newscaster along the coast of Mississippi. The damage caused by the hurricane was shocking. Everyone in the room watched the weather reports without comment. Cherrelle was the first to move.

"Cory, could you help me get our things back together? We are going to the Superdome. I don't feel safe staying here. I'd rather we go there." She started moving around the room, picking up their things. Cory went to help her.

"I'm with you." Chalice said.

"I'll go wake your mother, so she can get the things together that she wants to take." Calvin stated. Everyone started moving at once, in a hurry to get moved before the hurricane hit. The weather reports made it seem as if it were just around the corner.

It took them just a few minutes to get everything together, including non-perishable food and water. They walked outside, keys in hand.

Cory spoke up, "If you all don't mind, I think we should all ride together in my truck. I think we can all fit, if somebody holds the kids. They may not be letting too many cars in and I wouldn't want you to leave your cars downtown."

"That's an excellent idea, young man," Calvin patted Cory on the back in thanks. He smiled to himself. He had always liked him.

Cory's Suburban had three rows of seats. Cory and PawPaw were in the front. Calvin, Theresa, and Cherrelle were in the middle seats, and Chalice, Image, and Darryl sat in the back with the kids.

As they drove away from the house, Chalice asked her mother. "Has anyone talked to Camille?" Her mother and Cherrelle turned towards each other simultaneously in shock. "Where was Camille?"

Camille was lying across her bed, silently nursing her injured arm. She was so stiff, she could barely move. The bedroom door opened and Byron walked in holding a tray containing two bowls of canned chicken noodle soup. At least it was hot. Camille attempted to sit up using her uninjured arm for support. After a few tries, Byron put the soup on the dresser and came to help her sit up.

"How do you feel?" He asked her.

In her mind, there were so many answers she could give him, but she politely answered.

"Better."

"I'm sorry, I did this to you, but you made me do it. You make me so mad sometimes that I lose control. Do you forgive me?" He attempted to kiss her. Camille turned her head, but answered his question.

"Yes. Can I go now? I was supposed to be at Big Mama's a long time ago. I know they're wondering where I am."

"Nope, we're going to ride this thing out together. You, me, and the baby."

Camille knew there was no use on begging him to change his mind, so she did what she knew to do. She prayed.

When the family got close to the Superdome, they realized they would have to walk the rest of the way to get closer. People were everywhere. There were so many people, the noise was deafening. Cory grabbed Cherrelle's hand. She grabbed PawPaw's hand who in turn grabbed her mother's hand. Chalice was holding on between her father and her mother. Image and Darryl were close behind them with a child in each of their arms and one on Darryl's back. They stayed close to one another as they winded their way through the crowds. There were lines of people and crowds of people surrounding the dome. There seemed to be no order, even with the police and what looked like the National Guard surrounding the building. As they passed through the crowds, Theresa had her eyes open, on the lookout for any signs of Big Mama. It looked like they were letting groups in at a time.

Cory turned to Cherrelle, "The Superdome holds about seventy thousand people. I don't know how many they will let inside, but I hope they'll let us in. Maybe we should put your grandfather and the kids up front, so they can see we have elderly and children with us." He looked up at the sky. It was starting to become overcast. He expected they would be allowed to go in pretty soon. He was right. Shortly after that, another large group of people was allowed to go into the dome. Cherrelle and her family were a part of it.

Once inside they were shuffled through the crowd. They looked around for a space large enough for the entire group to stay together. DJ scrambled from his father's back and stopped in his tracks. His mother, struggling to carry the baby, tried to pull him forward. He refused to budge. "Come on, DJ. We have to keep moving." He didn't seem to hear her. He moved away from his mother, moving quickly away from her. "DJ!" she called out. Darryl heard his wife's voice and turned around to see what was going on. He saw his son disappear into the crowd. He handed Daisia to Cory and went after him. With all this commotion, the rest of the family realized something was wrong. They stepped to the side so the crowd would not continue to push them forward. Image worriedly looked for her husband and son through the thick crowd.

DJ was really moving. He moved liked he was on a mission. Darryl had a hard time keeping up with him, with the crowd of people continuing to swell. DJ saw his goal directly in front of him. He ran forward and buried his face in her skirt, "Big Mama, we thought you was lost!" Bessie reached down and hugged her great-grandson. She was so happy to see him. She couldn't believe he was here. "DJ," she whispered. Darryl walked up and joined in the hug. Big Mama had been so good to him, even with what had happened with Cherrelle that he just had to hug her. He could not believe she was there, in front of him. "Big Mama, everybody is going to be happy to see you. Come on." DJ wouldn't let go of Big Mama's hand. "I'm not gonna lose you again," he told her. Darryl, DJ, and

Big Mama moved through the crowd at, what felt like, a snail's pace. When they approached the family, the first to see them was Image, searching frantically for her family. She gave a yelp and started moving in their direction. Cherrelle heard her cousin and turned to find out what was going on now. She saw Big Mama as well. "Big Mama!" she called. Everyone turned and started moving towards Big Mama as fast as they could. Big Mama couldn't get a word in edgewise. Everyone was talking so fast and all at once.

"Big Mama, where have you been?"

"Oh Big Mama, we missed you."

"Mama, what happened?"

"Bessie, my Bessie." When they heard Clarence calling his wife, they parted to let him through. He grabbed his wife, pulled her close, and hugged her like he would never let her go. When he finally did, everyone else had a chance to hug her too. Cherrelle turned to Cory, so overcome that she wanted to cry. She put her face into his shoulder while Cory held her tight.

"Oh, Cory. I am so afraid. I don't want to be here."

Cory looked at his watch. It was after four o'clock. He looked into Cherrelle's frightened eyes as he held her face between his hands. "Guess what. I keep saying how rich I am, well now is my chance to prove it to myself. We don't have to stay here. Tell everyone to follow me."

The entire family quickly followed Cherrelle's instructions. The police barricading the building attempted to stop them. Cory stepped up and told them, "We have alternate transportation. Are you telling us we do not have the option to leave?" The policemen stepped aside. They walked out to the Suburban and headed to the airport.

Cherrelle had never been aboard a private plane before. It was large enough for everyone to be comfortable. "Wow", Cherrelle told Cory, "I guess you really are rich." She leaned over and kissed him as the plane headed to Houston. Everyone looked down and watched the rows of cars that stretched as far as the eye could see, until they were too high up to see anything on land any more. Cherrelle lifted her eyes to heaven and whispered, "Thank you, Lord." She closed her eyes and drifted off to sleep.

[44]Oatmeal Bars
[45]Salmon Croquettes
[46]Homemade Biscuits
[47]Shrimp Creole
[48]Banana Pudding

CHAPTER TWENTY-FOUR

WHAT'S GOOD FOR THE GOOSE

When night fell, Camille looked sadly at the television as the weather station gave more details about the upcoming hurricane. She was sure that her family had left her by now. Why hadn't they come for her? No one had called or tried to contact her at all. Of course she had no idea of knowing that Byron had taken the battery out of her cell phone and removed the phone plugs out of the wall. All she knew was that she must be as worthless as he said, because no one even cared enough to call and see if she was dead or alive. Byron came in from the bathroom. He sat on the sofa and turned the volume on the TV up.

"It looks like it's heading this way. We got enough food?"

Camille nodded.

"Good, I'm going to bed." He walked out and closed the bedroom door.

Camille curled up on the sofa and pulled the quilt up to her chin. She continued to watch the news reports. She finally drifted off to sleep at about midnight.

A loud wind woke Camille. The television was still on and thankfully they still had reception, although it was not good. The weatherman was saying that the storm had not hit New Orleans directly, but instead had made landfall at Buras. But that was so close, and the hurricane was so big, that they were still sustaining wind damage. The biggest cause for concern, the weatherman was saying, was the flooding that was beginning to be seen in parishes along the coast. Camille wasn't really worried. Although they lived in a two story apartment complex, their home was on the second floor. She could not imagine water getting up to where they were.

A few minutes later, the electricity shut off. It is still very early in the morning, almost six o'clock, and Camille is left in the dark, but it should begin to get light soon. The hurricane may have affected the outside light though because it seemed to be totally pitch black.

Camille felt helpless. She didn't even know if she had a flashlight or a battery operated radio. As a matter of fact, she knew she didn't have those things. She lay back on the sofa and closed her eyes.

A few minutes later, Byron came out of the bedroom.

"What's wrong with the TV?"

"The electricity went off. We are going to have to wait until it gets light to find out what's happening."

Byron walked over and looked out of the window. Wind gusts were still blowing things all over the place, mostly wood, paper, and street signs, but the most amazing thing he noticed was how high the water was getting.

"It's dark outside but you can still see a little bit. Come and look at this."

Camille got up and looked out of the window. She could not believe her eyes. There was water as far as the eye could see. It was still slightly dark, but it was getting lighter and you could see the water. It looked like it was still rising. Camille moved to sit in an inside room. The only room available that has no windows is the bathroom. She goes there to settle in through the rest of the storm. Byron goes in with her.

After an hour or so, Byron makes a move.

"I'm hungry. I'm going to go out to the kitchen and bring us something back to eat."

When he stepped out, Camille took advantage of the time to use the bathroom. She had been holding it for some time and was glad when he left.

He came back shortly. He had made a couple of sandwiches.

"I'm glad we're eating now. Water has come into the apartment. That means the apartment below us is totally flooded. We may have to go up to the roof."

Camille's heart began to thud loudly as she realized just how dangerous this situation was. Winds were still howling outside. They sat to wait it out.

It had been quiet for a few minutes. Camille figured the eye must have passed by and now they were on the other side of it, by the sounds outside.

As soon as it was quiet outside again, Byron opened the door. Water was everywhere. Even on the second floor, water was already at their ankles. Byron and Camille looked at one another. Camille realized this was the first time she had ever seen fear on Byron's face.

"Let's get to the roof before it is too late. I do not want to drown trapped in here."

Camille threw on jeans and a T-shirt. She also slid her feet into her tennis shoes and grabbed a raincoat. She was ready to go. Byron was already ahead of her. Thankfully there were stairs leading to the roof, so they didn't have to do any climbing. There was a very small space along the side of the roof, so they had to walk single file along the area. When she looked out, Camille got dizzy. Water was everywhere. It was getting higher and higher. At one point, a rolling wave of water sloshed against her foot. The water seemed to be more than twelve feet high. There was no place to sit, so they leaned against the roof, with nothing between them and the water but a small railing.

After a while, Byron became restless and he turned to get more comfortable. In the small space, he lost his footing and tumbled towards the edge. He reached out and held on to the railing for dear life, his legs fully immersed in water and bumping up against the building. He was being strongly pushed and pulled by the current from the flood.

Byron reached out for Camille to help him, the fear in his eyes palpable.

"Help me. I can't swim."

Camille very carefully reached for his outstretched hand, concerned about her own safety and footing. When she reached out, a sharp pain ran up her damaged arm, still aching from the pain she had received from him earlier. She pulled her hand back to nurse the pain in her shoulder just as he let go to reach for her hand. As she pulled her arm back, she saw Byron slip from the roof and fall into the water. He screamed a blood curdling sound that she felt she would never forget. She heard the heavy splash, but couldn't move from her position on the roof. After a couple of seconds, she slowly moved closer to the edge. She looked over into the water and saw Byron come up and go down. He came back up, but he didn't have a chance. The water was over his head and when he went down again, he did not come back up. Camille turned away and moved back from the railing on the roof. She cried and prayed all day long, and far into the night. Eventually she fitfully slept, standing up, propped against the roof.

Camille stayed on the roof for more than thirty-six hours before she was finally rescued. Weak and exhausted from being in one spot for so long, with no food or water, had taken its toll. When the helicopter from the Air Force Reserve team approached, she didn't have the strength to try to get its attention, but thankfully they saw her. They lowered the basket, and the volunteers secured her in it before they slowly moved her up and into the whirling machine. They took her to the airport with the other survivors and after a few days of rest, food and water, Camille is strong enough to make the trip with many other survivors to Ellington Field outside of Houston, Texas. They take her to the Astrodome with the other survivors.

CHAPTER TWENTY-FIVE

THE MILK OF HUMAN KINDNESS

Cherrelle, Cory, Theresa, Calvin, PawPaw, Big Mama, Chalice, Darryl, Image, and their three children were exhausted when they finally arrived in Houston. Cherrelle's sublet of her apartment had been released, so they all went there to rest and watch for news of the hurricane. Darryl put the kids down for a nap. Big Mama went into Cherrelle's bedroom to rest as well. Everyone who stayed up was shocked at the news reports.

Day after day they watched the injustices that the people of New Orleans and other cities along the coast had to suffer at the whim of Katrina and the government. People were stranded and homes were destroyed. It was the worst thing they had ever witnessed. What was even worse, were the deplorable conditions the people had to put up with in the Superdome. Every day Cherrelle thanked God and Cory for getting them out of there.

They could very well have been there.

More than anything else, when they watched the news reports and saw the sea of people gathered as far as the eye could see, they looked for signs of Camille and other family members who were missing. Only Cherrelle, Chalice, and Cory had brought their cell phones. Everyone else had rushed out so fast, they left them at home. When they attempted to contact other family members, they either got no answer or the disconnected, circuits busy message.

"Cory, I wonder if I'll ever see my sister again. And she was expecting my first niece or nephew." Cherrelle was distraught. She didn't talk to her mother about it because she didn't want to upset her any more than she already was.

Cory took Cherrelle's hand. "We are going to use our faith in this one, just like we have for every other situation in our lives. I know that God will get us through this, just as He has before."

Cherrelle nodded. "Cory, will you pray with me?"

He held both of her hands. As he started praying, Theresa walked in and joined the circle. Calvin was right behind her. Before Cory finished the entire family had gathered hand in hand, united in spirit and purpose, to have the desires of their hearts answered.

"Heavenly Father. We come before you humbled in your presence but strong in faith. We honor you, Father. We know that we can do nothing without you, but we can do all things through Christ, which strengthens us. Thank you Father, that your angels are encamped round about all of our relatives as they go through this storm. We thank you Father for allowing us to make it through safely. We come before you Father asking for traveling grace and mercy for our family members and friends. We thank you Father for the kindness of strangers and friends alike during this period of our lives. We know, Father that you know our end from our beginning and you only have thoughts of good towards us and not evil, so we thank you Father, that this situation will work out for the best and all things will work together for the good. Thank you Father that family members will become closer and that love will abound. We lift you up and we lift up your name. In the mighty name of Jesus. Amen."

When he was done, everyone hugged one another, with tears in their eyes. Cherrelle hesitated only a second before briefly hugging Darryl and Image.

Camille moved slowly into the Astrodome from the bus that dropped them off from Ellington Field. She was still a little stiff. She looked around in awe. There were already almost five thousand people inside. She found a spot for her cot along a wall and settled in.

Cherrelle was watching more news about what was happening to the evacuees, or as the family liked to say, the survivors in Houston.

"Cory, do you think we could go over and volunteer at the Dome? They also need volunteers at George R. Brown."

"I think that's a good idea. It would help us if we could help someone else. It looks like there might be more people at the Astrodome than the other place. How about if we go there? They might need us more. We'll get up early in the morning and go."

Cherrelle nodded and turned up the volume. The news media was explaining how Houston Independent School District had recruited hundreds of volunteers to help the people get settled in and help their children get registered for school. There were also volunteers from the Red Cross and local churches. Now the plan was to help those people find housing during the time they would be in Houston because they couldn't stay in the Dome forever.

Cherrelle changed the channel. Another channel was showing the deplorable conditions of the Superdome in New Orleans. The roof had a big tear in the top of it. She shook her head and changed the channel once again. It was too depressing to watch.

The next morning, Cherrelle, Chalice, and Cory went to the Astrodome to volunteer. When they arrived, they were assigned to work with the Red Cross. People were everywhere, survivors and volunteers alike. People were lined up cot to cot, with their supplies next to them. There were children everywhere. There was even a room for children who had no known adult with them, those who had been separated from their families in the rush to get them on the buses and out of New Orleans. The poor things, all of the children, were being kept busy by the volunteers to the best of their ability. They had paper and pens for drawing, but not a lot of crayons, coloring books or toys for the children. Cherrelle and Cory made a note that they needed to stop by the store and buy some of these things to bring tomorrow.

Cherrelle was assigned to a certain section in the Dome for handing out supplies and being a general assistant. She saw people who looked familiar, but none of them were her relatives.

"Hi", she said to one young women she had seen at church in New Orleans. "Do you know my sister, Camille? Have you seen her since you've been here?"

Ramona was so happy to see someone she even remotely knew that she broke down and cried. When she settled down, she said she hadn't seen Camille.

"I'll keep an eye out for you. I know how hard it is to lose a family member. I hope nothing bad happened to her. They said so many people died back there. Thank God I'm here." Cherrelle smiled at her and patted her hand as she got up to go. "I'm glad you're here too. I'll see you later."

Eventually Cherrelle found Cory and Chalice, and they got ready to go. It was such a hard day emotionally for all of them, they were exhausted. They walked slowly through the front doors of the Astrodome on their way to the car. A few minutes later, Camille walked out of the bathroom and settled back on her cot.

"It is amazing what good attitudes everyone has in the midst of this tragedy," Cory mused. "It kind of makes you feel good to know we helped so many people today."

Chalice agreed, "I was so upset yesterday, thinking about all we had lost. But today I feel so much better. One thing helping people in need does is put everything in perspective. When I see how much people have had to put up with and they are still strong, people who really have every reason to be angry, but are not, it makes you realize you can't sweat the small stuff. At least we are alive. We could be living like that. I want to go back tomorrow."

Cherrelle was so overcome with emotion, she couldn't say a word. All she knew was that she had to go back the next day to see what else she could do to help.

The next morning, Cherrelle, Cory, and Chalice got ready to go back to the Dome once again to volunteer. They were so blessed, and they wanted to help others have an easier time.

When they got to the Dome, they noticed that there were even more volunteers than the day before. Cherrelle was assigned to a different area of the Dome than she was the day before. Before she went to her assigned area, she and Cory wanted to stop by the children's area and drop off the toys and other things they had purchased. They passed by the tables set up by the local school district. They were helping students get enrolled in and registered for school. They stopped and watched one family get registered.

"Good morning," the bright eyed volunteer said to a mother and daughter. The child looked like she was thirteen or fourteen years old. "I'm going to help you register your daughter for school, and I'll need you to fill out some paperwork for me. What grade are you in?" She asked the girl.

"I'm in the twelfth grade." She told her without pause.

Mary, the volunteer, frowned slightly and looked at the young girl again. The students did not have to have records to register because many people had rushed out of the hurricane's path and had not had an opportunity to get birth certificates or any other records, so the volunteers were told to take the word of the parent and the child. She turned to ask the question of the girl's mother, who had been busy filling out some of the forms.

"What grade is your daughter in?"

"What grade did she tell you?" The mother asked.

"She said the twelfth, but she looks so young."

"If she said she's in the twelfth, then put her in the twelfth."

The volunteer stressed to the student. "You do realize you will be tested to see if you are in the right grade. If they don't think you should be there, they might put you in the grade they think you should be in." She was hoping the young lady would relent, but she did not. When she refused to budge, Mary completed the card and wrote twelfth grade at the top. She provided additional information to the mother, including information on which bus to take to be picked up for school.

Cherrelle and Cory walked off. They didn't want to laugh, but they did realize the young lady probably really didn't want to be in school.

This time Cherrelle was assigned to an information booth. She was given brochures and other information to read about local churches and other charitable organizations that were helping the Katrina survivors. The citizens and churches of Houston came through in a big way, and there was plenty of food, water, and clothes for everyone. There were also plenty of volunteers. From what she was reading, she could tell that Houston area churches had compassion for the hurricane survivors and did what they could to support the new, even if temporary, residents of Houston.

New Light Christian Center Church set up "Louisiana Love Relief" and asked its members to donate new or gently used clothes, shoes, and other items to be given to the survivors. The church also helped the survivors get settled in a residence, a church, and employment, and guided civil agencies and other organizations with culturally sensitive issues. Dr. Hilliard and his wife, Dr. Bridget, also set up Operation Church Reconnect

- where the church helps pastors connect with their displaced member in the city and open their doors, encouraging others to do the same, to allow New Orleans pastors to use the building for their church meetings.

Wheeler Avenue Baptist Church set up and found housing for displaced residents. These residents were provided with food, shelter, and clothing for months. Many of the members of the church volunteered to allow families to live with them until the survivors could get back home. Dr. Cosby encouraged his members to have compassion for others during their time of need.

Catholic Charities assisted families with one or two nights stay and provided money for food, gas, or transportation to help survivors reach their final destinations. They had plans to move to a long-term case management program. The plan was for the program to be managed by staff members, volunteers, and caseworkers hired from New Orleans.

Other organizations who provided assistance and relief to the survivors were the Houston Area Urban League; Houston NAACP; Greater St. Matthew Baptist Church; New Deliverance Church, and many, many more. "Wow", Cherrelle thought as she finished reading the information. "No wonder I love Houston so. I'm going to miss it when I go back home." She paused, "Where did that come from? I am home." She shook her head to clear it.

The lady standing in the booth next to her was reading the information as well. "The City of Houston is really being generous. I am so proud of them, us. But we believe in the cause and I'm glad I'm here." She stuck out her hand and smiled. "Hi, my name is Camille."

Cherrelle slowly put her hand out as well. "I'm Cherrelle. I have a sister named Camille." More quietly she said. "I haven't seen her since before the storm. We're from New Orleans as well." She began to tell Camille about how her family had ended up in Houston without her sister. The family was devastated. They had tried to contact Camille, but she was not answering her phone, and they had no way of knowing how to reach her or if she was even still alive.

Cherrelle, Cory, and Chalice had gotten to the Astrodome fairly early to volunteer, so before they split up, they decided to take a lunch break and come back to the dome later to continue working. Cherrelle looked at her watch and saw that it was close to the time for her to find them so they could go. She bid goodbye to Camille and moved along to find them. She walked into the entrance of the room filled with cots. People and their belongings were everywhere. She slowly scanned the room looking for Cory and Chalice. She didn't know if they would be on the floor assisting someone or where they might be, so she carefully looked around the room. As she turned around, not ten feet in front of her was Camille. She was sitting on a cot, with her legs crossed and her eyes closed. Her head was resting back against the wall. She looked so sad and so tired. Cherrelle didn't waste any time. She quickly ran over to her sister and hugged her so hard, she almost lost her balance. Camille jumped, not expecting to be attacked. They told her she needed to keep her wits about her, and she was about to scream when she recognized the perfume her sister always wore. It had to be her. Joy rose in her so strong, she could not believe it. Her prayers had been answered. Cherrelle moved her face from her sister's shoulder and kissed her on the forehead and cheek. Then she hugged her tighter.

Tears flowed down both of their cheeks as they realized they had found one another.

Cherrelle hugged her little sister and cried, asking her. "Where were you? We tried to call you and couldn't find you." All Camille could do was cry and thank God she had been found. She had been so forlorn, thinking that she was all alone in the world. Now she had found her family, and they did care about her after all.

Cherrelle helped Camille gather her few belongings. They went to the volunteer station to find out what to do to check out. They didn't want to just walk out. There had to be a process for this.

Once she had helped Camille check out, and they returned the cot, Cherrelle pulled out her cell phone to call Cory and Chalice. She told them where to meet her and that she had a surprise for them. As they went to the designated spot, Cherrelle passed by her volunteer station. Camille was still there.

"I found my sister", she told her. "I found Camille." Camille, the volunteer was so happy for her, that tears rolled from her eyes as she smiled and waved.

Cherrelle still couldn't get over finding her sister. She couldn't stop saying, "thank you, Lord." Camille couldn't believe it either. She had been sitting there praying at the very moment her sister found her. God had surely been good to her. Cherrelle turned to look at her sister. It seemed as if she had gotten bigger since she had last seen her. She rubbed her sister's belly. Camille didn't usually like the rubbing, but she was so happy to see her sister, she didn't care. Chalice was the first to arrive. She could not believe her eyes. She hugged her sister as they rocked back and forth for several minutes. "Let's go tell Mama and Daddy. They have been so worried about you."

Cherrelle stopped her. "We can't leave without Cory." She turned around. "Here he comes now."

When Cory saw Camille, even he hugged her. He knew how worried Cherrelle and her family had been about her. Cherrelle grabbed Camille by the hand. "Let's get you out of here. Are you hungry? How have you been surviving? I know you like your comfort."

"Let's just say, a hot meal and a hot bath, not necessarily in that order, are just what the doctor ordered."

CHAPTER TWENTY-SIX

BEST THING SINCE SLICED BREAD

At Cherrelle's apartment, Theresa and Calvin were wondering where Camille could possibly be. Theresa sat near the window as she had countless times when Calvin was missing earlier, cell phone and cordless phone nearby.

"I really miss her, but she's probably with Byron. I hope he's taking good care of her." Theresa and Calvin had not originally approved her decision to marry Byron, but he was her choice, and they tried their best to make him feel a part of the family. They had both heard the rumors about him and other women, but they never discussed it with Camille. They didn't want to hurt her.

Calvin told her, "Wherever she is, we know God is watching out for her."

"Do you think we could feel it if something really bad happened to one of our children? Some people think that's so."

"Who knows? All I know is that we will see her again. I am very confident of that fact."

They heard a car drive up and four car doors slam. Theresa and Calvin looked out of the window and noticed not three, but four people walking towards the house. "Camille!" Theresa said to herself. At least it looked like her. From this distance, she couldn't tell. They had parked in Cherrelle's designated parking spot. Theresa ran to the front door and opened it before the group got to the foot of the stairs. She ran half way down the flight of stairs to the first floor landing. They waited for her to reach her missing child so she wouldn't slip on the landing in her haste to reach Camille. When she reached her, all she could do was hug her for a very long time. Calvin was right behind her.

"My baby, my baby. I've missed you so much. What happened? Why didn't you meet us at Big Mama's?"

Camille sighed, "It's a long story. Can I take a hot bath and get something to eat first? Then I'll tell you all about it."

"Of course," Theresa told her as she wiped her eyes.

They all made their way up to Cherrelle's apartment and helped Camille get settled in. Cory put her things down in the den. Cherrelle ran a bath for her younger sister, putting her best bath salts and soaps in the water. While she was doing that, Theresa headed to the kitchen to make one of Camille's favorite dishes.

Camille soaked a very long time. It had been so many days since she had actually had a bath. She had been able to wash up at the airport and in the Astrodome, but that wasn't really bathing. Even when the water she was in turned tepid, she added more hot water so she could stay a little longer.

Chalice, Cherrelle, and Big Mama helped Theresa make the meal. Cherrelle was put in charge of making the Crab Cakes[49], Chalice cut up the sausage and chicken for the Jambalaya[50], Big Mama cooked the fresh green beans, and Theresa made the Peach Cobbler[51]. She made sure to bake her crust for a while first so it would be firm under the filling. Image came in and volunteered to make the French bread and set the table. She was really happy to hear the news of Camille being home.

Camille stepped out of the tub and looked at the big bump that was her stomach. She was about six months along. She thought she felt a movement, but wasn't sure. She placed her hand against her stomach and at that moment vowed to love this baby. It was unfortunate that his daddy was gone, but it was done, and she was still here. She thought about the best way to tell her family about Byron. She figured the best way was to tell the truth.

The family sat all over the living area of Cherrelle's apartment, some at the table, others on the sofa, and some even on the floor. When Camille came out of the bathroom, everyone had questions for her.

"Can we just eat first, and then I'll tell you. It might be too hard to take and too hard to say on an empty stomach."

Everyone fell in with Camille's wishes and held their curiosity until the meal was over.

Darryl and Image put their kids to bed and came back in to where everyone was listening to Camille's story.

Cherrelle sat next to her sister and asked her, "Where were you? We called and there was no answer. After a while, we were so caught up in looking for Big Mama, that we, well we didn't forget about you, but we figured you were probably fine and would eventually show up. By the time we figured you weren't coming, it was too late, and we were being ordered out of the area."

"What happened to Big Mama?" Camille asked, turning to look at her grandmother.

"We'll tell you that later. Tell us what happened to you and how you ended up at the Astrodome."

"Well, remember when you called and said to meet at Big Mama's so we could get out of the path of the storm?" Camille began. Everyone nodded.

"A few minutes after that, Byron came home and wouldn't let me leave. He threatened me and made me a prisoner in our apartment. When the storm came, the water got so high it started coming into our apartment. We climbed on the roof to get out of the way of the water and to keep from being caught inside with no escape." A tear came to her eyes as she remembered her ordeal.

"Byron and I stayed on the roof for several hours as the water got higher and higher. It even started sloshing on the roof. There was very little room for us to maneuver," Camille's eyes were focused on a distant object, as if she could see the events she was describing right then.

"I don't know what made him move around like that, but he lost his footing and slipped from the roof. I..." Her words caught in her throat as she attempted to go on. Tears flowed.

"I...I tried to help him, but the pain in my arm was so great from earlier, that when I reached out, I couldn't help him. The current pulled him away and he was pulled under. I heard him scream...scream for help. I couldn't do anything but watch him disappear." She closed her eyes. "I'll never forget it."

"He got what he deserved for putting his hands on you," her father growled. "He better be glad he can't pay for what he did to you."

"Calvin!" Theresa exclaimed. "That's not a very nice thing to say. We shouldn't speak ill of the dead."

"Good riddance to bad rubbish," Big Mama said.

He turned to his daughter. "How are you now?"

"Better," she said quietly.

"How did you get off the roof?" Chalice asked.

"I spent almost two days on the roof. Eventually, I was rescued by a helicopter. They lifted me from the roof in a basket. I was so weak; they took me to the airport where they had a makeshift hospital. After I got better, they put me on a plane to Houston and shuttled me on a bus to the Astrodome."

Cherrelle reached her hand out and took her sister's hand in hers. "How's the baby?"

"I don't know. I haven't had a chance to get checked out, but I think I felt something today."

"Oh, that's wonderful."

"Yeah."

"But I want to take you to a doctor as soon as possible so we can get you checked out, okay? You've been through a lot. As a matter of fact, you need to rest now." She helped her sister get settled into bed.

Later that night, Cory and Cherrelle went for a walk. She had so much on her mind. She thought back over the last year and how lonely she was before going back to New Orleans and how fulfilled she was now. She looked up at the sky. It was a beautiful, starlit night. There seemed to be not a cloud in the sky. They walked hand in hand and didn't say a word. When they got back to the apartment door, Cherrelle turned to Cory and kissed him. "Thank you for being in my life. You are so good to me and for me." She held his hand and got down on one knee. "Cory, will you marry me?"

"You know I will." He reached in his back pocket. "I keep

this with me every minute, every second, every hour of the day in the hope that you would change your mind." He pulled out a four carat diamond ring in a platinum setting and pulled her up from her knee. Tears fell from both of their eyes as he slipped the ring on her finger and kissed her lips. They went inside to tell everyone the good news.

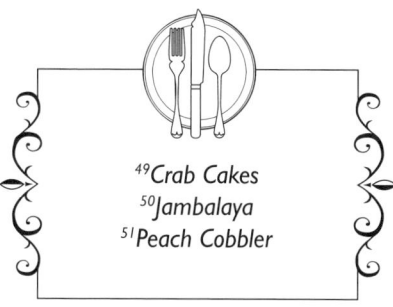

⁴⁹ Crab Cakes
⁵⁰ Jambalaya
⁵¹ Peach Cobbler

CHAPTER TWENTY-SEVEN
LIFE IS A BOWL OF CHERRIES

A year later...

It was a struggle, but they were able to pull it off. There was still too much damage to New Orleans to have the family reunion there this year, so, after finding most of the displaced family members, the event was held in Houston.

Reunion letters had gone out informing the family about the change.

Theresa and Big Mama were in the kitchen. Theresa was doing most of the cooking now, but Big Mama was able to "supervise".

"Make sure you stir it real good," Big Mama told Theresa.

They were making one of several dishes for the Friday night gathering.

"I am so excited. I talked to Bertha today. She and her family just got in from California. Everyone is starting to check into the hotel," Theresa said to Big Mama.

Big Mama nodded. She had been waiting for this day herself. She would get a chance to see her brother and his wife and all her nieces and nephews. When they finished wrapping up their dishes, they got ready to head over to the hotel where they would be spending the weekend.

At the hotel registration had begun, and the domino tournaments were already in full swing. They had started before registration was even set up. Others had started setting up the card tables for bid whist and spades competitions. Someone was in the front of the room setting it up for the getting-to-know-you games.

When Theresa and Big Mama got there, they started setting the tables to hold the casseroles. Cherrelle walked in with Cory. He was carrying her casserole dish for her. He put it down, gave her a kiss and went over to watch the domino tournaments and try to find a partner. Cherrelle started helping her mother and grandmother get things set up and arranged.

When they were done, they sat back and admired the food spread before them. Everyone had certainly come through. There were all kinds of dishes on the table – Broccoli Casserole[52], Squash Casserole[53], Shrimp Casserole[54], Cornbread Casserole[55], Red Beans and Rice[57], and Italian Sausage Pasta[58], to name a few. The main dessert was a sheet cake with chocolate icing[58], but there were even Pralines[59] to remind them of home and a Dirt Dessert[60] for the kids.

Theresa looked over at her daughter. She was radiant. Cherrelle and Cory were expecting their first child any day now. She felt that Cherrelle was finally at peace with herself. After they announced to the family that they were getting married, Cory and Cherrelle wasted no time in arranging the wedding and tying the knot. The wedding was within two months of the announcement. Camille was the matron of honor and Chalice was the maid of honor. After much discussion between Cherrelle and Cory, Darryl was allowed to be the best man. That act alone assured Theresa that her daughter was well and truly whole.

Camille walked over. Cherrelle really wanted to hold her first nephew, but the doctor had warned her against heavy lifting, and he was a hunk.

She rubbed his cheek, "How's my boy?" He smiled up at his aunt from the comfort of his mother's arms. His toothless smile tugged at her heart. She smiled, leaned over and gave him a kiss.

"How are you doing?" Camille asked her.

"I need a seat, but other than that, I'm fine." Cherrelle looked around the room and found a table with an empty chair. More family members were beginning to arrive.

Camille looked towards the door. "I need to help. Can you watch Andrew while I help out? I'll put him in his stroller. He likes to sit in it, and it reclines as well. It's time for him to take a nap anyway. He sleeps in it all the time." She had named him after the soldier who helped her from the roof. She had never forgotten his name.

Cherrelle sat down next to Charles and Caroline, her cousins from Houston. She was happy to see they had gotten back together. They seemed to be so happy now. Caroline was also expecting another child. Their oldest son, CJ was on the other side of the room, playing with some cousins. She hugged them both, and they caught up on what had been happening in each others' lives, including what happened to Big Mama the day of the storm.

"She said she was on her way to the store. I don't know what makes her think she should be walking to the store, but anyway, she was on her way there, and the police picked her up to help her get home before the approaching storm," Cherrelle told them. "Apparently she could not remember her address, and they did the next best thing. They took her to the Superdome, and that is where we found her."

"Amazing," Caroline said.

"Yes, God is good," Cherrelle agreed.

Cherrelle looks around the room. Children are running, laughing, playing and connecting with one another. Adults are laughing and reminiscing about the good old days - slapping dominoes, playing cards, having fun. Cherrelle is truly at peace with herself, with her family and with God. "Thank you, Lord." She looks over at her handsome husband, her true soul mate.

Cherrelle thought back to her first conversation with her grandmother about participating with the family reunion. She had started out hating the thought of a family reunion, because of her unfulfilled dreams and past hurts. But those things were a part of her past now, not her future. People might remember what she used to be like, but the old Cherrelle is gone. Now, Cherrelle felt she had an opportunity for new beginnings with her family, filled with laughter and shared memories, picking up where they left off and making new ones.

Cherrelle realized she would not have had this opportunity if her grandmother had not insisted that she be a part of the family again and get connected. She thought about the last year and a half of her life. She had been existing then, now she was living a full and productive life. Before the night ended, Cherrelle, with her husband by her side, asked the family to stand and give her grandmother a round of applause and a toast.

"To Big Mama!"

And her water broke.

Allysa Correlle was born fourteen hours later, a beautiful, healthy baby girl. She wasn't able to attend the reunion, but she was the talk of the family. And Cherrelle couldn't be happier.

52Broccoli Casserole
53Squash Casserole
54Shrimp Casserole
55Cornbread Casserole
56Red Beans and Rice
57Italian Sausage Pasta
58Cake with Chocolate Icing
59Pralines
60Dirt Dessert

Living with No Regrets

RECIPES BY
Earnestine Bryant Wagner

*Be Blessed
Earnestine Wagner*

CREOLE SMOTHERED CHICKEN *Footnote 1*

1   Chicken (cut up)
2   tablespoons soy sauce
2   tablespoons hot sauce
½   teaspoon salt
2   tablespoons oil
½   cup onion (chopped)
½   cup green bell pepper
½   cup parsley
1   bunch green onion
2   large cloves garlic (minced)
½   cup Sherry

In a large bowl, marinate chicken with the 2 tablespoons hot sauce and 2 tablespoons soy sauce 30 minutes to 1 hour.

In a skillet, place the 2 tablespoons of oil. Brown chicken in oil and remove from skillet. Sauté onions, bell peppers, green onions and parsley in skillet until soft. Stir in garlic and add sherry. Bring to a boil. You may need to add water. Return chicken to skillet and simmer covered until tender. Serve over rice.

GLAZED CARROTS *Footnote 2*

1   lb carrots with tops or
1   pack baby carrots
¼   cup brown sugar
1   tablespoon butter
1   cup water
Pinch salt

Peel, wash and cut carrots in one inch length. Or place baby carrots in a medium sauce pot. Cover with brown sugar, pats of butter, pinch salt and pour in water. Cover and bring to a brisk boil and lower heat to medium. Simmer until most of the water has cooked out and a glaze has formed. Turn carrots over in glaze.

TURNIP GREENS *Footnote 3*

1   smoked ham hock
½   jalapeno pepper (optional)
6   cups water to cover
1   tablespoon sugar
2   bunches greens
Salt to taste (if needed)

Bring ham hock, jalapeno pepper and sugar to boil in the water covering the ham hock. Reduce heat and simmer about 1½ hours or until ham hock is almost tender. Add cleaned and washed greens. Bring to a boil and simmer 25-30 minutes until greens are tender. If adding turnip roots, peel, cut in ½ inch cubes and add to greens. Cook another 10 minutes or until roots are done.

SHRIMP ETOUFFEE
FOOTNOTE 4

- 2 sticks butter or margarine
- 1 onion (chopped)
- 1 cup green onions (chopped)
- 6 ribs celery (chopped)
- ½ cup parsley (chopped)
- 4 tablespoons Tony Chachere's Instant Roux Mix
- 1 cup water
- 4 tablespoons salsa (optional)
- 2 cans stewed tomatoes
- 2 pounds shrimp
- ¼ pound Velveeta cheese

Clean shrimp and set aside.

In a large heavy skillet or sauce pot, sauté the onions, green pepper, celery and parsley in the butter until it is soft. Add tomatoes and salsa. Simmer over low heat 15 – 20 minutes. Add Velveeta. Stir roux in the cup of water and add to the tomato/vegetable mixture. Simmer another 10 minutes. Stir to prevent sticking. Add shrimp and continue cooking over low heat 15 minutes. Serve over rice.

FRIED CATFISH
Footnote 5

- Catfish
- 2 cups corn meal
- Seasoning (Tony Chachere's, Zatarain's, Tex Joy Steak Seasoning, Lawry's)
- 1 cup flour
- Black pepper
- Oil for frying

Cut fish in strips and wash. In a bowl, place the corn meal, flour, your favorite seasoning, and black pepper. Mix well together. Place mixture in a paper bag. Shake fish pieces in corn meal mixture. Remove fish from bag; shake off excess mixture and deep fry until brown. Turn over once. Fish is done when it floats. Remove and drain on paper towels.

JALAPENO CORNBREAD
Footnote 6

- 1 cup cornmeal
- 1 cup flour
- 1 tablespoon baking powder
- 1 can cream style corn
- 2 tablespoons sugar
- 1 teaspoon salt
- 2½ cups milk
- 3 eggs (beaten)
- 1 onion (finely chopped)

1½ cups sharp cheddar or Monterey Jack cheese (grated)

3-5 jalapeno peppers (chopped)

½ cup melted shortening or vegetable oil

Mix together cornmeal, flour, baking powder, sugar and salt. Stir in milk, eggs, and oil. Beat well. Fold in corn, peppers, onions and cheese. Bake in a well greased 9x13 inch pan at 400 degrees 40-50 minutes or until tooth pick inserted comes out clean.

DIRTY RICE Footnote 7

- 1 large bell pepper
- 6 ribs celery
- 1 yellow onion
- 1 bunch green onions
- ½ cup parsley
- ½ pound chicken gizzards
- 1 pound ground beef
- 2 cups rice
- 1 pound chicken liver
- Salt and pepper to taste

Chop or grind bell pepper, celery, yellow onion, green onion and parsley. Set aside. Use a food processor to grind together chicken livers and gizzards.

In a medium skillet, brown the ground beef. Add the ground liver and gizzards. Cook until liver and gizzards are brown. Add the chopped vegetables and simmer in skillet for 25 to 30 minutes.

Cook rice in separate pot until done. Add rice to meat mixture and season to taste.

OKRA AND TOMATOES & SAUSAGE Footnote 8

- 1 pound link sausage
- 2 pounds okra (fresh or frozen) cut up
- 1 medium green pepper (chopped)
- 1 small onion (chopped)
- 2 cans tomatoes
- Salt and pepper to taste

Cut sausage in ¼ inch pieces and brown over medium heat. Add okra, onions and bell pepper. Cook until soft, 10-15 minutes. Add tomatoes. Season to taste and simmer 10-15 minutes longer or until desired doneness.

TARTAR SAUCE
Footnote 9

2   cups mayonnaise
¼ - ½ cup onions
    (finely chopped)
2   tablespoon balsamic vinegar

½   cup sweet pickle
    relish
1   tablespoon horseradish

In a bowl, combine all ingredients. Cover with plastic wrap and refrigerate for an hour before using.

SWEET POTATO PIE
Footnote 10

2   medium sweet potatoes
¾   cup sugar (more if desired)
1   stick butter

2   eggs
¼   teaspoon cinnamon
½   teaspoon nutmeg

Boil sweet potatoes in water until easily pierced with a fork. Drain and place potatoes in mixing bowl. Add sugar and butter and beat with electric mixer until smooth. Beat in eggs and add cinnamon and nutmeg. Mix well. Bake pie crust at least five minutes before adding filling. Pour filling into pie crust and bake at 375 degrees for 40-50 minutes, or until filling is set. If crust start to become too dark before filling is set, cover edges of crust with foil.

BUTTERMILK POUND CAKE
Footnote 11

2   sticks butter
1   teaspoon baking powder
3   cups sugar
1½ cups buttermilk

4   eggs
1   teaspoon baking soda
3 ½ cups flour
2   teaspoons vanilla extract

Heat oven to 325 degrees Fahrenheit. Grease and flour a large tube pan. Cream butter and sugar until light and fluffy. Add eggs one at a time, beating well after each. Mix milk and soda, set aside. Sift flour and baking powder 3 times. Add flour alternately with buttermilk mixture to the first three ingredients until all is used. Add vanilla extract. Bake for 1½ hours.

SMOTHERED STEAK
Footnote 12

- 1 large steak
- 1 onion (chopped)
- ½ cup cooking oil
- Garlic powder
- Flour
- Water
- 1 clove minced or sliced garlic
- Salt and pepper to taste

Cut meat into serving size pieces. Sprinkle on garlic powder and season well with salt and pepper. Flour meat on all sides and brown in hot oil. Remove meat from oil when brown and remove excess oil. If a thick gravy is desired, add extra flour; 3-4 tablespoons to small amount of oil and sediments. Add chopped onions and stir with flour until onions are clear or slightly brown. Add water and simmer a few minutes. Return steak to skillet or pot and add fresh garlic. Reduce heat to low. Cover and simmer meat until tender. If gravy becomes too thick, add additional water. Serve over hot steamed rice.

MUSTARD GREENS
Footnote 13

- 2 - 3 bunches Greens
- 1 small jalapeño pepper (optional)
- 1 - 2 ham hocks
- Salt to taste

Boil ham hocks while preparing greens. Cook until almost done.

Clean and wash greens until water is clear. Add greens and jalapeno pepper to boiling ham hocks. Cook on medium until tender. Do not add salt until done. The ham hocks may provide enough seasoning.

CORN BREAD
Footnote 14

- ⅔ cup yellow corn meal
- ⅔ cup all purpose flour
- ⅓ cup sugar
- ½ teaspoon salt
- 1 cup milk
- 1 tablespoon baking powder
- 1 egg
- 3 tablespoons shortening (melted)

Heat oven to 470 degrees. In a medium bowl, mix dry ingredients together. Add milk and beat in egg. Melt shortening in a square baking pan and pour into cornbread mixture; leaving a small amount in pan for the top of bread. Pour batter in pan and top with shortening remaining in pan. Bake for 11-12 minutes until golden brown.

CHITTERLINGS *Footnote 15*

10 pounds chitterlings	1 bay leaf
1 large onion (cut in half)	3 tablespoons vinegar
4 cloves garlic (chopped)	Salt and pepper to taste
1 jalapeno pepper (cut in half)	

Clean and wash chitterlings. Place in a large pot and season with the onion, garlic, jalapeno pepper, bay leaf, vinegar, salt and pepper. Cover with water and boil over low heat until tender. Cook until most of the water is gone. Stir to keep from sticking. You should have a nice thick gravy.

COLLARD GREENS *Footnote 16*

4 strips thick sliced bacon	2 teaspoons sugar
2 bunches greens	1 cup water
½ jalapeno pepper (optional)	Salt to taste

Clean, cut and wash collard greens. Leave greens in water until ready to drop in pot. In a large pot, fry bacon. When bacon is ready, lift the greens by hand full and drop in the pot with bacon and bacon fat. Add jalapeno pepper, sugar, small amount of water, cover and simmer until tender. Season to taste with salt.

CANDIED YAMS *Footnote 17*

4 Medium Sweet Potatoes	½ teaspoon nutmeg
¾ cup granulated sugar	1 cup water
½ cup brown sugar	1 stick butter
½ teaspoon cinnamon	

Peel and cut potatoes length wise. Place in a medium sauce pot. Pour white sugar, brown sugar, cinnamon and nutmeg over potatoes. Pour water over all. Cut butter in pats and place on top of everything. Cook over medium heat until potatoes are soft and syrup is desired consistency.

SHERRY CHICKEN   Footnote 18

1 fryer chicken (cut up)	½ can water
1 pound mushrooms	1 small onion (chopped)
1 stick butter	1 clove of garlic (minced)
1 cup sherry	1 cup sour cream
1 can cream of mushroom soup	1 tablespoon minced parsley

Salt and pepper to taste

Season the chicken with salt and pepper, and brown in the stick of butter. Remove chicken and set aside. Sauté mushrooms, parsley and onions in remaining butter about 3 minutes. Add garlic during the last minute. Remove pan from heat and add cream of mushroom soup, water and sherry. Cook the mixture over medium heat about 5 minutes. Stir to prevent sticking. Add sour cream and simmer 1-2 minutes.

Prepare a baking pan or casserole dish for chicken. Pour ½ the sherry/mushroom in dish. Return chicken to dish and pour the remainder of the sherry sauce over chicken. Cover and bake at 350 degrees for 1 hour. Serve over rice.

CHICKEN TETRAZINI   Footnote 19

1 fryer chicken	2 stalks celery
2 cans cream of mushroom soup	1 green pepper
	2 tablespoons parsley flakes
2 cups cheddar cheese	
1 pound package spaghetti	1 can mushrooms
1 stick butter	1 jar pimentos
1 onion	2 cups chicken stock
2 cloves garlic	Salt and pepper to taste

Boil chicken, remove bones and cut in bite size pieces. Break spaghetti into thirds and cook as per package directions. Sauté vegetables in butter until soft. Add soup, stock and mushrooms. Simmer a few minutes. Add pimentos and chicken. Mix with cooked spaghetti and season to taste. Sprinkle cheese on top and bake at 375 for 30 – 35 minutes.

SEVEN LAYER SALAD *Footnote 20*

½ head lettuce
1 small onion-thinly sliced
1 cup coarsely chopped green pepper
2 stalks celery-chopped
1 cup small green peas (drained)
1 ½ cup Miracle Whip
2 tablespoons sugar
1½ cup grated cheese
5 strips of bacon, cooked and crumbled
Strips of ham, turkey, and chicken (4 ounce each)

Place 1/2 of lettuce on bottom of glass dish. Add onions, green pepper, celery and peas.

Top with remaining lettuce. Mix salad dressing and sugar and spread on top. Sprinkle on cheese and crumble bacon. Top with strips of ham, turkey and chicken.

Refrigerate at least 4 hours before serving.

PECAN PIE *Footnote 21*

1 cup light brown sugar
½ cup white sugar
1 tablespoon flour
2 eggs
1 teaspoon vanilla
2 tablespoons milk
½ cup butter or margarine melted
1 cup pecans

Heat oven to 375 degrees. Mix together sugar and flour. Beat eggs thoroughly, add milk, vanilla and butter to beaten eggs. Add egg mixture to flour and mix well. Fold in pecans and pour into an unbaked pie shell. Bake in preheated oven 40-50 minutes until filling is set.

CHICKEN SALAD *Footnote 22*

3 cups cooked chicken (diced)
3 eggs (boiled and chopped)
2 tablespoons chopped onion
¼ cup green pepper (chopped)
¼ cup red bell pepper (chopped)
1 rib celery
1 tablespoon sugar
¼ cup sweet pickle relish
1 cup mayonnaise or Miracle Whip
Salt and pepper to taste

In a large bowl, place the chicken and eggs. In a medium size bowl, mix the remaining ingredients. Stir well to blend together. Add a portion of the mayonnaise mixture to the chicken and eggs. Fold in to determine the desired consistency. Fold in the remainder as desired.

For a more gourmet salad, add chopped apples and pecans.

MARINATED CUCUMBER & TOMATO SALAD *Footnote 23*

- 3 medium cucumbers
- 2 ripe tomatoes
- 1 small red onion
- ½ cup cider or red wine vinegar
- 2 tablespoons balsamic vinegar
- 3 tablespoons olive oil or salad oil
- ¼ cup sugar or you may use artificial sweetener
- ½ teaspoon dried oregano
- 1/8 teaspoon salt
- Fresh ground pepper

Wash cucumbers and tomatoes. Peel cucumbers, leaving a scant amount of the peel and slice in ¼ inch circles. Slice tomatoes and cut into wedges. Cut onions in thin circles forming rings. Put prepared vegetables in a large salad bowl.

Combine oils, vinegars, salt, sugar, oregano and pepper with wire whisk and mix well until salt and sugar dissolve. Pour liquid mixture over vegetables and toss to coat. Cover and refrigerate at least an hour before serving. Toss two of three times while marinating. Serve using a slotted spoon.

CREAM CHEESE POUND CAKE *Footnote 24*

- 3 sticks butter
- 1 8-ounce cream cheese
- 6 eggs
- 3 cups sugar
- 3 cups cake flour (sift flour 3 times if not using cake flour)
- 2 teaspoons vanilla extract

In a large mixing bowl with electric mixer, beat butter and cream cheese. Add sugar and mix well. Add vanilla. Add a small amount of flour, then an egg, one at a time, alternately with flour. Beginning with flour and ending with flour. Grease and flour a tube pan. Bake in tube pan 1 hour and 25 minutes at 325 degrees.

SEAFOOD BOIL *Footnote 25*

- 4 to 5 pounds shrimp
- 1 dozen crabs
- 1 large onion (quartered)
- 1 bulb of garlic (cut in half)
- New potatoes
- Corn-on-the-cob (1½ -2 inch length)
- Sausage (1 - 2 inch length)

5 to 6 ribs celery
3 - 4 quarts water
   (May need more water
   based on the amount of
   corn and potatoes used).

3 Lemons (quartered)
Tony Chachere's Creole
   Seasoning (to taste)
Zatarain's Shrimp &
   Crab Boil

To a large cooking pot, add 3-4 quarts water, bag Zatarian's Shrimp boil, Tony's Creole Seasoning, lemons, garlic celery and onions. Bring to a rolling boil. Add the potatoes and the corn to the pot. Boil about 10 minutes then add sausage. Boil another 10-15 minutes before adding the shrimp and crabs. Add seafood, adding crabs before the shrimp and boil about 3 minutes. Allow seafood to remain in water 10-15 minutes after boiling, giving seasoning a chance to set in.

CHICKEN SEAFOOD AND SAUSAGE GUMBO   Footnote 26

1 Chicken, boiled
1 package dried
   powdered shrimp
1 cup chopped onion
1 cup chopped bell pepper
3 ribs chopped celery
½ cup chopped parsley
3 garlic cloves, Minced
1 10 to 16 oz. package
   sliced okra
3 quarts chicken broth

2 packages sausage
   (14-16 ounce each)
1 cup Tony Chachere's
   Instant Roux Mix
1 pound medium shrimp
   (peeled and deveined)
1 pound crabmeat or
   crab fingers
1 to 2 teaspoons
   Gumbo File'
   (optional)

Creole seasoning and pepper to taste

In a large pot, cover chicken with 3 – 4 quarts of water. Boil chicken until tender. Remove chicken from pot and set aside to cool. Use broth from boiled chicken for the gumbo. Add dried shrimp powder and vegetables to the broth and boil. In a large measuring cup or bowl, mix the roux with enough water to make a smooth liquid paste. Stir into the pot of vegetables. Simmer on low heat for 30-35 minutes. Cut sausage in ½ inch pieces and sauté or cook in oven. Drain and discard grease from sausage and add sausage and crab fingers to the pot. Continue boiling over medium to low heat for 30 minutes. Remove chicken from bones and cut in bite size pieces. Add shrimp and chicken to pot and simmer another 10 minutes.

BARBECUE BRISKET
Footnote 27

1   beef brisket
Italian Dressing
Garlic powder

Salt
Pepper
Paprika

The night before cooking, marinate brisket in Italian dressing. Refrigerate and turn over in dressing several times. The next day, when ready to cook, remove from marinate and season with garlic powder, salt, pepper and paprika.

Build fire by assembling a pyramid of charcoals. Use a commercial lighter fluid and carefully pour the fluid on the pyramid. Allow fluid to soak in to the charcoal. Use a long match to ignite the charcoal. When charcoals are white on the edge, spread them out. To add extra flavor to meat, use chips or chunks from one of your favorite woods. Example: hickory, oak, pecan etc. Soak wood chips or chunks before placing on charcoals. Place meat on rack and cook over slow fire for hours, until desired doneness.

If meat appears to begin getting too brown, wrap in foil and punch holes in foil.

BARBECUE RIBS
Footnote 28

2 slabs ribs
Your favorite barbecue spice
   Or

Salt
Garlic powder
Freshly ground black pepper
Red pepper (optional)
Paprika

Remove the white membrane from the under side of rib. Wash, pat dry with paper towel, and rub a generous amount of barbecue spice over ribs. If not using barbecue spice, sprinkle with garlic powder, salt, pepper and paprika. Place in refrigerator, allowing seasonings to soak in. Build fire by assembling a pyramid of charcoals. Use a commercial lighter fluid and carefully pour the fluid on the pyramid. Allow fluid to soak in to the charcoal. Use a long match to ignite the charcoal. When charcoals are white on the edge, spread them out. To add extra flavor to meat, use chips or chunks from one of your favorite woods. Example: hickory, oak, pecan etc. Soak wood chips or chunks in water before placing on charcoals. When ready to cook, place meat on rack and cook over low fire until tender. When done, brush with barbecue sauce and cover with foil to keep it moist.

BARBECUE CHICKEN   *Footnote 29*

1 large fryer	Pepper
Your favorite barbecue spice	Paprika
Or	Garlic powder
	Salt

Clean, cut in half and wash chicken. Rub barbecue spice generously all over chicken or sprinkle chicken with garlic powder, salt, pepper and paprika. Refrigerate while preparing the pit for cooking. Build fire by assembling a pyramid of charcoals. Use a commercial lighter fluid and carefully pour the fluid on the pyramid. Allow fluid to soak in to the charcoal. Use a long match to ignite the charcoal. When charcoals are white on the edge, spread them out. To add extra flavor to meat, use chips or chunks from one of your favorite woods. Example: hickory, oak, pecan etc. Soak wood chips or chunks in water before placing on charcoals. Let seasoning soak in the meat at least an hour before placing on the pit. When ready to cook, place meat on rack and cook over low fire until tender and juices run clear. When done, brush with barbeque sauce and cover with foil.

BARBECUE SAUCE   *Footnote 30*

1 – 24 ounce bottle ketchup	3 tablespoons chili powder
1 ketchup bottle of water	2 tablespoons garlic salt
½ cup vinegar	1½ tablespoon sugar
1 teaspoon lemon juice	1 tablespoon butter
2 tablespoons black pepper	3 tablespoons yellow mustard

In a medium sauce pot, simmer the ketchup, water, vinegar, lemon juice, chili powder, salt, pepper, sugar and butter about 15 minutes, stirring often. In a small bowl, place the mustard and some of the sauce. Mix well until smooth. Return to pot and simmer another 20 minutes.

STRAWBERRY GLAZE
Footnote 31

1 cup sugar
3 tablespoons corn starch
1 cup water

½ teaspoon vanilla
Red food coloring

Combine sugar and cornstarch in a heavy saucepan. Mix well and add water. Cook over medium heat until glaze thickens. Add vanilla and enough food coloring to make a bright red color.

OATMEAL COOKIES
Footnote 32

1 cup shortening
1 cup granulated sugar
1 cup brown sugar
2 eggs
1 teaspoon vanilla
1 teaspoon cinnamon

1½ cups flour
½ teaspoon salt
1 teaspoon baking soda
3 cups oatmeal
1 cup pecans (optional)
1 cup raisins (optional)

Cream together shortening and sugar and add eggs. Stir in vanilla and cinnamon. Sift together flour, soda and salt and fold into the creamed mixture. Stir in oats and nuts. Place dough in spoon size portions on a slightly greased cookie sheet. Bake at 350 degrees for 8 to 12 minutes.

DEVILED EGGS
Footnote 33

1 dozen eggs
⅔ cup Miracle Whip Salad Dressing
¼ cup sweet pickle relish

2 tablespoons mustard
1 teaspoon sugar
½ teaspoon fresh ground black pepper

Paprika for garnish

Boil, peel, and cut eggs in half lengthwise. Remove yolks and place in a bowl. Set egg whites aside. Mash egg yolks with pastry blender or fork. Add salad dressing, stirring well to form a smooth mixture. Add remaining ingredients and mix well. Stuff the egg whites with cake decorator or spoon. Garnish with paprika.

FRUIT PUNCH
Footnote 34

- 3 cups lemon juice
- 2 (46 ounce) orange juice
- 1 (46 ounce) pineapple juice
- 6 quarts water
- 3 cups sugar
- 3 quarts ginger ale

Mix together all liquid ingredients except ginger ale. Add 2 cups sugar and test for desired sweetness. Add the rest of sugar if needed. Mix all ingredients well.

Add cold ginger ale when ready to serve.

LASAGNA
Footnote 35

- 1½ pounds Italian sausage (about 6-7 links)
- 2 cloves minced garlic
- 1 tablespoon basil
- 2 teaspoons dried parsley
- 1 can whole tomatoes
- 1 jar Prego (traditional)
- ½ Prego jar water
- 8 lasagna noodles
- 2 cups Mozzarella cheese
- 1½ pound carton cottage cheese (3 cups) small curd
- 2 eggs, beaten
- ½ cup parmesan cheese
- 2 tablespoons dried parsley flakes

Directions

Remove Italian sausage from skin and sauté until brown. Drain fat. Add garlic and simmer another couple minutes. Add tomatoes, basil, parsley and Prego. Rinse Prego jar with water and add to sauce. Simmer about 45 minutes. While sauce is simmering, boil lasagna noodles according to package instructions. Drain and rinse in cool water. Lay flat on foil

Mix the 3 cups cottage cheese with 2 beaten eggs. Add the parmesan cheese and the 2 tablespoons parsley. Mix together well.

Assemble:
1. Lay 4 cooked lasagna noodles in bottom, overlapping as you go.
2. Spread ½ cottage cheese mixture evenly over noodles.
3. Layer half the mozzarella cheese
4. Spread about half of meat over mozzarella cheese.

5. Repeat the process – noodles, cottage cheese, mozzarella, and finish with meat.
6. Sprinkle parmesan cheese over meat.
7. Pop in oven and bake at 350 degrees for 25-35 minutes until hot and bubbly.

GARLIC BREAD
Footnote 36

1 loaf French bread	Paprika
1 stick butter (softened)	¼ cup parmesan cheese (optional)
Garlic powder	Parsley

Preheat oven to 350 degrees.

Cut bread in half horizontally. Spread butter on the cut side of each half. Sprinkle evenly with garlic to cover each half. Follow with paprika and sprinkle evenly to cover each piece. Sprinkle parmesan cheese if desired. Garnish by sprinkling parsley over each piece. Slice diagonally 2½ - 3 inches each. Place, garlic side up on a cookie sheet and bake approximately 8-10 minutes or until lightly brown.

MEAT LOAF
Footnote 37

2 pounds lean ground beef	1½ cups bread crumbs
1 small onion (chopped)	3 tablespoons Worcestershire sauce
1 small bell pepper (chopped)	2 eggs
2 cloves garlic (minced)	2 cans tomato sauce
1 rib celery (chopped)	2 cans water

Salt and pepper to taste

Mix together all of the ingredients except tomato sauce and water.

Shape in a loaf and place in a rectangle baking pan or dish. Bake in a 350 degree oven for 15 minutes. In a saucepan, add the tomato sauce and water. Bring to a boil and pour over meat loaf. Bake an additional 40 - 45 minutes or until desired doneness.

MASHED POTATOES *Footnote 38*

3 large baking size
   russet potatoes
1 stick butter

1 cup evaporated milk
   (Pet, Carnation, etc)
Salt to taste

Peel, cut and wash potatoes. Place potatoes in a pot of water and bring to a boil. Cook until tender when inserted with a knife or fork. Remove from heat and drain. Use a potato masher or electric mixer. Add butter while potatoes are still hot. Mix or blend well. Add enough evaporated milk to achieve the desired smoothness. Season with salt.

STIR FRIED GREEN BEANS *Footnote 39*

1 - 2 pounds
   fresh green beans
3 - 4 large cloves garlic
   (pressed or minced)

Soy sauce
2 - 3 tablespoons olive oil
   or any cooking oil

Wash and remove ends from green beans. Use a wok, a large frying pan or a large pot. Place the oil in pan and heat on medium high. Add green beans and garlic. Splash on soy sauce to coat beans. Constantly stir the beans. Cook for 10 to 15 minutes.

LEMON BARS *Footnote 40*

¼ cup powdered sugar
½ cup (1 stick) soft butter
1 cup flour
2 tablespoons
   fresh lemon juice

1 cup sugar
2 eggs
Zest from 1 lemon
2 tablespoons flour
Pinch salt

Preheat oven to 350 F. Cream powdered sugar with butter. Add 1 cup flour and salt. Mix well. Press into a well greased 9 inch square pan. Bake 15 minutes.

Beat eggs. Add sugar, lemon juice, zest and 2 tablespoons flour. Pour over baked crust. Bake 20 minutes more. Let cool and cut in to squares.

CHICKEN SPAGHETTI CASSEROLE *Footnote 41*

- ½ stick margarine
- 1 onion, chopped
- ½ cup bell pepper, chopped
- 2½ cups chicken broth
- 1 can mushrooms, sliced
- 1 can cream of mushroom soup
- 1 can cream of chicken soup
- 1 chicken, cooked and deboned & cut in bite size pieces
- 2 cups grated cheese
- 1 pound package spaghetti
- Fresh ground black pepper

Sauté bell pepper and onions in margarine. Add chicken broth, mushrooms, cream of mushroom soup and cream of chicken soup. Heat thoroughly and add 1 cup cheese. Fold in chicken and cooked spaghetti. Place in casserole dish and top with remaining cup of cheese. Bake in 350 degree oven until cheese is bubbly and melted.

BUTTER ROLL DUMPLINGS *Footnote 42*

- 2 cups flour
- 1 stick soft butter
- 3 teaspoons baking powder
- ⅛ teaspoon salt
- ¾ cup water
- 3 cups milk
- 1 teaspoon vanilla extract
- 2 teaspoons cinnamon
- 1¼ cups sugar

Mix the flour, baking powder and salt, add water to form dough. Roll out dough, on floured surface, to about ¼ inch thickness. Spread dough with the stick of butter. Mix sugar and cinnamon together. Sprinkle 6-8 tablespoons of sugar mixture over butter. Cut rolled dough into about 2 inch lengths and place in baking dish. Stir together the milk, vanilla, 1 tablespoon flour mixed with the 1/3 cup sugar cinnamon mixture and bring to a boil. Sprinkle the remaining sugar mixture over dough. Pour the boiling mixture over all. Dough will rise to the top. Bake at 350 degrees for 35-40 minutes.

BEIGNETS
Footnote 43

½ cup butter
1 tablespoon sugar
¼ teaspoon salt
1 cup water
1 cup + 1/8 cup flour

1 teaspoon baking powder
1 teaspoon vanilla
4 eggs
Oil for frying
Powdered sugar

Sift together the flour, salt and baking powder and set aside.

In a medium sauce pan, heat butter, sugar, salt and water to boiling. Remove from heat and add flour mixture all at one time. Add vanilla. Stir well until ingredients are thoroughly combined. Add eggs one at a time, beating vigorously after each until dough is smooth and shiny.

In a heavy skillet or deep fryer, heat about 2-3 inches of oil. When oil is nice and hot, drop dough, by heaping teaspoons, into hot oil. Fry beignets, a few at a time, until golden. Remove with a slotted spoon and drain on paper towels. Sprinkle beignets with powdered sugar.

OATMEAL BARS
Footnote 44

1 stick butter
½ cup brown sugar
¼ cup granulated sugar
1 egg
¼ teaspoon nutmeg
2 cups oatmeal

½ teaspoon vanilla extract
¾ cup whole wheat flour
½ teaspoon baking soda
½ teaspoon ground cinnamon
pinch of salt

NOTE: be sure to use quick cooking Oatmeal

Preheat oven to 350 degrees. In medium bowl, beat together butter & sugar until light and creamy. Add egg and vanilla, and beat well. In a separate bowl, whisk together flour, baking soda, cinnamon and nutmeg. Add flour mixture to butter mixture and mix until just blended. Fold in oatmeal.

Press dough into an ungreased 8X8 baking pan. Bake for 30 minutes. Cool, then turn out onto cutting board and slice into bars.

SALMON CROQUETTES
Footnote 45

1 can salmon	1 teaspoon Worcestershire sauce
2 eggs	½ cup corn meal
1 small onion	½ cup flour
1 teaspoon black pepper	1 cup oil
¼ teaspoon red pepper	

Mix salmon with eggs, onions, pepper and Worcestershire sauce. Make 6-8 patties. Mix together flour and cornmeal. Roll patties in meal mixture. Fry in oil until brown. Turn one time.

BAKING POWDER DROP BISCUITS
Footnote 46

2½ cups flour	1 teaspoon salt
⅔ cups shortening	1½ cups milk
2 tablespoons baking powder	

Preheat oven to 450 degrees.

In a large bowl, mix together flour, baking powder and salt. Cut in shortening until mixtures resemble course crumbs. Add milk to form soft dough. Drop by tablespoon onto an ungreased cookie sheet or baking pan. Bake about 10 minutes or until golden brown.

SHRIMP CREOLE
Footnote 47

1 pound shrimp	1 teaspoon basil
2 tablespoons cooking oil	4 twigs fresh parsley
1 bunch green onions, chopped	1 teaspoon oregano
1 medium bell pepper	1 tablespoon paprika
2 ribs celery, chopped	2 large cans tomato sauce
3 cloves garlic, minced	2 bay leaves
1 large can tomatoes	Salt and pepper to taste

Peel and clean shrimp, set aside to drain. Wash bell pepper, green onions, celery, parsley and garlic. Cut up in small to medium size pieces. In a pot with a cover, add cooking oil and the cut up vegetables. Sauté a few minutes then add the tomatoes, tomato sauce, ½ can water, the paprika, oregano, basil, bay leaves and salt and pepper. Cook for 35 minutes covered. Add shrimp and cook over low heat ½ hour longer. You may need to add a little more water. Remove bay leaves and serve over rice.

BANANA PUDDING *Footnote 48*

1 cup sugar	1 teaspoon vanilla flavor
3 egg yolks	¼ - ½ stick butter
2 tablespoons flour or cornstarch	3 ripe bananas
2 cups milk	1 bag or box vanilla wafers

1. Mix sugar and flour together
2. Beat egg yolks and stir in milk until smooth
3. Add egg mixture to sugar
4. Bring to a boil over medium-high heat, stirring constantly; cook until thickened.
5. Add vanilla and butter and remove from heat.
6. In a bowl or casserole dish, layer the wafers and bananas.
7. Pour pudding over all.

CRAB CAKES *Footnote 49*

2 cups lump crab meat	1 - 2 slices white bread, torn into small pieces
½ stick unsalted butter	
½ small onion	1 tablespoon sherry (optional)
2 eggs	
3 tablespoons mayonnaise	1 tablespoon lemon juice
2 teaspoons Worcestershire sauce	½ teaspoon freshly ground black pepper
1 cup butter cracker crumbs	⅛ teaspoon cayenne pepper
Salt to taste	

Remove any shells from crabmeat. Keep as many lumps as possible.

Place about a tablespoon of the butter in a skillet on medium heat and sauté the onions until soft. In a medium bowl, whisk together eggs, mayonnaise, Worcestershire sauce, sherry, lemon juice, cayenne pepper, black pepper, salt and cooked onions. Fold in crab meat and add cracker crumbs and torn pieces of bread. Shape into cakes and place in refrigerator 30 minutes to an hour. Melt the remaining butter in a non stick skillet over medium heat and cook until golden. Turn over one time. Cook each side approximately 3 minutes each.

CHICKEN & SAUSAGE JAMBALAYA *Footnote 50*

This recipe needs a large pot and may be cooked over a butane burner out doors, or on top of the stove indoors, and serves 15-20 people.

2	chickens, cut up and seasoned	5	cups long grain rice (Note: a portion of water to rice is 2 to 1)
1½	cups vegetable oil		
2	pounds sausage (cut in ½ to 1 inch pieces)	5	cloves garlic (minced)
		4	pounds onions (chopped)
2	one pound cans tomatoes	1	bell pepper (chopped)
1	bunch green onions	10	cups water

Salt, black pepper and red pepper to taste

1. Brown seasoned chicken in hot oil, preferably in black iron pot or cast iron pot.

2. Next, brown sausage well.

3. Remove meat and most of the oil and add onions, garlic, bell pepper and green onions. It is extremely important to brown these vegetables well. You may have to add a little water from time to time to keep them from sticking.

4. Now put the chicken and sausage back in the pot along with all the water and tomatoes. When the mixture comes to a rolling boil, add the rice. When it reaches a good boil, lower the fire a little and let the water boil out. Stir well, lower the fire and cover. After about 15 minutes, stir well once more and cover. Do not keep stirring, leave undisturbed over a low fire for 45 minutes.

Jambalaya may be made with various combinations of meat and seafood.

PEACH COBBLER　　　　　　　　　　　　　Footnote 51

Pie Crust

3 cups all purpose flour	1 egg
1¼ cups shortening	6 tablespoons ice water
1 teaspoon salt	1 tablespoon vinegar

   In a mixing bowl, place flour and the salt. Cut in shortening using a pastry blender or fork. In a small bowl, whisk the egg and add the water and vinegar. Mix well. Pour over crumbled flour mixture and press together. Flatten to about 1½ inches. Wrap in plastic and place in refrigerator.

Cobbler Mixture

2 pie crust recipes (make 2 of the above pie crust)	1½ cups sugar
	½ cup flour
	1½ teaspoon fresh nutmeg
3 large cans peaches (29 oz can)	1¼ stick butter

   In a heavy pot, place the peaches with juice. Mix together the sugar, flour and nutmeg and stir in pot with peaches. Cook over low heat. When peaches begin to thicken, add the ¼ stick butter and continue to simmer until desired consistency.
   Preheat oven to 350 degrees. Roll out one of the crusts and place in a 10.5 X 14.75 X2.25 inches baking dish or pan. Prick bottom and sides of crust with a fork and bake crust 8-10 minutes before adding peaches. Add peaches and cut the remaining stick of butter in pats and place over peaches. Roll the second crust and place on top of butter and peaches. Use a knife to place ½ inch slits in top crust. Bake until golden brown; approximately 40-50 minutes.

BROCCOLI CASSEROLE　　　　　　　　　Footnote 52

1 pound broccoli	1 can cream of mushroom soup
3 cups cooked rice	
½ cup chopped onions	8 oz cheese whiz or ½ lb Velveeta
2 tablespoons butter	
½ teaspoon black pepper	

   Steam broccoli until tender, drain. Sauté onions in butter. Add the soup, cheese and pepper. Simmer until smooth. Fold in broccoli and rice. Pour into a baking dish and bake at 350 degrees 25-30 minutes or until hot and bubbly.

SQUASH CASSEROLE *Footnote 53*

1½ - 2 lbs yellow squash	2 cups bread crumbs
½ stick butter	¼ - ½ pound Velveeta
1 small onion	salt and pepper to taste

    Cook squash in small amount of water, drain. Sauté onions in 1 tablespoon of the butter and add to the drained squash. Add the cheese salt, pepper and 1 cup bread crumbs. Melt the remaining butter and mix with the remaining cup of bread crumbs. Pour casserole in baking dish and top with buttered bread crumbs. Bake at 350 degrees until brown and bubbly.

SHRIMP CASSEROLE *Footnote 54*

1 stick butter or margarine	1 can cream of mushroom soup
2 medium onions (chopped)	½ cup water
1 green bell pepper (chopped)	3 cups cooked rice
½ red bell pepper (chopped)	1 can Ro-tel tomatoes
3 cloves garlic (minced)	3 cups cleaned shrimp (cut in half)
3 ribs celery	buttered bread crumbs
¼ cup chopped parsley	
3 slices bread	

    Sauté peppers, onions, celery, garlic and parsley in butter. Add shrimp and ro-tel tomatoes. Simmer a few minutes and add soup and water. Simmer a few minutes more and add the 3 slices of bread, crumbled. Fold in cooked rice and pour into a greased casserole dish. Top with buttered bread crumbs and bake in a 350 degree oven for 30 minutes or until top is brown.

CORN BREAD CASSEROLE   *Footnote 55*

1½ cups corn meal	⅓ cup cooking oil or melted shortening
½ cup flour	2 cup grated cheese
2 teaspoons baking powder	1 small onion (chopped)
½ teaspoon salt	1 jalapeno pepper (chopped) *optional*
2 eggs	1 pound ground beef
1 cup milk	
1 can cream style corn	

salt and pepper to taste

Sauté ground beef with salt and pepper. Drain and set aside. In a large mixing bowl, stir together the corn meal, flour, baking powder, salt, milk and eggs. Add cream style corn and shortening to corn bread mixture. Pour half the mixture in a hot greased pan. Sprinkle the ground beef over the corn bread mixture and layer the onions, jalapenos and cheese. Top with the remaining corn bread mixture and bake at 350 degrees 35-45 minutes.

RED BEANS AND RICE   *Footnote 56*

1 ham bone	¼ cup chopped bell pepper
½ pound ham	¼ cup chopped parsley
1 pound dried red beans	½ teaspoon basil
1 large onion (chopped)	2 bay leaves
1 cup green onions (tops and bottoms)	Salt and cayenne pepper to taste
¼ cup butter	

Kidney beans will do, but small dark red beans are better. Put them in a large heavy pot or bowl with enough water to cover. Soak overnight. In the morning, rinse and add enough water to cover. Bring to a boil and add all other ingredients. Reduce heat and simmer for at least 3 hours. Be sure beans are not old. They should become creamy, but most will remain whole. Add cold water as needed. Goes well with smoked sausage and sliced onions.

Cook your best pot of long grain rice and serve over the rice.

ITALIAN SAUSAGE PASTA *Footnote 57*

- 1 (12 ounce) package wagon wheel pasta
- 1 pound Italian sausage
- 2 tablespoons olive oil
- ½ cup onion (chopped)
- 3 cloves garlic (chopped)
- ½ teaspoon fresh ground black pepper
- 2 (14 ounce) cans stewed tomatoes
- ¼ - ½ teaspoon red pepper flakes (optional)
- 1 (8 ounce) package cream cheese
- ½ teaspoon salt

Bring a large pot of water to a boil and add salt. Cook pasta in boiling water 8-10 minutes or until al dente. Drain

Heat olive oil in a skillet over medium heat. Remove casings from sausage, crumble and cook sausage and pepper flakes until done. Stir in onions and garlic and cook until tender. Chop tomatoes and add to the meat mixture. Stir in black pepper and cream cheese. Simmer about 8-10 minutes. Stir cooked pasta into sauce and heat thoroughly. Remove from heat and serve.

SHEET CAKE WITH CHOCOLATE ICING *Footnote 58*

- 2 sticks butter
- 1¼ cups sugar
- 2¼ cups flour
- 5 eggs
- 2¼ teaspoons baking powder
- ¾ cup milk
- ¾ cup water
- 1½ teaspoon vanilla extract
- 1 box Butter Cake Mix
- ¼ cup vegetable oil

Preheat oven to 350 degrees. In mixing bowl on medium speed, beat butter. Add sugar and cream until smooth. Add flour alternating with eggs. Add baking powder and milk. Empty cake mix into mixture. Add vanilla and water. Continue on medium to high speed until well blended. Add vegetable oil and mix well. Grease and flower a 17.3 X 13.5 inch pan. Bake 30-35 minutes. Cake is done when toothpick inserted in center comes out clean.

CHOCOLATE ICING

⅔ cup cocoa
½ of 8-ounce cream cheese (softened)

2 teaspoons vanilla extract
½ stick butter (softened)
3½ cups powdered sugar
⅓ cup + 1 tbsp evaporated milk

In a medium bowl, cream butter and cream cheese. Add cocoa and vanilla. Alternate powdered sugar with milk. Cream until smooth. Spread on cake when cake cools.

PRALINES
Footnote 59

2 cups white sugar
⅔ cups evaporated milk
⅛ teaspoon soda

1 teaspoon salt
1 teaspoon vanilla
2 cups pecans
½ cup butter (1 stick)

1. In saucepan, mix sugar, milk, salt, butter, and soda. Stir well. Bring mixture to a boil. Cook to soft ball stage.
2. Add vanilla and pecans. Beat until stiff.
3. Drop from spoon onto waxed paper or well buttered dish.
4. Enjoy

DIRT DESSERT
Footnote 60

2 large package Oreo Cookies
2 8-ounce packages Cream Cheese
2 cups powdered sugar
3 cups milk

2 3-ounce packages Vanilla instant pudding
2 teaspoons Vanilla
1 16-ounce Carton Cool Whip (thawed)

Grind cookies, set aside. Cream together cream cheese and sugar. Mix pudding according to package directions using 3 cups milk. Add to cream cheese mixture. Fold in along with cool whip and vanilla.

In a 10 in. foil-lined flower pot, layer cookie crumbs then creamy mixture. Beginning and ending with cookie crumbs. Refrigerate for a day before serving. Just before serving, cover the stem of an artificial flower with foil and insert in middle of pot.

Reading Group Guide for
Discussion Questions

1. How would you feel if someone in your family basically stole your intended from you and married them?
2. Do you feel that Cherrelle was justified in refusing to serve as chairman of the family reunion committee?
3. If you had been jilted at the altar or betrayed by a loved one for any reason, would you be able to forgive them?
4. Why do you think Camille remained in an abusive relationship? Do you know anyone like that? Why do they stay?
5. Chalice moved from one relationship to another. Why do you think she attracted the type of men she found?
6. Do you think Cherrelle, Camille, and Chalice all have low self-esteem? If so, why?
7. Hurricane Katrina was a devastating storm that forever changed America. How did Hurricane Katrina affect or impact your family?
8. Should Cherrelle and Cory have helped Darryl and Image get away from the storm?
9. How was the family affected by Big Mama's Alzheimer's? Did it cause the family to have to make any major adjustments?
10. Do you feel it was important for the family to understand that a family reunion is like a business? If you participate in putting on a family reunion for your family, how do you ensure that things are done fairly for everyone?

Suggestions

1. Have each person in the book club prepare one of the foods in the cookbook and bring it to the meeting.
2. Have each person in the book club bring their favorite recipe and share it with one another – bring the dish for tasting.
3. Use the suggestions for the family reunion to give you ideas on planning your own family reunion.
4. Ask each person in the book club to tell what they did during Katrina or how they helped the survivors.

Living With No Regrets

Cherrelle Elliot has been betrayed by both family and friends. On the day of her wedding, her fiancé jilts her at the altar and marries her first cousin. She is devastated to find that her family members have accepted the relationship without regard to her feelings when she sees her ex-fiancé, cousin, and their new child being admired at the family reunion. Her grief and embarrassment cause her to leave her home city of New Orleans and move to Houston.

After years away from New Orleans, Cherrelle's grandmother asks her to chair the family reunion committee, but she refuses. Reassigned to New Orleans to work on a new project for her company, she is forced to take a matured look at her family, and Cherrelle realizes that some things have changed. Her grandmother is in the early stages of Alzheimer's, her sister is being abused by her husband, and her father is missing to name a few. The only things that make life in New Orleans bearable are the foods that remind her of the love of her family and an unexpected reunion with Cory, a childhood friend she secretly had a crush on.

Her grandmother's disease forces Cherrelle to take over the family reunion, but plans are interrupted when Hurricane Katrina roars through, causing havoc for the family as members are separated from one another.

Living With No Regrets is a story of how Cherrelle and her family deal with betrayal, forgiveness, family, love, reunion planning, Alzheimer's, and spousal abuse. Recipes to the meals that routinely bring the family together are included.